D1459501

04564947

BENEATH THE WORLD, A SEA

BENEATH THE WORLD, A SEA

Chris Beckett

Published in hardback in Great Britain in 2019 by Corvus,
an imprint of Atlantic Books Ltd.

10 9 8 7 6 5 4 3 2 1

A CIP catalogue record for this book is available from the British Library.

Hardback ISBN: 978 1 78649 155 8
E-book ISBN: 978 1 78649 156 5

Printed and bound in Great Britain by TJ International, Padstow, Cornwall

Corvus
An imprint of Atlantic Books Ltd
Ormond House
26–27 Boswell Street
London
WC1N 3JZ

www.corvus-books.co.uk

THE CORPSE SERVANTS

The figure of the Palido appears in village folklore across the entire Submundo Delta. He has immensely long, stilt-like legs, skin that is completely white and a pointed tongue. He's usually depicted at least twice as tall as normal human height, stick thin, with elaborately curled moustaches, in a top hat and a brightly coloured waistcoat. He can fly through the air, make himself invisible, and be in two places at the same time. He can also raise corpses from their graves to run errands for him. The corpse servants whisper the Palido's messages with shrivelled grey lips.

There are many versions of the story, but in all of them, the Palido tricks the first Mundinos by opening some sort of door for them.

'Enter, my friends!' he purrs, stooping almost double to bring his smiling face level with theirs. 'Enter, and you will come to a place of peace and plenty.'

They hesitate.

'My dear friends, there is no need to worry,' says the Palido. His moustaches twitch, his long thin arms beckon them forward, his narrow pink tongue runs over his lips. 'As a token of my friendship, I will give you piglets and chickens to take with you, and tobacco plants, and maize, and tools, and a whole big sack of sweet potatoes. I will even give you goats.'

They look at each other. They accept the gifts. They step through the door.

But the door leads into a cage, just big enough to hold them all. It's a cage, but it's also a coffin, and the corpse servants laugh as they dig a hole for it. 'Ha ha!' they hiss to one another. 'Now the dead are burying the living! The dead will walk while the living lie where no one will ever find them.'

The corpses are immensely strong. They dig so fast and so deep that the coffin drops right through the earth, for the ground of one world is the sky of the world below.

Hyacinth Young, *Myths and Legends of the Submundo Delta*

I. THE POLICEMAN

(1)

'Because the truth is'

Because the truth was *what*? It was obvious that he'd just written the words – the notebook was open on his lap, his pen poised over that final S – but Ben had no idea what he'd been about to say. And why was the sun suddenly shining? And what was that strange scent, like nothing he'd ever smelt before? Only seconds ago, or so it seemed, he'd been sitting here on deck in the warm darkness of a tropical night with green rain forest passing by in front of him, dimly illuminated by the deck lights of the boat. It had been seven days into the four-week river journey to the Submundo Delta, and his excitement and anxiety had been mounting as he approached that band of territory surrounding the Delta that was known as the Zona de Olvido.

The Zona de Olvido. The Zone of Forgetfulness. That, of course, was the explanation, but though he had known in advance of the Zona's unique quality and understood perfectly well that once you'd passed through it and come out again, no trace of your time there remained in memory, the actual experience was so sudden, so total, so shocking, that it took him several seconds to grasp what had happened. It was like a cut between two scenes on a cinema screen.

He had been in that green forest at night but now the sun was shining and he was right in the middle of something else entirely. He looked up from his notebook and there it was, the Submundo Delta, the Delta Beneath the World.

The trees, if they could be called trees at all, came in shades of pinkish purple without the slightest trace of green, and grew in a mass of spirals and helices, constantly recurring at many different scales of magnitude. Huge, magenta leaf stems the size of arms uncoiled from the branches, and then themselves unfurled smaller spirals from bead-like nodes along their lengths, these spirals in turn releasing rows of still smaller ones. And the branches were spirals too, spirals branching out from spirals, giving the effect of some kind of ornate three-dimensional calligraphy in an unknown and untranslatable language. They hung over the water, these branches, their tips curling back on themselves in yet more spirals, and put out delicate, helical flowers – if flower was the right word – that were dazzlingly white except for their bright pink mouths. On a wooden hut that stood at the water's edge, a faded mural depicted grinning skeletons digging a grave, watched by a little group of living human beings confined inside a cage, while, beneath the grave, a many-armed creature waited, its round head covered in eyes. The air was thick and humid and that strange pervasive aroma wafted from the forest, a hint of burnt sugar in it, and honey, and bitter lilies, but something else there too so completely unfamiliar that Ben could find nothing to compare it with. The sky was covered in white, translucent cloud through which burnt a huge white sun, seemingly much larger than in the world outside, and with tiny flashes of pink and blue and green glinting around its edges, as if it was ringed with diamonds or splintered glass.

Spitting out fumes and bilge water, the boat chugged steadily onwards through all this strangeness, the river twisting and looping like the one viable path through some vast maze, with countless side channels to tempt it off its course. Some of these channels were navigable and marked with rusty signs bearing arrows, crosses, exclamation marks or the names of villages – Ca' do Santos, Bom Presago, Al' do Mortos – but most of them were clogged with purple water plants and one was blocked by the half-submerged wreckage of a Dakota plane, its exposed wing and fuselage covered with the twisted filigree pattern of some white and glistening growth.

Ben was entranced. The coils and spirals stirred something inside him that was close to nightmare, but that was part of the appeal. Half an hour had passed before he thought, with a tiny twinge of unease, about the vanished days in the Zona.

He had absolutely no memory of it, but he knew that, while still inside the Zona, the boat had stopped at the inland port of Nus at the confluence of the River Lethe with the River Rhee, and had remained there for several days while the captain negotiated the sale of part of his cargo, and the advance purchase, to be collected on his return, of a consignment of rubber from the surrounding rain forest.

And Ben knew that – odd as it might seem for a place that no one outside could remember – Nus had a bad reputation. At the beginning of the journey, a leaflet had been given to each of the boat's four passengers, with a small map showing the approximate position of the Zona, and the way this mysterious band of territory completely encircled the Delta. 'The Company respectfully reminds its passengers,' the leaflet read, 'that everything that happens to you within the Zona, including Nus, will no longer remain in your memory once you emerge from the Zona again, and continue on into the Submundo Delta. You should be aware that this creates many legal challenges. Crimes, which are likely to occur, may be impossible to investigate, and wrongs cannot easily be righted. You are strongly advised, therefore, to remain on board throughout our time at Nus, when there will be an armed guard on deck at all times.' A programme of movies would be provided, the leaflet said – they would be projected on to the wall of the boat's tiny dining room – meals would be served, and the bar would be open all day. It was up to each passenger to decide whether or not to accept the company's advice, but no liability whatsoever would be accepted for the safety of any passenger who chose to ignore it. The boat would continue its journey at the allotted time and any passenger not on board would have no choice but to wait for the next boat that had berths available.

Given that he was a very responsible and dutiful man, Ben assumed that he'd followed the company's advice. He had had no reason to go ashore in Nus and his professional insurance would not have covered it, for this was a business trip, after all, and his work lay not in the Zona but in the Delta itself. It was a little disappointing, admittedly, to come to the conclusion that he'd probably just stayed on board, but if he considered the alternative possibility that, freed from the fear of future scrutiny, he might have made the decision to ignore the company's advice, disregard the conditions of his insurance and go ashore, he experienced a twinge of something that felt like the tiny tip of a whole deep iceberg of dread.

But anyway, never mind all that. He was in the Delta now and in front of him were magenta trees with spiral leaves and flowers with bright pink mouths. This was where his work would be. This was the point of his journey.

He was sitting in a canvas chair on the starboard side of the small foredeck set aside for passengers. At the front of the deck, standing and leaning on the railings, was another passenger called Hyacinth who had told him, way back before the Zona, that she was an anthropologist, and that she'd made this journey several times already. She was in her middle thirties, roughly his own age, and he'd discovered that, though based in New York, she was, like him, a Londoner. She sometimes read interesting-looking novels by foreign authors, but she spent a lot of time just looking out at their surroundings with a quiet absorption he rather envied. From time to time she'd take out a sketchpad and make a drawing.

Right behind Ben, on the port side of the little deck, sat a middle-aged Dutch couple: Mr and Mrs de Groot. Both of them were plump and pink and usually glistening with sweat, him wearing pebble spectacles that enormously magnified his moist and weary eyes, her in very dark glasses for which, apparently, there was some medical necessity. Mr de Groot had told Ben he used to work for the United Nations in Geneva, and had learnt of the Delta there, the UN being responsible, of course, for the administration of the Delta Protectorate.

'We have so many hopes for this place,' Mr de Groot told him now, when Ben looked in their direction. His wife had some kind of chronic illness, and in the first part of the journey, back when the forest was green, she had often complained of headaches and nausea, and seemed to be constantly troubled by the weather, so that her husband was forever fetching aspirins and glasses of water, or helping her with cardigans or parasols. 'We have spent many years looking for something that might reduce her suffering. And I hope, I very much hope, that this place might possibly be the—'

But at this point his wife turned her blacked-out eyes towards him and spoke to him in Dutch, and he jumped up to fetch something for her from their cabin.

As he disappeared below, two strangers stepped out, a man and woman, walking over to lean on the railings to Ben's left. He had no recollection of ever seeing them before.

'Hi, I'm Jael,' the woman said, turning towards him. She was American and in her thirties. She wore dungarees without a T-shirt, and she was almost freakishly good-looking with a mass of wavy red hair.

'I'm Ben,' he told her. 'I guess you must have come on board at Nus?'

'I guess so,' she said, examining his face with slightly narrowed eyes.

'So, I suppose ...' He stumbled on his words slightly, unnerved not just by her piercing gaze, but by the reminder of those missing days inside the Zona. 'So I suppose we must have introduced ourselves before.'

'Yup,' she said, her gaze still unflinching. 'That's how it is with the Zona. You and I may have become bosom chums in there for all we know, or we might have been deadly enemies. We don't know.' She glanced down at the red notebook that was still on his lap. 'Or not unless one of us wrote it down. I never keep a diary in Nus myself. I think it defeats the point. But it looks like maybe you did?'

He stuffed the notebook into the satchel in which he carried things he might want on the deck. 'Just a few notes,' he said.

'Which may or may not be lies,' she observed, still studying his face in a way that made him feel that every word he spoke was being carefully weighed and classified. She smiled. 'That's the thing with Nus, isn't it? You can lie to your future self as easily as to anyone else.'

'I suppose so,' Ben said, trying to laugh, though it didn't seem much of a joke.

'And this is Rico,' she said.

Her companion turned towards Ben. He too was film-star good-looking with long slim limbs and a certain feline grace that Ben found instantly fascinating. But his beautiful face had a ravaged and weather-beaten look.

'Yeah, hi, Ben,' he said. He was also American. 'Crazy Rico at your service.' And he bowed extravagantly and completely unsmilingly, as if he was one of the Three Musketeers.

Ben didn't take to the two of them. He felt he knew their type and that he had encountered people like them all too often in the police: druggie, alternative types who tried to intimidate you with their weirdness and unpredictability.

At dinner that night, when all six passengers and the captain ate together, Jael made no secret of the fact if the conversation bored her, zoning out completely, or whispering and giggling with Rico. But when a topic interested her, she spoke with great enthusiasm and erudition, her sharp, always slightly narrowed eyes darting from one face to another as she made her points. And having spoken, she would listen, very intently, to anything that was said to her in reply. Rico was much quieter but would suddenly say odd things or laugh loudly at unexpected moments when no one had said anything funny.

Later, when Ben returned to his cabin, he found on his cot a carbon-copy of a disclaimer document that he'd been required to sign in Nus, absolving the shipping company of any responsibility for injuries or losses that he might suffer while visiting the town.

Next to it lay a purple notebook on the cover of which was written, in his own hand, 'Time in Nus. June/July, 1990.'

In fact, there had never been any chance of his missing out on such a place, a place so hidden that he would be concealed there even from his own future self, but he didn't know that yet, and this unexpected evidence of his reckless choice was deeply disturbing. He didn't open the purple notebook, though he himself had presumably been the one who had laid it on the bed, but instead sealed it closed with two stout elastic bands and shoved it into the bottom of his suitcase along with another notebook – blue, and entitled 'Journey to Nus' – which he could remember beginning to write, but knew must also contain entries from days he had no recollection of, and the red one which he'd abandoned earlier that day. He didn't want to read words he could no longer remember writing, or hear in his head the voice of a self he had no knowledge of. For what might that other self say? What might he choose to hold back?

(2)

'Why are you going to the Delta anyway, Ben?' Rico asked Ben at breakfast. 'Have you told me already and I've forgotten, or are you keeping it a secret?' He gave a loud shout of laughter and then, before Ben could answer, held up his hand to stop him speaking. 'Don't worry, dude, I know! No need to tell me. You're going there for the same reason every fucker goes there. To fall apart.'

It wasn't just Ben that didn't like Rico and Jael. Hyacinth tensed whenever they were near and Mrs de Groot's level of agitation would rapidly increase. Sometimes in the dining room her husband would look at Ben or Hyacinth with his huge magnified eyes, as if appraising what support he would have if it ever became necessary to forcibly remove the two of them. But luckily for the peace of mind of the other passengers, for the rest of that tortuous journey through the coils of the Lethe, Jael and Rico invariably took themselves off after breakfast to the cargo hatch at the back of the boat. Only rarely visiting the deck, they'd lie around all day up there with their cigarettes and drugs, her in the bottom half of a faded yellow bikini, him in khaki shorts. Sometimes Rico would strum on a guitar, not very well and not even properly in tune.

The de Groots were often absent from the deck as well, for when Mrs de Groot had one of her many attacks, she had to retire to the darkness of her cabin with her husband in attendance, and this just left Ben and Hyacinth. Hyacinth was very self-contained, apparently happy to read, or draw, or lean on the railings and watch the forest going by in her calm, absorbed way. Sometimes, when she'd sketched a twisted tree or a channel choked with vegetation, Ben would ask to see the results and she'd pass them across with a shrug. The drawings were very good. They evoked a kind of nostalgia for this strange place: a curious thing when the boat was still in the midst of it, with scenes right there in front of them, hour after hour, that were just like the ones she drew.

'So this is it,' Ben said softly on the afternoon of the second day, trying to anchor himself in this place which still seemed too peculiar to fully believe in. 'The Submundo! The Submundo Delta.'

Hyacinth looked over at him and smiled. 'You have to remind yourself it's real, don't you? I've been to the Delta seven times now and I still have to.'

From the cargo hatch to the rear came the sound of Rico's unhinged laughter.

'Of course Delta is really a misnomer,' said Mr de Groot, who was just returning to the deck after settling his wife into one of her drugged sleeps. He was a man who took comfort in facts, and liked to recite them whenever a chance presented itself. 'The appearance is of solid ground with channels passing through it, but actually the water continues beneath the forest as well. It would be more accurate to call it an inland sea with trees growing up from the bottom of it. They put out side roots above its surface and these roots join together to create the dense mat that gives the impression of solid—'

He broke off, hearing a faint cry from his wife in their cabin below. With a sigh, he went back down to her.

There were just five crew on the boat. The captain, Korzeniowski, with his thick grey beard, dined with the passengers every night, and was courteous but completely unsmiling; Lessing, the engineer, never spoke to any of the passengers, and when they saw her at all she was usually fixing something or smoking by herself at the back of the boat in her blue overalls or making notes in a grimy little book; the cook and the two other hands were all Mundinos, local men from the Submundo itself, speaking to each other in their own idiosyncratic Portuguese Creole. (Hyacinth was fluent in this language and would sometimes chat to them but, though Ben had taken intensive Portuguese lessons before he set out, he quickly realized he was going to have to unlearn most of what he'd so laboriously acquired.) At night, when the boat was moored to one of the crumbling jetties that punctuated the banks of the Lethe, all five of the crew took turns to keep watch on deck, as they had apparently also done at Nus. But this time it wasn't to protect the passengers and cargo from criminals, but to fend off any duendes that might otherwise disturb everyone's sleep by climbing on board with their suckered hands and feet.

Down in his tiny cabin, Ben rather enjoyed listening to the footsteps of the allocated member of the crew pacing the boards over his head. It was a soothing sound, and there were very few other sounds at all, for there were no night birds in the Submundo to cry or scream and the local creatures were completely silent. But sometimes creaks and groans came from the forest's roots and branches and Ben would sleepily wonder about the source of these pulses of tension passing through that enormous woody mass. Were they the result of wind blowing through the canopy, perhaps, or rainfall in the surrounding mountains changing the flow of water through the submerged trunks? Or was it the tugging of the moon, whose light crept in through his porthole to shine on the neatly folded clothes he laid out each night for the next morning?

The Lethe was truly serpentine. You might pass some distinctive landmark – a half-collapsed jetty, a rusty signpost – and apparently leave it far behind you as you chugged slowly onwards through the river's twists and bends, only to find yourself looking through a narrow neck of forest at that very same jetty or sign, and realize you were only a matter of yards away from a stretch of water you'd been through several hours before.

Two or three times a day, the boat came to riverside settlements – clusters of simple, usually flat-roofed cabins, joined on to one another, propped up by poles above the water, and often decorated with brightly coloured murals. The many-armed and many-eyed water creature was a constant theme. So were the skeleton gravediggers, lowering their caged victims into the ground. And often a sinister white-faced figure stood watching in waistcoat and top hat, stick-thin and immensely tall.

From time to time the boat moored at the jetties of these villages to take on fresh vegetables or a few chickens, which the cook, rather than buy for cash, would barter for small items specially brought for the purpose, such as knives, enamel mugs or plastic buckets. The Mundino people, so Ben had learnt from the material sent to him from Geneva, had Iberian, African and Native American origins, and had been shipped into the Delta back in the 1860s by a wealthy Portuguese aristocrat called Baron Valente with the idea that, if any of them were fortunate enough to survive, they and their descendants would be useful in the future as a ready-made labour force when the time came to open up this remote and unexplored region to civilization.

'In much the same way,' Mr de Groot observed over dinner one evening, snuffling with the amusement that his store of facts provided him, 'sailors in those days would leave goats or pigs on uninhabited islands, so there would be a food supply in the future in case of need.'

Every Mundino settlement was surrounded by vegetable gardens, shockingly bright green against the pinks and purples of the ever-encroaching forest. Chickens, pigs and small children wandered about and, in an open space in the centre of every village – a sort of town square, separated from the river by at least one row of cabins – there invariably stood a carved representation of the Mundino god, Iya. The wood was rubbed with fat to preserve it, which made the images shiny and black, and even shinier black stones – pieces of obsidian from the Montanhas de Vidro at the northern edge of the Delta – were set into them to form the small pointed nipples and eyes.

On one occasion, Ben walked over to the central square in one of the larger villages and just stood there looking up at Iya's stone eyes and her strange fixed smile. Children were pestering him for sweets or pens, but he did his best to shut them out of his mind, absently patting curly heads, and gently detaching his fingers from sticky little hands that took hold of his. And, as he looked up at the god, it struck him, not for the first time, that it was impossible to look at the image of a face without, at some level, seeing it as alive. He'd first noticed this with a teddy bear he'd had as a child. Even when he was much too old to really believe it, he could still not completely rid himself of the idea that the thing's glass eyes could see. It was as if there was a primitive layer of the brain which took everything to be whatever it seemed to be.

'She watches over them,' Hyacinth said, coming to stand beside him. She was wearing a white T-shirt with her sunglasses tucked into the top, and was holding her sketchbook at her side. 'She protects them against the duendes, and against floods, and she sees everything they do, good or bad, and stores it in her mind for the final reckoning.'

Suddenly the children stopped tugging at Ben and Hyacinth and went running and shouting across to Rico. He'd brought his guitar and now, perching himself on the veranda of a hut in a single graceful movement, he proceeded to bash out songs and gurn for them, while Jael, all by herself, danced a little dance in a floaty green dress.

Hyacinth raised her eyebrows slightly but said nothing.

'Do you think they kill duendes in this village?' Ben asked her.

She laughed at the naïvety of the question. 'Oh, for sure! They do in all the villages. For them it's just like killing rats.'

Presently, the captain rang his bell and they returned to the boat. The de Groots were already in their cabin, and Jael and Rico resumed their normal station on the cargo hatch, so Hyacinth and Ben had the deck to themselves again as they left the village behind.

'I don't know why I haven't asked you this before,' he said, 'but what exactly is your reason for coming to the Delta?'

She smiled. 'I don't blame you for not asking,' she said. 'Jobs, goals, objectives … It all seems a bit trivial, doesn't it, compared to this?' She gestured to a mass of white helical flowers, like tiny twisted saxophones, their bells opening towards the boat in a blast of silent crimson. 'I think I told you I'm an anthropologist – yes? – but perhaps I didn't explain more than that. I'm based at Columbia University in New York, but I have a small research grant from the Protectorate to study the folk beliefs of the Mundino people. How about you?'

'Well, as you know I'm a policeman …' Ben began and hesitated. He remembered announcing this over dinner on the first leg of the journey. As a rule he enjoyed the slightly chilling effect this news typically produced, but in the context of a river boat travelling towards the Submundo Delta, the effect had been more of slightly absurd incongruity. In the faces of all of them – Hyacinth, Korzeniowski, the de Groots – he'd seen the same unspoken question: *A London policeman? Here?*

'Yes, you did tell us,' she said. 'But why do they need you in the Delta? I didn't quite get that.'

A large flock of bright blue iridescent birds had suddenly appeared. They hovered briefly around the mouths of the flowers, stabbing into the naked upturned bells with long red tongues, and then headed off up the river ahead. Of course they were not *really* 'birds', Ben reminded himself, and the helices with their upturned bells were not *really* 'flowers'. Life in the Delta was different. The birds had teeth. The flowers, as Mr de Groot liked to inform him from time to time, had no stamens and no known reproductive function, though they secreted a kind of golden milk, which could sometimes be seen dripping into the water from their lips, to disperse in creamy clouds.

But now Ben spotted a more familiar-looking animal in the trees ahead: a large green lizard, a bona fide reptile, leaning down from the top of a branch shaped like a musical clef, to watch the boat approach. He wondered how it got here, so far away from anything remotely of its kind.

'Why do they need a British policeman?' he said. 'It's a good question, but there's a particular problem that I've been recruited to assist with. I shouldn't really say more than that.'

She nodded. 'A particular problem, which you can't discuss. How mysterious! But let me guess. Would it by any chance be to do with duende killings?'

As she obviously knew, after a campaign by the small research community in the Delta, the UN had decreed that the beings known as duendes, unique to the Submundo, should be categorized as 'persons' under Protectorate law, meaning that they were entitled to the same protections as human beings. Hyacinth was quite right in guessing that his appointment was a direct consequence of that decision, strange and rather daunting as that now seemed to him, so far away from that dreary office in Geneva where he'd been interviewed, but he smiled and told her he wasn't yet at liberty to discuss his role.

'You should try drawing those birds,' he said to change the subject. It seemed that the creatures were interested in the lizard. They were hovering around it, and the boat was catching up with them.

'That would be hard,' she said. 'They don't keep still for one thing. And there's something about them, isn't there, that really isn't of this world? It would be hard to get down on paper, I think. Those teeth, and the way the beak almost seems to mock.'

'But they're only animals after all,' Ben said.

'You think so? I don't know *what* they are, myself. I don't think anyone does. But I can't look at any of this without thinking about how it must have seemed to those first inhabitants when they were dumped here. Imagine what that must have been like! They were all alone. No one else would come into the Delta for sixty years. They thought they'd been buried somehow in some hidden world beneath the world they knew, a world under an enchantment, with its own giant sun and moon.'

The few books about the Submundo that Ben had managed to find were all written from the perspective of the scientists and explorers who had rediscovered the place in the 1920s, and so it was their reactions that he was familiar with. He'd never thought before about how the first Mundinos must have felt when they found themselves here back in the 1860s, but now he remembered the shock of emerging from the Zona, and asked himself what that might have been like if you had no idea where you were or what to expect. 'They wouldn't have remembered how they got here, would they?' he said. 'It must have been very scary.'

They were passing the green lizard when suddenly one of the bird creatures darted forward and bit it. With blood running from the side of its head the frightened animal opened its red mouth to hiss and show its teeth, but another bird darted forward, and then another, each attacking from a different direction so that the lizard didn't know which way to face and was unable to defend itself. Bleeding and torn, the creature backed off towards the trunk, but they cut off its retreat and kept on harrying it until eventually – it was some way behind now and Ben had to lean over the railings to see – it lost its grip and dropped into the water. The birds hovered over it in a swarm, watching the dying animal sink into the Lethe in a cloud of its own blood, and then, in what seemed a single movement, they darted back to their golden feast.

'Yes it must,' Hyacinth said. 'It must have been absolutely terrifying.'

She and Ben lapsed into silence, surrounded by that strange aroma that was a little like caramel and honey and bitter lilies, but was mostly like nothing else at all.

'I should warn you, Ben,' Hyacinth said after a few minutes, 'it's hard to see projects through in this place. People think they've come here for a particular reason, but somehow the momentum dissipates, and what was going to be a straight line becomes a meander and then, as often as not, it fizzles out completely.'

(3)

In the middle of the Delta, a cluster of small extinct volcanoes formed a kind of island, rising up out of the hidden sea. The main channel of the Lethe came right up to it, widening into a kind of lake, and looping round its northern tip before continuing westward towards the remote and impassable Valente Falls. A wall enclosed a harbour kept clear of weeds and lilies. A couple of launches were moored there, as well as a modest-sized tanker and a small, white two-person submarine with its name painted along its side in large blue capital letters: SOLARIS.

Behind the harbour was Amizad, the Submundo's only town, with its red-tiled roofs and white church tower, its very ordinariness strange. The crew threw ropes to Mundino dockhands. Hyacinth slung her bag over her shoulder. The de Groots emerged from their cabin. Ben thought Mrs de Groot seemed a little more cheerful than she had been at the beginning, and she smiled at him as her husband helped her down the gangway to a waiting taxi, an unexpectedly sweet, almost conspiratorial smile. Hyacinth strode off by herself into the town. Rico and Jael simply settled down on the jetty as if they had nowhere to go, him strumming some chords on his guitar.

Ben had a delegation to meet him. '*Wonderful* to see you, Inspector Ronson,' said the Chief Administrator, a squat, Australian woman called Katherine Tiler. 'I hope you had a pleasant journey.'

'Or what you can remember of it anyway,' said Da Ponte, the Chief of the Protectorate Police, thickly moustached, glossy with a sheen of sweat, and also very short.

The small stature of the two of them reinforced in Ben a growing sense that he'd arrived in Toytown. They had a car waiting, also small, and a driver – they insisted on Ben taking the front seat for his long legs – who took them along two shortish streets to the hotel where he'd be staying. The two-storey buildings had plastered walls that were either whitewashed or painted in pink or pale blue. They looked European, though which part of Europe exactly, Ben couldn't say. A few were crumbling and empty.

The Hotel Bem-Vindo stood on the town's small central plaza, facing a brick clock tower that had been built to commemorate the establishment of the Special Protectorate. The Town Hall, where the administration was based, stood on the adjoining side of the square to the hotel's right, and there was another hotel opposite, and a couple of cafés. As Ben climbed from the car, a little mechanical man in traditional Mundino dress came out of a door at the top of the clock tower, bowed and banged four times on a bell with a hammer before disappearing inside with a whirr. Just like Toytown, Ben thought, or perhaps a film set, its very familiarity and ordinariness made bizarre by the presence just across the water of life forms so unlike the life of the rest of Earth that they were thought by many to have arrived five hundred million years ago on the same asteroid that created the Submundo basin.

Ben's two hosts insisted on walking him into the reception of the hotel.

'So looking forward to working with you!'

'No rush at all in the morning, obviously.'

'You'll need your sleep. That journey takes it out of you.'

'Shall we say an eleven o'clock start?'

They were very keen to come across as friendly and pleased to see him, but it seemed to Ben that they overplayed this, like a cheating husband trying too hard to act the part of a loving and attentive spouse.

He turned away from them. The lobby of the Hotel Bim-Vindo also served as its bar but was completely empty. Fussy, fake antique furniture stood unused. The barman polished glasses. Mrs Martin, the proprietor, greeted them excitedly. She was an Englishwoman, it seemed, who had at one time been married to a local man. She was thrilled to see one of her compatriots, and rather obviously also thrilled that he should turn out to be a good-looking youngish man. (Ben was thirty-five, and he *was* good-looking, with his thick black hair, his blue eyes, and his slender, toned, physique.)

'You feel so cut off here sometimes,' she said. 'What with planes not being able to get in, and no phones or TV or anything. It sometimes feels as if all the world's going on without you. And it's *so* nice to hear a proper English voice.'

She came out from behind the reception counter to show him up to his room, which was also fussily ornate, with elaborate mirrors, big, heavy velvet curtains, and sepia-tinted photographs in heavy gilt frames. One of the pictures showed Baron Valente posing with twenty of his so-called 'pioneers', a tall, handsome white man in a richly embroidered waistcoat, one hand resting paternally on the head of the small, frightened-looking boy on his right, the other on the head of a tense little girl whose face was too blurred to make out at all.

The porter laid down Ben's bags and left. The room was warm and a little stuffy, with the strange bitter-sweet smell of the forest somewhere in the background behind the furniture polish and pot-pourri. Desperation and loneliness oozed from Mrs Martin. ('Nicky! *Do* call me Nicky!' she cried.) Ben had a sudden strong sense that, if he'd made the smallest move in that direction, she would have very willingly laid down with him right then on her hotel bed. In fact, it seemed to him that, short of saying it out loud, she was actually telling him just that. Here in the Submundo, he was to discover, even in the centre of Amizad, unspoken signals were louder than they were in the world outside. At times this was exhilarating, at others claustrophobic: everything and everyone felt a little too close, as if they had come right to the threshold of his inner self.

Mrs Martin wanted to chatter, but she finally left him, and he opened up his cases and began to unpack. As he stacked shirts in a drawer, the photo of Valente caught his eye, and he went to have a closer look at it. The Baron's gaze was direct, confident and sure of his own rightness. All the other faces looked wary and confused, and almost all of them were blurred, as if they hadn't understood that an image was being made of them or that they needed to keep still. The picture next to it showed the clock tower in the square in the process of construction, seen more or less from the same perspective as he would have now if he looked out of his window. Or at least, so Ben thought, until he read the inscription beneath it. 'Nus town square, 1933', it read and he felt a sudden chill. This wasn't the Amizad clock tower, then, but an identical one inside the Zona de Olvido, which he must surely also have seen and stood in front of, as alive and conscious as he was now.

Beneath his shirts he found his three notebooks – blue, purple and red – where he'd shoved them to the bottom of his case. He weighed them in his hand for a moment, his notes from oblivion. All he remembered of their contents was the first part of the first notebook, and the final four words of the last: 'Because the truth is'. He had a momentary impulse to toss all three of them into the wastepaper basket so the maid would remove them in the morning and that would be the end of them. But he knew he wouldn't be able to leave them lying there so instead he put them in the left-hand drawer of the fancy Louis XIV-style desk, laid a few small things on top of them – a paperback, a pack of cards, a waterproof torch – and pushed the drawer closed.

II. THE ANTHROPOLOGIST

(4)

Back in the seventies, when Hyacinth was a teenager in North London, there was a little wood behind her parents' house. She thought of it as a wood, at any rate, and 'the wood' was what she and her friends always called it, but in reality it was an old bombsite from the war, which for some reason – a legal dispute of some kind – had never been redeveloped. And so, in the thirty years or so since a German flying bomb had exploded there, trees had grown up, not to full-size, but certainly well past the sapling stage: sycamore, yew, rowan, ash, holly. The sloping strip of uneven ground had once been a terraced street called Diski Row, which had climbed towards the larger, busier road that still ran along the top of the hill. Every house in the row had been wrecked by the bomb, and the passing of time had finished the job. Now there was a mesh panel fence round it with rusting Keep Out signs, and barbed wire along the top.

But in various places holes had been wrenched in the fencing and, alone or with friends, Hyacinth would slip inside almost every day and head to a favourite spot among the trees which couldn't be seen from anywhere outside. Usually she and her friends had the whole wood to themselves, but they weren't the only ones who knew about it. Other people came there to have sex, smoke dope or drink cheap booze, and it was also used for small-scale fly-tipping, solvent sniffing, and masturbating over pornographic magazines. Each of these activities left behind its own distinctive archaeology so that, along with rusty fridges, broken TVs and spilling sacks of rubbish, there were broken cider bottles, glue-smeared polythene bags, used condoms (whose contents, she learnt, shrank and turned yellow as it dried), empty cigarette packets with neat little rectangles of cardboard torn out of them, and little autumnal drifts of flesh-coloured torn-up porn. (Hyacinth was puzzled about these drifts. Why not just leave them in the wood if you didn't want to take them home? It was only when she'd learnt a little more about male lust and the way it switched off like a light when it had performed its function, that she realized how the wood's little tribe of wankers, having reached their climaxes, would suddenly make the humiliating discovery that the focus of their excitement was nothing more than ink on paper.)

Already in a way an anthropologist, Hyacinth was curious about all these different human tribes who shared her hiding place and, in her mind, they were as much parts of the life of the wood as were the trees that had taken root there, or the foxes and cats that she and her friends sometimes came across when they crawled in through the fence to lose themselves in clouds of oily, aromatic smoke. They saw rats occasionally too, and squirrels, and even a couple of times a small deer, while in early spring the stagnant pools that formed in the footprints of the demolished houses would fill up, first with groaning masses of copulating frog flesh, and then with tadpoles you could scoop from the slime in soft writhing handfuls. The wood was a coalition. It didn't belong to any one of these human and non-human organisms but was a sanctuary for them all, even the sad pervert with the glass eye, who once offered Hyacinth and one of her friends a whole pound note if they'd let him see their knickers.

She felt comfortable there. Back at home she could never tell when her mother's fragile veneer of normality would fall away and she'd lash out suddenly in bitter, tearful rage, while her father hid in the tiny attic room he called his study, knocking back sherry by the tumbler-full and doing supposedly important things with books and paper that no one else would ever give a damn about. Their only child, wherever she went inside the house, she was surrounded by the poisonous force fields that thrummed and crackled between the two adults through the hollow, drab brown rooms. But in her wood, with the foxes, the birds, the tadpoles, and perhaps with a friend or two from equally inhospitable homes, she could do what she pleased and feel sane.

One warm summer day Hyacinth and her friend Tiff found a red ants' nest under a curved fragment of rusty metal which the creatures had used to provide themselves with a solar-heated roof. Tiff turned the metal in her hands. 'What is this anyway? It's quite…. Ow!'

An ant had bitten her and she flung the metal to the ground, but Hyacinth picked it up and shook off the remaining ants. 'Wow! I know what this is, Tiff! It's a piece of the bomb that made this place!'

The two of them had smoked a fair amount of grass. Squatting down with their find, they developed the idea of the bomb as a kind of blind creator god, of which this scrap of metal was a precious relic, and ended up spending the rest of the afternoon constructing a little shrine around it with stones and twigs and chunks of rubble. But as they were emerging from the wood towards evening, they met some young workmen who were bringing up new fencing to replace the damaged panels. The workmen were only a year or two older than Hyacinth and Tiff. They were friendly and weren't particularly bothered by their trespassing. But perhaps they were a little resentful that these posh-voiced girls could spend the afternoon taking drugs and daydreaming while they lugged mesh fencing around North London in a stuffy van, because there was a certain grim satisfaction in their voices as they told Hyacinth and Tiff that their company was about to clear away the remnants of Diski Row to build a block of flats.

So the wood was going to be cut down, bulldozed, covered in concrete, and reconnected to the ordinary London streets that surrounded it. Hyacinth grieved, but not that much. She knew she was beginning to outgrow the place, and she was old enough to understand there wasn't the slightest chance of saving it. This wasn't some piece of ancient woodland, after all, or the last refuge of some endangered species. It was just a lacuna in the fabric of the city, opportunistically taken advantage of by herself, her friends and sundry other life forms. She took some comfort in the thought that, when her wood had gone, all the elements of the coalition that had made it what it was would still exist, ready to take the next opportunity whenever it came.

And that included her. She would find a new refuge, she told herself, perhaps in America, where she was already planning to continue her studies after school, far away from her mother and father. She had no inkling, of course, that one day she would find the Delta, but her wood had given her faith that something would turn up.

It always was a *something* for her, a something or a somewhere, never really a *someone*.

•

This was her seventh time in the Submundo Delta but she still loved the river voyage, even though on some previous trips this enjoyment had been marred by having to share the deck and the dining room with other returnees who affected to be irritated by the length of the journey, or the fact that they couldn't charge their laptops, or the time it was keeping them from their important work. She always found this maddening. Could those people not *see*? Could they not *feel*? Were they so blinkered by the dreary goals trained into them by a society obsessed with its need for control and mastery, that they couldn't appreciate the loosening, the opening out, the rising to the surface, that came with that moment when you realized you'd forgotten the last few days and you were there in the midst of the Delta? You could loathe the place, she could see that, you could fear it, you could be repulsed by it, you could long to be somewhere else, but she couldn't understand how anyone could get bored of it for to her this was the one place on Earth where her emotional responses didn't diminish over time. In fact, sustained intensity when you were in it was one of the Delta's many strange psychic properties, the counterpoint to the effect that occurred when you passed through the Zona the other way and emerged in the world outside. You could still remember that you'd been there – the Submundo wasn't like the Zona – but it was hard to hold on to the *feeling* of the place, and even harder to convey it to other people, who always seemed oddly indifferent to the fact of the Delta's existence.

But to her relief, no one this time was complaining about the length of the journey, or the lack of electric sockets, or the wasted time. Jael dallied on the cargo hatch with the increasingly lobotomized-looking Rico, the two of them clearly returning from one of the regular trips to Nus which they claimed to find energizing.

The unhappy Dutch woman, Mrs de Groot, languished in perpetual pain like a tragic Fisher Queen maimed by some forbidden spear, tended by her loyal but impotent knight. And the other passenger, the British policeman Ben Ronson, was very obviously, and rather endearingly, entranced. He was actually quite nice-looking too, with his thick black hair cut in a boyish, old-fashioned, Second-World-War sort of style, and his startlingly naked blue eyes whose apparent defencelessness he himself of course couldn't see. She found him pleasant to talk to. He had nice manners. He even listened to what was said to him.

After she'd learnt what he did for a living, Hyacinth had dimly remembered reading about some work he'd done in London on forced marriages or some such culturally sanctioned crime. She supposed that, from the perspective of the world outside, where the Delta shrank to a small grey dot on a map which an obscure, not very interested committee in Geneva was supposed to administer, duende killings fitted rather neatly into that same category – crimes committed by a community that didn't consider them to be crimes at all – making Ben an obvious choice to look into them. But of course he had no idea what he was letting himself in for, or what kind of place the Submundo was, and she could see that, rather touchingly, he hadn't even noticed the effect the Delta was already having on him – that opening up, that rising from the depths, that shaking off of old and calloused skin – though it was utterly obvious in his face and his posture. He was still at the stage where he was putting it all down to the novelty of the experience and nothing more.

There was a lot of time to spare and the forest did open you up. Once, while she was drawing, Hyacinth told him about her wood in London, how it had been a refuge to her, and how, absurd as the comparison might seem, what the wood had meant to her back then was something akin to what the Delta meant to her now. He seemed puzzled, but listened and asked questions. It turned out that, when they were growing up, he and Hyacinth had only lived a mile or two apart, and they soon established that he knew all the streets that surrounded Hyacinth's wood, though he couldn't place the wood itself.

'I used to go to Scouts over there,' Ben told her when she mentioned one of these streets, and she almost laughed out loud at the news that he'd been a Scout in his teens – it seemed so fitting somehow – but she saw him flinch in anticipation as he saw the signs of laughter in her face, and she managed to contain it.

'But you must have seen the wood then!' she told him. 'The Scout hut was pretty much opposite the top of it!'

'I vaguely remember a metal fence with bits of crumbling brick wall behind it.'

'That was it! That was the top end of my wood.'

'Oh, I see. I suppose I didn't really think of it as a wood.'

She could tell he was completely bemused by the idea that anyone could feel this sort of attachment to a patch of waste ground.

'Didn't you have somewhere like that?' she asked. 'Some special place that was just your own, where the grown-ups didn't go?'

But he laughed uneasily and said he didn't, he'd always been too busy with 'school, and football and generally getting into trouble'.

In Hyacinth's experience people who talked in that way about 'getting into trouble' were never the type you could imagine getting into any kind of trouble at all, much in the same way as people who said, 'Don't mind me, I'm just crazy,' were always exceptionally conventional and sane. And what kind of trouble could Ben have possibly got into, she wondered, when something as mild as her illicit use of a bombsite as a hiding place from the adult world seemed to strike him as inexplicably weird? When she pressed him a little more about his childhood, he talked about the cinemas he used to go to, the schools he attended, and the football team he supported, but seemed to find it difficult to come up with anything more than these shells and containers.

'To be honest, I can barely remember it,' he said, 'which is probably because it was so boring and average. Nothing at all like yours, by the sound of it.'

III. THE POLICEMAN

(5)

It was his first night for a month in a decent bed and Ben had promised himself a long sleep, but he actually woke very early and decided to go outside for a walk. Mrs Martin – he hadn't yet brought himself to call her Nicky – was already up and eager to know what he'd have for breakfast, but he told her on this occasion he'd take coffee in the town.

'Well, if you're sure.' She looked dismayed. 'We have fresh croissants and coffee all ready.'

'Much appreciated, but I need the air this morning, I think, before the day gets too warm.'

One of these days, he found himself thinking as he emerged into the warm moist air outside, if he wasn't very careful, when he was tired and discouraged, or had been made to feel that he didn't know what he was doing, he would take from Mrs Martin what she was so obviously offering him. He would let her kiss him, and tell him how wonderful he was. And she'd offer him more and more, dote on him, mother him, tend to him, and at the same time, if that's what he seemed to want, submit to him as if she was a helpless child. And it would feel great for about half an hour and then he'd feel sick.

He walked down to the waterfront, through streets that were still very quiet: a little grocery shop here, a small café there with a single customer sitting at the bar. In the harbour, the boat that had brought him was still docked, along with the submarine and a couple of other vessels. To the east, beyond the harbour wall, the smooth water of the Lethe, here almost half a mile wide, flowed on round the northern end of the rocky island on which Amizad was built. Looking in that direction, the forest was in the distance, the far shore, another place entirely. But just to the south of the town, Ben knew from the little town map that was provided in his room, it came right up to the rock itself, and you could simply walk straight out into it.

On a bench in the middle of the quay, he spotted Hyacinth, sketching in charcoal in a large pad.

'Good morning. Drawing already?'

'Hello there, Mr Policeman. Yes, it's a nice way to start the day.'

He sat on the bench beside her. 'I'm not really a policeman, you know.'

He wondered immediately why he'd said it, for he'd always despised people in authority who tried to wriggle out of the role they themselves had chosen to play. And Hyacinth seemed to feel the same because she frowned and said nothing at all, still scratching away at a detail of the water at the southern edge of the harbour.

'Well, I *am* a policeman, of course I am,' he corrected himself, 'and very happy to be one. What I meant was that it wasn't my life's ambition. I have other interests. I considered other careers. Like many people, I studied for a degree and then looked around for something I could do, and this just happened to come up.'

She laughed. 'Well, you seem like a policeman to me. I saw you that way even before you told me what you did.' She glanced down at the drawing she'd been working on. 'I'll tell you what. If you've got ten minutes, I'll draw you.'

Well, why not? Ben thought. He settled into a more sustainable pose, and she flipped over a page and began to draw again. 'So what have you got on today, Ben?'

'Nothing until eleven, when I've got a meeting with the police chief here and the Head Administrator.'

'Da Ponte and Tiler. Ha.' She scratched away with her charcoal, making a series of long curves. 'Good luck with that.'

'You know them?'

'I've met them a few times. This is their world. They've been here a long time. Everyone has to develop their own way of coping with the Delta if they're here for more than a few months, and they've both learnt to manage by keeping very very still.' She paused, held the pad further away from herself to see the effect.

'I've got to admit,' he said, 'that my understanding of this place is so limited that I do wonder what a meeting's going to achieve.'

'Well, cancel it, then,' she said, resuming her scratching. 'They won't mind. In fact, I'm sure they'd rather you cancelled it altogether. There's a call box just over there, look. Dial one for Administration. Leave a message. Then I suggest you go out into the forest. Meet some Mundinos. And hopefully a duende or two. I promise you, until that's happened, you'll have no idea at all what you're talking about.'

'Because of this disturbing effect they're supposed to have?'

She was taking another pause, holding out her picture and looking back and forth with sharp critical eyes between the picture and his face. '"Supposed to have",' she repeated. 'Ha! There really are things you need to experience before you do anything else.' She made a mark, considered it, rubbed at it with her finger. 'Oh and by the way,' she said, 'everyone here knows that you're here about the duende killings, so you can probably afford to relax that whole "need to know" thing.' She glanced at him, scratched away at the paper, glanced at him again. 'Tough assignment. How to stop people you know nothing about from killing a creature you've never encountered.'

'That's about it, I'm afraid,' he said, thinking he'd take her advice and put the meeting off for a day.

They sat in silence for a while, him looking southwards along the quay, her glancing back and forth between his face and her page, sketching, pausing, sketching again. It was an odd thing to have his face examined quite so closely, simply as a physical object.

'Oh look,' he said presently. 'There's Jael and Rico.' The two of them had arrived and sat down four benches away. They had cakes of some kind in a paper bag. Rico had his guitar. He stretched out his arms and his long thin legs, graceful and fluent as a cat, and as he did so he glanced across at Ben and winked. Ben looked away uneasily.

'Yeah?' Hyacinth adjusted some detail in her drawing and didn't look round. 'Keep your head still, please. You've moved.'

'They're a strange pair.'

'Sure are.'

'Just a couple of drug-addled hippies, I suppose.'

'Bit more than that.' Hyacinth opened a box and selected a finer piece of charcoal. 'Jael's work was once going to be the next big thing in science. Jael Tarn. Have you not heard of her?'

'Do you know what, I think I have. I think I read something a few years ago. It's just that ...'

'I know. You don't expect to see a famous scientist acting like she does. She used to work on the interface between biology, subatomic physics and psychology. It was very original stuff. But she came down here and chucked it all in. Decided it was beside the point.'

'And Rico?'

She shrugged. 'He *is* just a drug-addled hippy, as far as I can tell. Can't say I get what she sees in him, but it seems he's useful to her.' She paused, held the picture at arm's length again, nodded. 'Anyway, here you are, Ben. I'm done. What do you think?'

She held up the pad and there he was, a little sterner in the face than he would prefer to see himself, a little more single-minded in the eyes, but she'd absolutely got those taut muscles in his cheeks and jaw, whose tension he could feel from inside, like steel cables. He was, unmistakably, a policeman.

The phone box was a British one, except that it was painted in pale United Nations blue and had been adapted for the American coins that were used in the Delta Protectorate. Ben put a dime in the slot, phoned in a message postponing the meeting, then headed off southwards through the town, thinking to walk out into the forest. There were a few more people on the streets now, about half of them local Mundinos as far as he could tell, and half international visitors like himself. He passed another café with four or five customers inside, and a butcher's shop, and a small, dark 'International Book Store'. In a shop called Fantini's, which was also a diner of sorts, he bought himself a French loaf, a bottle of lemonade and some cooked chicken.

'*Obrigada, senhora,*' he said to Mrs Fantini, trying out the Portuguese he'd been mugging up on since he took his post.

'*De nada,*' she told him, with a smile that struck him as sly, though not unfriendly. On the wall behind her a miniature

Iya hung from a nail, watching Ben blankly with her little stone eyes.

Almost at the end of the town (it was only a dozen streets wide), there was a little place with a prettily painted shopfront that sold ceramic ornaments. Ben was surprised by this – was there really a market for such things in Amizad? – and, out of curiosity, stepped inside. There was a shelf of quaint Mundino characters in traditional dress, and a row of ceramic clock towers – the little town's Eiffel Tower – but what caught his eye were the figurines of duendes in various sizes. At this point, he'd still only seen duendes in photographs – and very blurry ones at that, for the creatures didn't photograph well for reasons not yet understood – but nevertheless he was startled by the way that they were presented here, with vulnerable, almost beseeching eyes, and hands stretched out as if offering friendship. He was turning one over in his hand when the owner of the shop came out of a back room where she'd been working, drying her hands on a piece of rag.

'That's ten dollars if you'd like it,' she said, and then, 'You must be the new policeman. How do you do? My name is Justine.'

He shook her hand. She was a Frenchwoman, a few years older than himself, quite tall and thin, with large eyes and delicate features, and somehow fragile, like her own creations. She wore green school sandals and had her hair in a single long plait that hung most of the way down her back.

'From what I've read about duendes,' he said, 'I never thought I'd see a cute one in a gift shop.' He realized at once that he'd said the wrong thing. She wasn't a confident enough person to be angry, but instead she visibly shrivelled. And Ben understood that, in her mind, this was *not* a gift shop, and that what he had assumed to be a sentimental and formulaic souvenir was to her a work of art, an expression of what she wanted to think of as her deepest or truest self. 'Beautifully made,' he added hastily. 'And how amazing that each one is different.'

She rallied a little. 'I try to bring out the life in them. I try to show that these creatures too are children of the same universe as ourselves.' Her eyes moistened slightly. 'The Mundinos butcher them in their thousands, you know. I do hope you're going to be able to help them. The poor things can't speak for themselves, so I make these little figures to do it for them.'

'That's … that's very commendable. I'll certainly buy one. But I'm going for a walk now, so perhaps you could keep it for me until my return.'

'With pleasure. Where will you walk?'

'I thought I'd go into the forest.'

She looked startled. 'On your own, on foot?'

'That's right.' He jiggled the model duende in his hand. 'Who knows, I might find one of these chaps for real.'

Soon after Justine's shop, the road, which had hitherto followed the waterfront, curved inland to avoid a small rocky outcrop that marked the end of the town and of the stretch of the River Lethe that came right up to Amizad. Having avoided this lump of rock – it was the core of a volcanic side vent – the road continued along the edge of the much larger Rock which was the island on which Amizad stood. But here there was no town and no Lethe. To Ben's right, in place of houses and roads, a waste of stone and earth, apparently completely bare of vegetation, rose up to the extinct volcanos that formed the crest of the island. Several research stations were visible near the top, along with the aerials and parabolic dishes that were busy measuring the perturbations in space and time that set the Delta apart from the rest of the planet. And to his left, where the river had been, there was now the forest, abutting directly on to the rock. He was right next to it at last. There were spiral magenta leaves above his head, white helices dangling down within his reach, opening their lovely pink bells.

A hundred yards further along the road he came to a track that headed straight out into the trees. He hesitated, feeling suddenly very nervous. But he knew there were no *real* dangers in the forest – no carnivorous animals, no venomous insects or snakes – and besides, the physical sensation of fear seemed very close indeed to the feeling of desire: so close, in fact, that it was hard to distinguish the one from the other. As he took his first step off the Rock and on to the forest track, he felt like a young boy on the way to his first sexual encounter.

The track was made of living wood. Feet and wheels going back and forth had worn through the thin layer of compost and down to the matrix of entangled roots beneath, polishing the roots themselves until they were shining and smooth. He stood there for a few seconds, just inside the threshold, and then began to walk, under those big magenta trees with their countless spirals, until the Rock was out of sight. In the warm, moist air, the aroma was almost overpowering – caramel and lilies, sweet and bitter, along with that other scent that had no name – and the whole place was extraordinarily quiet. No birdsong, no hum of insects, only sometimes the faint groaning and creaking from the wood itself that he'd listened to in his nights on the boat. Away through the trees, patches of sunlight revealed ponds, pools and channels, each one silent and alone, or so they appeared, though in reality all of them were simply openings into one continuous sea.

The track crossed a channel on a rough wooden bridge. Pinkish underwater weeds undulated gently in the slow northward flow towards the main channel of the Lethe, each a kind of necklace of bead-like, spiral-bearing nodules with only a superficial resemblance to plants in the world outside. According to the briefing notes that Ben had read, there were two theories about the life of the Delta. One: it was of extraterrestrial origin. Two: it was of terrestrial origin but completely unrelated to the rest of life on Earth, having arisen separately from inanimate matter.

Fifty yards off a single punt was being slowly poled away from him by someone who didn't look back, pushing the boat steadily forward through purple reed-like growth.

Later that morning, near a hand-painted sign that indicated a Mundino village to the south, he passed three women and a little boy carrying firewood, and then, a mile later, two men repairing a canoe on the banks of a small channel. They all greeted him pleasantly, but, so it seemed to him, with that same slyness that he'd noticed in the shopkeeper, Mrs Fantini. And he felt there was something dreamy about all of them. They were immersed in their own world, waist-deep in it, as the trees were waist-deep in their secret sea. They seemed happy enough to stir from this state, to respond, to act, but happy too to return to it when the need for action had passed.

But perhaps this impression was just a reflection of how he himself was feeling. There was a remarkable intensity about that first walk. Often he'd stop because it seemed to him that some particular combination of tree trunks, spiralling branches, pools, light and shade formed a kind of hieroglyph which, if only he studied it for long enough, would yield up some sort of secret. Several times he made diversions to sunlit pools he saw through the trees because they seemed like stages in a theatre, waiting for some mysterious performance to begin. And even though no one appeared and nothing happened, that very absence of action or actors seemed more charged with significance than any play he'd ever seen.

Once he passed an old woman, completely naked, sitting all by herself with her feet in the water on the far side of a lake. She was surrounded by a cloud of those white helical flowers, which, one by one, she was slowly pulling towards her mouth to suck out the honey-milk. He called out '*bom dia*' to her, and she looked in his direction with a small smile, but it wasn't a smile of greeting, more the sort of smile that sometimes comes to a person's face on noticing some pleasing detail in a landscape. She didn't seem to notice the golden milk that was dripping from her chin.

Soon after that a large flock of those iridescent bluebirds arrived, at least a hundred of them, hovering above him, their wings whirring. They alighted on the branches of nearby trees to watch him in complete silence from among the profusion of entwined magenta spirals. Then suddenly they seemed to relax, as if in the exact same moment every single one of them had concluded that he wasn't something that required their attention. After a few seconds they flew away again, all at once.

He was on his way back, but still a few miles from the town, when the shadows began to lengthen and the pools and channels to glow with a faint phosphorescence. The sun went down quickly at that latitude. In the rapidly deepening dusk, now about a mile from Amizad, and shortly after recrossing the bridge, he noticed three people up ahead of him, silhouetted at the side of the path, watching him approach. He'd passed another group about half an hour previously – young Mundino labourers taking time out to unwind and smoke on the way back to their village from a job in Amizad – and he assumed these would be more of the same.

But, though he'd quite enjoyed his previous encounters with the locals, this time he was wearied by the prospect. It felt tiresome, having just settled back into a delightful solitude, to have to put on his social mask again, and perform his allotted role. For the fact was that, whatever Hyacinth might say or think, the role he played didn't really feel like *him* at all. He felt at sea in the world and the discipline she had seen in his face was the result of a constant effort to focus his will on visible and achievable goals. But Hyacinth was subtle, he thought, and, though she seemed to quite like him in an amused sort of way, he was sure she'd never be really interested, however much he'd like to touch her, to reach her skin, however much he longed to break out of this cage of muscle and bone in which he'd somehow confined himself. For he couldn't break out into the world as others did, and why would someone like Hyacinth be interested in a man like that?

These thoughts, oddly urgent for some reason, and strangely loud, were rushing through his mind as he drew nearer to the three figures beside the path. For God's sake, he reprimanded himself, why was he thinking of Hyacinth at all, when really he hardly knew her? And why did he so constantly worry about the impression he made on women anyway? It's not as if he really wanted to *be* with a woman. Women always let him down, and anyway, as soon as a woman actually took an interest in him, he—

But then he realized for the first time that he'd been mistaken in thinking that the figures watching him approach were Mundino labourers. They weren't Mundinos, they weren't men or women, they weren't human beings at all.

He would have liked to have turned and walked quickly away from them but where they were sitting was the only way he knew back to Amizad, so he had no choice but to go straight past them. He walked very slowly, refusing to listen to the babble inside his head, and about ten yards away from them, he stopped to give them a chance to move away. Given that the locals killed them on sight, he thought, surely they'd want to take the opportunity of removing themselves from the reach of a human being? But they didn't. Still squatting side by side, the three of them watched him. He could see their little black button eyes now, their identical V-shaped smiles. The one in the middle was stroking the ground with its long fingers, the others were completely motionless. He did not want to face them. He found them repugnant. He loathed their rubbery flesh, their lack of anything resembling humanity, and, if he'd had an axe with him, or a crowbar, or a shotgun, he would cheerfully have smashed their mindless mockeries of smiles. And yet in spite of this strange eruption of violent rage, some part of his normal outer self was still present, like a solitary flagbearer in the chaos of a battlefield, reminding him that, whether he liked these creatures or not was beside the point: he was a policeman, they were entitled to their lives, and he was here in the Delta to protect them.

The three duendes watched him silently. He could see pink blotches on their grey rubbery skin now, and rows of tiny grey flecks within the pinkness. He was looking straight at their mask-like, noseless faces, their shiny round black eyes. And something behind those eyes was looking back at him.

He felt dizzy. The cacophony in his head was deafening now: voices, emotions, phrases, images, banal fragments of songs blaring out, one on top of another. If you go down to the woods today, you're sure of a … Hateful, disgusting creatures. He'd love to smash them to pieces, smash and stamp and slash, let out all that rage, smash down the wall, climb up out of his grave … But no, no, no, not really. What was the point? It was all shit anyway. He'd still be no good. No one was any good. She wasn't going to be any different, of course. Every bear that ever there was … They never blinked, did they? Not so much as a flicker. Their eyes stripped you naked, somehow – a bare bear, ha ha, bare bear, bare bear – they stripped you down to the bone.

Something inside of him was keeping up a constant din of meaningless babble, and bad puns that reduced words to empty sounds, and mocking challenges to every apparently genuine thought or feeling, each one of which was immediately contradicted, peeled away, rendered meaningless. There was something hysterical about this, something manic, as if in thousands of chambers all round him lurked shapes and forms – memories, objects of desire, nightmares – that, without this racket to distract him, he would have no choice but to look out at and see. And meanwhile beneath him, as the black unblinking eyes watched his approach, an enormous pit descended through hundreds of storeys into a dreadful realm of pure abstract form.

He was right next to the duendes and they were watching him.

'Good evening,' he croaked, and carried on, forcing himself not to look back until he was a good fifty yards past them. They were still there. He could just make out the silhouettes of their heads. Even now they were watching him.

'Mummy's good boy,' said a voice inside his head. It was his own voice, but he heard it as if it was someone else. 'Mummy's boy. Mummy's good good boy. No bad thoughts at all.'

•

It was completely dark when he arrived back in Amizad. He'd been walking with only the light of a big half-moon and the glow of pools and channels through the trees, from which, a couple of times, he'd seen strange, shadowy creatures emerging. But it was still only half past eight in the evening and, as he passed her shop near the edge of town, the potter Justine was just shutting up. He didn't want to see her. He didn't want to have to look into her eyes, but, as he tried to hurry past, she spotted him and came out with the figurine he'd bought earlier.

'Hello! Mr Ronson! How was your walk in the forest? Don't forget your little duende!'

So he took the simpering symbol of human–duende under-standing and threw it into the harbour on his way back to the hotel.

(6)

Please don't think for a moment,' said Katherine Tiler, 'that we don't understand the gravity of the problem, or the need to ad-dress it. All Ernesto and I are asking for is some sensitivity to the cultural context, and some understanding of the resource constraints.'

The postponed meeting was happening. The room was dim and brown and, in spite of the open windows and the two fans slowly revolving overhead, uncomfortably hot and stale. Feeling himself beginning to sweat already, Ben sat at one end of the table, Katherine Tiler at the other. To Ben's left, was the police chief Da Ponte. The small stature of both of them made Ben feel unnaturally large.

He had papers in front of him, a digest he'd compiled himself from a series of reports that had been sent to him by the Protectorate Agency, and a list of queries he'd wanted to clear up. His notepad and pen lay ready beside them. He cleared his throat. A huge distance seemed to separate Ben as he was now from the Ben that, back in May, had convinced an interview panel in another dim and woody room in Geneva that he was the one for this job.

'To restate the current position,' he said, 'now that the agency has determined that duendes should be regarded as persons, the practice of killing them is equivalent to murder under international law, and it simply can't be ignored any longer. We need to get a handle on this problem. We need a much better picture of just how many duendes are being killed. We need to build a new culture in which duende killing isn't acceptable. And, of course, we need to start arresting and prosecuting perpetrators. I appreciate your resources are stretched, and probably we need to address that, but I hope you can see that doing nothing is not an option.'

They regarded him in silence: not a hostile silence exactly, but a bland, polite silence, waiting to make sure he'd finished.

'I think it was a good idea of yours to go into the forest yesterday,' the Chief Administrator finally observed. 'I think it's important to really get to grips with local conditions before jumping to any conclusions.'

'You're not the first to say that.'

Tiler inclined her head in acknowledgement. 'I'm not surprised. This is a very strange place, as you will have gathered already, and nothing works in the way it would do in the world outside. I'm still learning, and I've been here for twenty years. Ernesto, of course, was born here.'

'Ha! I was indeed,' said Da Ponte, 'but even I don't understand it. Did you encounter any duendes during your wanderings, Inspector?'

'Yes, I did.'

'Ah.' Da Ponte seemed almost to smirk under his large moustache. 'And how did you find the experience?'

'It was disturbing, of course. But I anticipated that.'

'You can begin to imagine, perhaps, how difficult it would be to have such creatures coming right into the village where you live, crawling up out of the water, climbing on your roof with their suckered feet, peering round the edges of your doors?'

'Indeed, but that's not a reason to kill them. Other ways need to be found to manage this. Fences round the villages, for example.'

Katherine nodded, slowly and a very large number of times, as if digesting a profound and difficult truth. Ben passed his hand over his slippery forehead. In the square below, someone shouted a greeting to a friend, and the sound coming through the open window served to emphasize the leaden silence inside the room.

'I had a few questions to ask you both,' Ben said, picking up the piece of paper with his list of queries.

But Katherine Tiler was already pushing back her chair. 'No problem,' she said, holding out her hand. 'Give them to me, and I'll arrange to have the answers left for you on your desk.'

He knew he should ask to go through them now. They were straightforward practical questions and she could probably answer a lot of them straight away. But somehow he lacked the energy.

'I should like to be informed of any new duende killings,' he told Tiler as she opened the door for him. 'I would like to be involved in the investigations. Can you please ensure that happens?'

'Absolutely,' she said. 'No problem at all. Isn't that right, Ernesto?'

'Of course.' Da Ponte sucked for a moment on his moustache, and glanced across at his boss. 'If you wish, Inspector, I can call you at the hotel as soon as a report comes in.'

'That would be good. Please do, regardless of the time of day or night.'

It occurred to Ben that Tiler had mentioned something about him having a desk here, and he should ask where it was but, now he had the option of an open door, he couldn't bring himself to delay things even for a few minutes more.

In the square, people were gathering at the café tables. They were outsiders rather than locals, scientists and administrators working at the various research stations on the slopes above the town: bright, able professionals, many of them quite young, who came from all over the world, though mainly, of course, from North America. In front of the Café Lisboa, the smaller and less popular of the two cafés, there was just one table left with no one sitting at it, though a coffee cup and an ashtray had yet to be cleared, and he decided to stop there, have a look through his papers over a coffee, and consider his next move. Or so he put it to himself anyway, though it was questionable whether he'd yet made a move at all.

His coffee had arrived, and he was leafing through his papers, making notes and just beginning to feel almost as though he was doing something useful, when someone sat down in the seat opposite. It was Jael, who he'd last seen on the quay with her boyfriend Rico. Ben was uneasy at once: there was something boundaryless about the two of them which he didn't feel comfortable with at all. She looked at him completely blankly when he greeted her. 'I'm Ben,' he reminded her. 'We were on the boat together.'

She nodded as she took out a cigarette. 'Of course! The policeman. Here to rescue the duendes.'

'I gather you're a biologist?'

'I was.'

'So what is your take on the origins of the lifeforms in the Delta? Extraterrestrial. Or terrestrial like us?'

She watched him intently for a moment, then blew out smoke. 'Why just those two options? For all we know, they could be a relic population of the original life of Earth and *we* could have an extraterrestrial origin.'

She glanced out into the square and waved. Her boyfriend was over there, Ben now saw. Rico looked as if he'd just returned from some errand. He gave Ben a thumbs-up and, in that graceful cat-like way he had, squatted down under the clock tower. What an obnoxious person he is, Ben thought with a sudden burst of anger, disliking Rico intensely even as he watched in fascination the way his slender limbs moved. He had met so many people like him in his police work, people who called themselves anarchists, lived in squats or housing cooperatives, claimed benefits, switched promiscuously from one sexual relationship to the next, and thought that just because they'd abdicated all responsibility for anything whatsoever that happened in the world, they were somehow morally superior to those like him who were actually trying to keep the wheels of the world turning.

'Rico and I aren't very interested in such questions,' Jael said, turning back to Ben with a brief, functional smile. He didn't like her either, but she was a very different kind of creature from Rico. He felt that whatever he said to her, she would be able to bat away without even making an effort, like a tennis champion facing some clumsy amateur across the net. 'Those sorts of questions tickle our curiosity, of course,' she said, 'but they're essentially trivial and answering them is really little more than a kind of stamp-collecting. It gives everyone a vague warm sense that our knowledge is growing and humanity is becoming ever more important, but it doesn't really get you anywhere at all.'

'But these days we're making huge strides in so many fields!'

She leant forward to look straight into his eyes and, very disconcertingly, did not look away again. 'Huge strides? Are we? Whoever "we" might be. Well, perhaps "we" are, but it doesn't matter how big the steps are if the distance is infinite, does it? The destination remains as far away as ever. People fill in the gaps between the things we know with pretty words or trivial facts so they don't have to see their ignorance stretching away to infinity, but that's how it is all the same.'

She examined Ben's face, seemingly amused by his obvious resistance to what she was saying.

'What Rico and I have found,' she said, 'is that you have to go another way entirely if you actually want to understand, and not just acquire pretty stamps to stick in your album.' Ben had looked a little away from her to avoid her gaze, but she now moved her head even further forward so that he was forced to look at her again. 'You have to start from the position that you already know how things are,' she said, 'and that you aren't an outsider in this universe. The Greeks had a word for it. *Alethia*. Unforgetting. Truth isn't something out there, in other words. It's something we already possess but have temporarily forgotten.'

Ben wasn't sure how to respond to this. Silly New Agey nonsense, it sounded to him, but he knew Jael would easily demolish any attempt he made to challenge it. 'I didn't realize Rico was a scientist too,' he said.

Jael laughed. 'Oh, he is, he is.' She glanced across at her boyfriend, who was sitting with the guitar on his lap, his head tipped back and his eyes rolled upwards, as if he'd temporarily forgotten where he was. 'He's a true scientist. Untarnished by any training whatsoever. How are you getting on with your enquiries?'

'Well, I've made a start,' Ben said warily.

She blew out more smoke. 'You can hardly expect the Mundinos to love the creatures, can you, when they climb out of the creeks at night and fuck with their heads? The Mundinos aren't philosophers, after all. Why would they be?' Still watching Ben's face, she smiled. 'Why, if you lived in a place like this, would you want to be something as dumb as a philosopher?'

'This … this fucking with their heads, as you call it,' he said. 'Have you any thoughts about how it works?'

She laughed, glancing across once more at Rico over at the clock tower. He was running his fingers over his guitar but not really playing it, and Ben realized he was just filling in time, waiting for Ben to leave so he could come over and join Jael.

She turned back to Ben. 'You've experienced it yourself by the look of you. Am I right?' She nodded. 'Okay, so you know what it's like. The locals think the duendes put nasty things into their minds, and I'm sure you'll agree that's understandable, but really all the duendes do is break down barriers. Things already inside your head – half-thoughts and feelings that you don't normally acknowledge – become as powerful as the things you normally choose to focus on.' She laughed. 'Which is unsettling, because it undermines your sense of being a consistent person and reveals all the sides of you that you've been busy denying or projecting on to others. Liberals find out they're really conservatives. High-minded egalitarians discover their elitist contempt for common people. Nice, well-behaved, respectful men discover their buried rage towards women.' She watched the policeman's face, clearly amused to see how uncomfortable she was making him, and trying to guess which item on her list in particular the duendes had uncovered in him. 'It's hard to cope with,' she said. 'Unless you're Rico, that is. They really don't bother him at all.'

Ben looked across at Rico who gave him another thumbs-up. A flock of those blue iridescent birds arrived in the town square, whirled round it twice, regarding everyone there with their small, hard, jewel-like eyes, and disappeared again in the direction of the Lethe. It made Ben notice for the first time that there were normally no birds there – none at all – unlike every other town square he'd ever been in. He thought perhaps he'd seen a pigeon the previous day, a single bedraggled pigeon that had strayed in from outside, but if so it was no longer here now, and perhaps he was remembering some other place and time. He laid some coins on the table and stood up to go.

A woman rose from a table at the other café and came hurrying over as Ben crossed the square, a youngish woman, with a long, serious face and black hair.

'Hi. My name is Mary Boldero. I'm a biologist at one of the research units here. I believe you're the policeman who's come to do something about the duende killings, yes? Great! My friends and I,' she gestured towards her table where a couple of bearded men and a woman with blonde hair were sitting, 'we wanted you to know that we are absolutely on your side on this. *Absolutely* on your side. Along with the entire scientific community here in Amizad. If we can help in any way at all, please don't hesitate to ask.'

She pressed Ben to join them. 'Just for a few minutes,' she insisted, when he seemed reluctant. So he walked over to the bearded men and the blonde woman, shook their hands and accepted the seat they fetched for him from another table.

'It's absolutely appalling what's going on,' one of the men said. 'If these were human beings we'd call it genocide. And, whatever you do, please don't listen to anyone who tells you it's an occasional problem. The fact is that duendes are being routinely slaughtered all over the Delta on a daily basis, and all because of ignorance, superstition and prejudice. The locals even boast about it if you give them half a chance. This is *nineteen ninety*, for God's sake!'

'And of course the police are all locals,' the other man said. 'You need to be aware of that, Inspector.'

'I'm sure he is, Charles,' Mary told him. 'This guy's not just any cop. You should see his CV.'

The man called Charles nodded. 'Of course. Apologies, Inspector, I didn't mean to tell you how to do your job.'

They were bright, highly educated people, Ben could see, part of a community of bright, highly educated people, used to being much sharper and better-informed than anyone they met from outside of their circle, and no doubt frequently frustrated, as clever people are, by the stubborn ignorance and resistance to logic of most of the human race. You met people like this in the police force too. Certain forensic scientists, for instance. Because they thought more quickly than other people, and saw things that others missed, they didn't always understand their own blinkers.

'We know almost nothing about the duendes,' Mary said, 'but we know enough to realize how amazing they are. They build these so-called castelos, for instance. You've probably heard of them? Architecture in miniature. Extraordinary, intricate, exquisitely beautiful structures.'

'You should see them, Inspector,' Charles said. 'Each one is unique. Incredibly complex. Detail within detail down to the microscopic level.'

'Of course the Mundinos kick them to pieces whenever they find them,' the second woman said.

Charles made a gesture of impotence and exasperation. 'It's just ignorance and superstition, of course, and we need to remember that. But still, you can't help wondering sometimes how the Mundinos can possible fail to see the beauty of it all.'

Mary sighed. 'It's just lucky they can't reach the underwater structures.'

'I guess you're aware, Inspector,' the other man said, 'that the duendes may be the offspring of trees?'

Ben laughed. 'No? You're kidding?'

'He's not,' Mary told him. 'You should come down in our sub sometime. You can see the duende larvae in their pods, hanging from the roots above. We don't understand how genetics works in the Delta lifeforms because there's no DNA equivalent, but it's increasingly looking like they and the trees they grow from may be a single dimorphic species.'

'That's incredible,' Ben said.

'Bear in mind that we aren't really looking at "animals" or "plants" here in the Delta,' Charles said. 'Parallel evolution makes it less obvious, but our usual categories just don't apply. And there are so many other mysteries to solve as well. It's incredibly frustrating that all this isn't better known.'

'Mysteries such as ...?'

'Well, basically life in the Delta just doesn't follow our normal assumptions at all,' Mary said. 'For instance: life everywhere else is opportunistic, but here there are dozens of ecological niches standing empty. Why do so few creatures come out in the day, for instance? Why are there scavengers but no predators? Really obvious opportunities are left untouched, while substantial energy goes into things with no obvious survival value at all.'

'There is just so much work to do here,' Charles said. 'So much to find out. So much to look at. And letting the Mundinos carry on killing the duendes and destroy their structures makes about as much sense as … I don't know … letting a bunch of homeless kids light bonfires in the Sistine Chapel or spray paint the walls, just because they've had a rough deal and we feel sorry for them. It's madness. It makes no sense whatsoever.'

'There are only a few thousand Mundinos,' Mary said. 'It's great you're here, Inspector, but could we not just pay them all compensation or something and move the whole lot of them back to Brazil? I mean, why do they need to be in the Submundo at all? They didn't choose to come here in the first place. What good does it do them or anyone else for them to remain here?'

There was a new guest at the hotel that night. A tanned, tall, very fit-looking American man, with penetrating grey eyes. Mrs Martin was all over him and, even though he didn't like her, Ben still felt a pang of jealousy.

'Hi, I'm Tim Dolby,' the American called out cheerily across the dining room, where he and Ben sat alone at their tables. 'May I join you? It would be easier to talk.'

He was wearing a white linen shirt open at the collar, and close-fitting black jeans. 'I'm an evil oilman,' he said, as he settled himself opposite Ben. 'You know, one of those guys that everyone says is bad, and everyone uses the stuff he gets for them.'

Ben asked him what had brought him there. Given the time it

took to get in and out of the Submundo, he assumed it must be important.

'Oh, just sniffing round, you know,' Dolby said, 'the way we evil oilmen do. No, but seriously, though, what a place! *What – a – place!* Can't believe that I've lost several days of my life. No recollection at all of that other town in the Zona there. Almost exactly like this one, if you look at the photos, same street plan and everything, but I have no memory of it at all. Mind-blowing, isn't it?'

He shook his head as if to rid himself of that particular set of thoughts, and composed his face into a serious and concerned expression. 'But that's enough about my little adventure! I hear *you're* actually here to do something useful. Trying to stop these duendes being killed, Mrs Martin tells me. She seems to be a big fan of yours. Rightly so. That's important work. Unique life forms, and, if this is the right word, a unique civilization. Absolutely vital that they're protected. It would be good to talk to you about it sometime. I really mean that. Seems to me you'll need quite a lot in the way of resources to see through a task like yours and my company has big pockets, and likes to help out where it can. Not *quite* so evil as people think.'

(7)

Hyacinth was by the waterfront again. She had her pad and the zip-up bag that held her pencils and charcoal, but hadn't yet started drawing. Ben was glad to see her. She was the one person in Amizad that he was fairly sure he liked.

'I thought you'd be out doing fieldwork in Mundino villages.'

'I thought you'd be out there saving duendes!' she said. 'You don't look very happy, Ben.'

'Things are a bit frustrating. But I expected that. I'll find a way. I always do.'

'I guess a post like yours is created to placate some interest group or other, isn't it? To tick some box for them? Some interest group far away from here that doesn't understand very much or even care very much, but needs to feel that it's doing something?'

'I suppose so.' He couldn't see why she thought this would be comforting.

'But you're not happy just to tick the box? You want to make a difference, yes? To feel that you're doing what you can to make the world a better place?'

'Well, of course. Isn't that what we're supposed to do?'

'Is it? I'm not sure. I do my job because I find it interesting and someone is willing to pay me to do it. I wouldn't do it if I thought it was harmful, but I don't think I take responsibility for making the world a better place. Apart from anything else, it would make me extremely anxious, seeing that it's pretty much impossible to act in this world without unintended consequences or unconscious motives.'

She opened her pad and began to draw. 'I wonder why the duendes don't just leave people alone,' Ben said. 'There must be so much forest where there are no humans at all, and I can't see that the Mundinos would worry about them if they didn't keep coming into their villages.'

'The Mundinos say that the duendes keep coming because they want to take over their minds.'

'Yes, but those are superstitions, surely? Duendes have never harmed anyone, not if you look at the science. Jael says that all they do is make you notice things in your head that normally you'd barely be aware of.'

'So you've been talking to Jael?'

'I ran into her.'

Hyacinth made a few more marks on her pad, frowned down at it for a moment, and then laid it down on the bench. 'All I'll say is that Mundinos have been living alongside duendes for more than a century. They must have learnt something, don't you think?'

'Of course, but that's not to say that—'

He was interrupted by loud shrieks. Mrs de Groot was racing along the quay, wearing nothing but a flimsy pink nightdress, and she was heading southwards, to where the road led round to the forest.

A teenage boy in a hotel porter's uniform was running after her, followed by two young women receptionists in smart suits and bare feet. 'Mrs de Groot!' they were both pleading. 'Please! Let us help you! Let us look after you! Really, Mrs de Groot. Please!' They were from the Bristol, Amizad's other hotel, just across the square from the Bem-Vindo. They must have kicked off their shoes to help them run.

Mr de Groot came after. He was trying to run too, but he was exhausted and dangerously overheated in his crumpled white tropical suit, his face red and pouring with sweat. He stopped to catch his breath.

'Be careful, Mr de Groot,' Hyacinth called out to him. 'You could hurt yourself. I'm sure those young people will fetch her back.'

He looked at her but didn't answer. He drew breath in great whooping gasps, his eyes magnified to double their size by his thick glasses, and then headed off again after his wife.

Ben looked at Hyacinth. 'What was going on there? Shouldn't we do something?'

She shrugged. 'This place has that effect sometimes. She'll tire herself out soon and then they'll bring her back. Meanwhile, she's having the time of her life. I'm worried about him if anything. He absolutely dotes on her, doesn't he?'

Although they'd been on a boat with him for a month, it had never occurred to Ben that the Dutchman doted on his wife. It had seemed to him that he saw her more as a burden he had to bear. But watching him go after her now, he understood what Hyacinth meant. The man's whole life was dedicated to his wife. In his eyes she was like some exquisite piece of china that he longed to hold, but knew would break if he ever once allowed himself to consider his own needs instead of hers.

Hyacinth was getting ready to go and, as she picked up her pad to put it away, Ben noticed that she'd been drawing him, several different rough outlines of him, superimposed on one another, so the effect was defracted, fragmented, incomplete.

'We should meet up properly one of these days,' she said as she stood up. 'Go for a forest walk or something like that.'

(8)

At three in the morning Police Chief Da Ponte called Ben in the hotel to say that a duende killing had been reported in a settlement called Espiritu, at the end of a side channel of the Lethe. His tone was completely different to any Ben had heard him use before, animated, friendly, keen to please. Did Ben want to go with him and investigate?

Ben splashed water on his face, pulled on his clothes and hurried down to the quay. Da Ponte shook Ben's hand warmly with both of his hands. The air was cool but not cold, the harbour and river still glowing faintly with phosphorescence. There was utter silence. A teenage boy was already in the boat, and started the outboard motor as soon as Ben arrived, causing a sudden eruption of crude, ugly noise. They climbed into the boat, a very basic aluminium thing that smelt of fish, with a single headlight at the front. The boy swung them out of the harbour, and turned northward to pass round the end of the Rock before continuing towards to the west. Phosphorescence sparkled round the bow like stars, and in the distance, channels and pools glowed softly through the dark trees.

'Finally …' Da Ponte shouted over the noisy motor. 'Finally, perhaps, we get somewhere, eh?'

He explained that several decapitated duendes had been found by one of his officers on a night patrol and the officer was waiting at the scene, having sent the boat back with the message.

The boy turned into one of the side channels. There was a rusted signpost with several bullet holes through it: 'Espiritu 8 km'. As the headlight swept across the bank, it revealed three small, vaguely deer-shaped creatures of a kind he'd seen a few times on the journey to Amizad: Hyacinth had referred to them as 'harts'. They didn't bolt. Unflinching in the bright light, their heads smooth and earless, they just stared out at the three people in the boat, with glittery, jewel-like eyes. Later, on another corner, the wing of a plane emerged briefly into existence as the beam swept over it.

A young police officer called Juan was waiting on the bank with a torch, which he waved as the boat approached. He had broad shoulders and a pleasant, open face, but Da Ponte seemed oddly off-hand with him, while continuing to be very friendly towards Ben. Juan pointed out the tree where three headless corpses hung, nailed up by their feet, with their long fingers trailing on the ground. Not having a hard skeleton as humans do, the creatures had deflated in death and resembled wetsuits hung up to dry.

Back on the boat, the teenager shut down the outboard motor. The resulting silence was shocking in its intensity, as was the darkness outside the beam of Juan's torch. The boat and the silhouette of the young boatman were still just barely visible because of the phosphorescence in the channel. Juan spoke in Mundino Creole, too quickly for Ben to be able to follow him at all.

'There is a young woman in Espiritu called Anita, who's known as a duende finder,' Da Ponte explained. 'We can all feel duendes when they're near, obviously, but these duende finders can detect them much further away. Often they are troubled people, you know? People not right in the head. And this girl, she felt them the night before last, creeping round the village, and she told the village chief, who is her great-great-aunt: a famous woman in these parts, Mama Elena. Elena organized a posse of men and woman to go with Anita and kill the creatures. It was led by her grandson. And, as you can see, they found them here by the water. The duendes were making a castelo, which the village people see as a kind of accursed thing. I expect you know that when Mundinos kill duendes, they always cut off the heads to take the power away from them, and hang up their bodies as a warning. Juan has a contact in the village who tells him things.'

'Ah, an informer,' Ben said, and the policeman Juan, who'd hitherto been completely glazed over, smiled at him vaguely, as if Ben had spoken to him. 'But where's the castelo?'

Juan didn't speak English, but he heard the word and immediately started scanning around with his torch until the beam found a small white jagged-edged object, a kind of stump, perhaps two feet wide and rising a few inches above the ground, surrounded by shards and chunks of the same material. Clearly there had been a substantially taller structure here, but someone had smashed it down. He picked up one of the pieces and handed it to Ben. It was part of a spiral, a little like the unfolding tip of one of those pink leaves, but made of some hard brittle substance, like shell, and with rows of tinier spirals ranged all along its length, each one nested into the last. When Ben made to put it in his pocket Juan immediately cautioned him. 'That's bad luck, senhor! It gives them power.' Da Ponte was about to translate but Ben waved his hand at him to show he'd understood and pocketed the thing anyway. How could you possibly police duende killings, he thought, if you allowed yourself to take seriously the superstitions on which they were based?

But still he did flinch when there was a sudden loud beating noise from the trees nearby. The two policemen laughed. Juan shone his torch on something with white triangular wings flapping away between the trunks, like an empty sack of white flesh that had somehow been brought to life.

'It's just a ghost ray,' the police chief told him.

Da Ponte, Juan and Ben pulled down the headless corpses and pushed them into bags brought for the purpose. Dawn was breaking, and they could hear the cockerels crowing in the village half a mile away as they returned to the boat. In the grey first light, they reached a little jetty and a row of cabins on stilts. The boy tied up the boat, and Juan led Ben and Da Ponte into the middle of the village. The usual statue of Iya stood on top of her pedestal, gazing out blankly over the roofs with her fixed smile, and there was a faded mural on one of the huts of laughing skeletons shovelling earth out of a hole in the ground. Villagers gathered to stare. Squat black pigs snuffled between the huts. A woman watched the new arrivals from across a cauldron where she was boiling up a kind of porridge, looking away quickly when she saw Ben notice her. There were exchanges in Creole, too fast for Ben to follow, but he heard Mama Elena's name mentioned and presently the old woman herself emerged from her hut.

Her eyes were yellow and bloodshot, their pupils clouded over with cataracts. She must have been almost completely blind, and she seemed to need two assistants to hold her up in order to remain standing, but it was obvious at once that she had huge authority. Juan, who clearly knew her quite well, was respectful to her to the point of deference, bowing and calling her madam, as he introduced Ben and Da Ponte.

'Ah, Ernesto Da Ponte.' The old woman nodded. 'The son of Elisa at Sao Jorga. I know all about you. You went to the outside and then came back.' She turned towards Ben. Her clouded eyes reminded him of the eyes of Iya in that they simultaneously saw nothing and saw everything. 'And this is the foreign policeman who got off the boat at Nus.'

Ben tried not to show it with the eyes of all the villagers on him, but he was badly thrown by this. How could the old woman know he'd got off the boat at Nus, unless someone there had written it down and then circulated the information back in the Submundo? And if that had happened, why had they gone to that trouble, and what else did they know about what had happened there? Perhaps they knew more about him than he did? But he pushed these worries out of his mind and made his face look stern. It was probably a bluff, he decided, a way of throwing him off guard, and he needed to hold on tightly to whatever authority he had. This was a murder investigation, after all.

'What do you know,' he asked, 'about the deaths of the three duendes yesterday, just a short way up the river?'

The old woman spent some minutes questioning other villagers before she answered this, and then spoke to Da Ponte at some length. It was all very theatrical but again, in spite of his dutiful hours repeating Portuguese sentences, Ben couldn't understand what was being said at all, other than the frequent '*não se*' which he knew meant 'I don't know'.

'She says she doesn't know anything about it,' Da Ponte finally said. 'This is the first she knows of it, and no one here knows anything about it either. She suggests some outsiders must have done it, someone from another village trying to make trouble perhaps, or maybe a foreigner. She says foreigners get up to all kinds of weird stuff when they think they're alone in the forest.' As she listened to her words being translated, the old woman's face remained utterly opaque. She knew he knew she was lying, Ben was sure, but she was confident he had no way of proving it and she was enjoying the power that gave her. When Da Ponte had finished, she chuckled, a sound that resembled the creaking of a rusty hinge, and said something which made Juan, very unprofessionally, laugh out loud. In fact, to Ben's disgust, even Da Ponte the police chief had to suppress a smile: 'She says what else do we want from her?' he translated. 'She says, are we telling her now that she must *like* the creatures?'

'Tell her of course not,' Ben snapped. 'We don't have to like them, and perhaps we'll never know them or understand them, but that doesn't mean it's okay to kill them, any more than it would be okay to kill a person we didn't know or like or understand.'

When this had been conveyed to her, the old woman snorted and then immediately snapped out another question.

'She asked how long you'd been in the Delta, Inspector,' Da Ponte said, 'and I told her you'd just recently arrived.' Then he spoke directly to the village chief in her own language.

'What are you telling her?' Ben asked. 'I'm not getting any of this.'

'I just acknowledged that you didn't have much experience of duendes as yet.'

Oh, thanks a lot, Ernesto, Ben thought. What purpose did it serve to concede that ground? Surely every policeman knew that, when questioning a suspect, you should give the impression that you know *more* than you actually do, and are completely confident of solving the case? 'Uh, okay,' he said, 'but tell her I might not know much personally, but I've read a number of the books that have been written by scientists who study the Delta.'

Mama Elena interrupted before Da Ponte could finish. A short exchange followed which ended up with the old woman cackling with laughter. The people watching laughed too and the policeman Juan smiled broadly without the slightest attempt at preserving any kind of professional distance. 'She asked me if you denied that duendes can get into people's minds,' Da Ponte said, 'and I told her of course not. So then she asked me how does science say they do that. I told her science hadn't figured that out, which was what made her laugh. "You tell me to listen to science," she said, "and then you tell me science doesn't know!"'

'Tell her science may not know yet how that works,' Ben said, 'but what science does know is that duendes don't really harm people. All those stories have been very carefully checked out. There are a small number of instances of people apparently losing their minds after being exposed to duendes for long periods. But in every single verified instance there's overwhelming evidence that the person concerned was already very ill in their head before they went anywhere near them. And please also point out to her that duendes were here long before people. Whatever it is that they do that makes people uncomfortable, it can't be intended for the purpose of upsetting human beings. They lived here for millions of years without any human beings at all.'

Da Ponte said something to the old chief which sounded rather shorter than what Ben had said to him, and then there was another fairly lengthy exchange. 'She still insists that duendes steal people's minds,' he relayed back eventually. 'She says she's seen it herself many times, and she says there wouldn't even be a village here if they hadn't kept the duendes away. I told her they're welcome to keep them away but they mustn't kill them. Then I told her that the Protectorate is really cracking down on duende killings now and we don't want to hear any more reports like this from Espiritu, or we'll have to start arresting people. I think she got the message.'

There was a satisfied, wrapping-up sort of tone in his voice and Ben suddenly realized to his amazement that the police chief considered their business there to have been completed. 'What? Are you saying that's it?'

'I think we've done what we can.'

'Are you serious? I can't believe you think that constitutes a murder investigation! What about the rest of the village? What about this girl Anita you mentioned?'

Da Ponte's face became hard and defensive. 'Trust me, I know these villages, and this is as far as we're going to get.'

The old woman turned her face towards him. She might not be able to see it with her eyes or understand the words in which it was expressed, but she could sense the tension between the two policemen, as she could feel the sun on the skin of her face, and she was clearly fascinated by it, as was the rest of the audience.

'They'll all say the same thing,' Da Ponte said. 'I promise you that. No way is anyone going to point the finger at any individual.'

'So let's search some huts. They use the heads for ritual purposes, don't they? So presumably someone's got them. Let's start with the old woman herself.'

Da Ponte was appalled. 'What? Search the chief's hut? You're kidding, right?'

'Of course I'm not. This is a murder investigation! She's the boss round here, so she's clearly a suspect. In fact, Juan's informer said she instigated it.'

Da Ponte stared at Ben for several seconds, then shrugged and turned to the old woman. 'I apologize,' seemed to be the gist of what he said, 'but the foreign policeman wants to look inside your hut.'

Her face became stony. So did Juan's. Da Ponte's too was taut with disapproval, but the old woman shrugged and gave a gesture which said, Let him get on with it.

Ben walked into the hut, with Da Ponte following. It was very dim inside and a second or two passed before he realized that, above the rug-draped couches, the walls were decorated with dozens of shrunken, inhuman faces.

'Jesus Christ! She's not even hiding the evidence!'

Da Ponte sighed. 'Inspector, it wasn't a crime to kill them until recently. For all we know, every one of these heads is perfectly legal.'

'Well, they shouldn't be legal, for God's sake! They should be impounded and banned! How can we make any progress otherwise?'

'As you know, Inspector, I don't make the laws. Perhaps that should be one of your recommendations when you write your report? It would need to get past the Legislative Council, of course, but, who knows, perhaps you can persuade them.'

'I don't get you, Da Ponte. I really don't get you and Tiler. Do you actually *want* to do anything about this problem?'

'Please. Not in here. We can talk later. It's a very serious matter, us being in here. Most people in the village will never have been in here, let alone people from outside. To these people, Mama Elena is like the Queen of England.'

'Okay. So what do we do now then? Why don't we interview this girl Anita?'

'There's no point, Inspector, as I've already said. She'll tell you the same as everyone else. Villagers take their lead from their chief. And do you want to make it completely obvious that Juan has an informer here? Now, can we please leave Elena's house?'

Shortly after they reached the broad main channel of the Lethe, they met a large motor launch, the *Jimmy G*, heading the other way. Dolby, the American oilman, waved across at Ben. The biologist Mary Boldero waved beside him.

Ben and Da Ponte were too annoyed with each other to speak on the way back to Amizad, Ben's annoyance exacerbated by an uncomfortable awareness that the police chief was probably right. Unless the Protectorate was going to increase the size of its police force and turn it into a force of occupation, how could it stop duende killings without the support of local leaders?

He arrived back at the hotel in the early afternoon, tired and discouraged. Mrs Martin was sitting at one of the tables in the lobby with a friend.

'Oh, Inspector, it's you! We were worried about you, rushing out in the middle of the night!'

He managed to stretch a smile over his face. 'That's police work for you, I'm afraid, Mrs Martin.'

'Nicky!' she reproached him. 'No need to be so formal!'

'Nicky,' he corrected himself. He realized the friend was Justine the potter. The two women looked out at him from the circle of their conversation in oddly different ways. Mrs Martin was eager to engage with him, eager for her friend to witness her engaging with him. Justine was wary, uncomfortable. Perhaps she could tell he didn't like Mrs Martin and wanted to distance herself, but she seemed almost to be reproaching him too, or to feel reproached. 'Hello, Justine,' he said.

'He calls you by your first name, I notice!' Mrs Martin pretended to be jokily jealous in order to hide the fact that she actually *was* jealous. 'So police work, was it? Do tell!' And to Justine: 'He's a sort of police superstar, you know. The Protectorate headhunted him to—'

'I really can't discuss my work, I'm afraid,' he told her.

'No, of course,' she said hastily. 'It wouldn't be professional. Anyway, you're all right, that's the main thing! The night porter said you went rushing out at three in the morning and we were worried maybe the forest had got to you like it did to that poor Dutch woman yesterday!'

He hadn't wanted to get into a conversation, but now he was curious. 'Do you know what happened to her?'

'They caught up with her at the beginning of the forest track,' Mrs Martin told him, clearly delighted to sense that she was finally holding his interest. 'She was too exhausted to carry on. Now she's back in her room in the Bristol. Dr McKenzie came from the hospital to give her a jab to calm her down. They're planning to move her over there later.'

'She shouldn't have been given a permit to come here,' Justine said.

'No, she shouldn't,' Mrs Martin agreed. 'There are supposed to be psychological tests these days.' She smiled bravely. 'The Delta is a dreadful place in many ways, Inspector. Everyone says how unique and interesting it is and how alive it makes you feel, but—' She broke off. 'Oh, don't mind me. I'm just having a moan. Justine knows what I mean.'

'Why do you stay if you don't like it here?' Ben asked.

Mrs Martin looked away from him and Justine towards the window on to the square. She had that brave glassy look on her face which some people affect when they are angry at their fate to the point of tears, and want you to notice that, but also want you to know that they won't give fate the satisfaction of seeing them weep. 'Justine and I are like a lot of us here, Inspector, even the ones who tell themselves they love it so much they can't tear themselves away. We've left it too late. This place changes you after a while.'

'How exactly?' Into his mind came a vivid image of a single spiral leaf, with its nodes like the vertebrae of a skeleton, from which burst smaller spirals, and from them, smaller spirals still. It was a grasping thing, like a claw or a tentacle.

'I suppose we all need something to hold us together.' She gave a brave, artificial laugh. 'Some sort of glue! And when you've been here for a long time, the glue becomes less strong. Oh, it's exciting at first. I mean, that Dutch woman, for instance. She didn't want to come back out of the forest and, from what I've heard, she fought tooth and nail to stop the doctor slipping in the needle. It took her husband and Derek the manager and two receptionists to hold her down, she was so desperate to get back out there. But you find out the downside as time goes on. I don't think I could face that awful forest at all any more. Let alone the world outside.'

She'd been looking out of the window all this time, but now she glanced back at Ben. 'It might be different if I had someone to look after me, someone strong.' Her eyes searched his face, an angler casting a line out just one last time into a bare stretch of water where there's never been a bite. Then she looked back out of the window. 'But on my own? No. The moment for that's long gone, I'm afraid.'

'I'm sorry to hear that,' he said, rather stiffly. She was closer to getting a bite than he wanted her to know. He disliked her so much that he found it hard to call her by her first name, and yet her palpable yearning to be held had a strong magnetic pull. He turned to Justine, who'd been silently observing all this. 'I wonder how on Earth the Mundinos manage, out in the forest all the time?'

Justine was about to say something, but the hotelier got in first. 'Don't ask me. I was married to one of them and I still don't know. Tough as boots, and completely mad.'

The receptionist came over at this point to tell him that there was a call for him from Katherine Tiler. He went up to his room to take it.

'I gather you had a frustrating time at Espiritu,' Tiler said. 'It's so difficult knowing how best to deal with these traditional leaders, isn't it? I thought I'd try to arrange a meeting on Friday, with some key people. Let's move this forward, shall we?'

Yes, she was like a cheating spouse, Ben thought as he put down the phone, a cheating spouse bringing presents so as to avoid questions about where she's been, or who or what she really cares about. But, although he saw that very clearly, he still couldn't bring himself to respond to anything more than the surface of what she'd said. It was easier to see things in this place, it seemed, but harder to act on them.

IV. THE POTTER

(9)

Justine first met Rico in France. It all seemed rather cloudy in her mind now, as if it happened to someone else completely, and many of the details she could no longer recall, but she was the daughter of a doctor and a civil servant. She had a conventional middle-class upbringing, with the usual emphasis on self-improvement. Pottery was one of her hobbies, encouraged by her parents, and she was praised for her efforts, but the idea of doing it for a living had never occurred to them or to her, for her talent extended no further than a reliable competence at reproducing the ideas of others. In much the same way, she was a competent pianist. Having received piano lessons from the age of seven, she could perform tolerably difficult works by famous composers in whatever manner was suggested to her by her teachers – and she was praised for that also, but she could not have devised her own interpretation of a piece, let alone compose an original piece of music of her own. In her family and indeed her social class, the acquisition of musical and artistic skills was highly valued, and her parents regularly paraded her accomplishments in front of others in the hope of praise. They longed for a prodigy, a daughter who their friends might see in some colour magazine – 'this brilliant young pianist', 'this rising star', 'this extraordinarily talented young woman for whom a meteoric career beckons' – but, while Justine's talents might enable her to play pleasing pieces and make more than adequate Christmas presents for aunts and uncles, that unfortunately was all. Her parents could barely conceal their disappointment. And when Ben threw her little duende out into the harbour without even thinking that she might be walking behind him, the way it made her feel was very familiar.

Growing up in Paris, she assumed she would follow some similar profession to her parents, marry, have children and, also like her parents, devote her life to accumulating the various accoutrements of bourgeois life, so as to allow her own children in turn to attain the necessary professional qualifications, and begin their adult lives with a similar financial head start as herself, so that they in turn could do the same again, and so on. In order to achieve this, it was apparently necessary to be constantly measuring oneself against others, worrying whether one was good enough or doing one's best, and at the same time ensuring at all times that the standard that one was using to make these judgements was the right one, and not in itself revealingly old-fashioned or low-brow or vulgar.

Although it was settled that she would follow a profession, she had no strong preferences of her own. Her parents proposed, therefore, that she should choose the law and she dutifully studied for the qualifications necessary to obtain a place in a reputable law school. When the time came, she studied there equally dutifully, carefully writing up her notes after each lecture in her beautiful long-hand with underlinings in green, red and blue pencil, drawn with a ruler to keep things neat. She acquired a boyfriend, also from Paris. His name was … what was his name? After all this time in the Submundo, she often forgot his name for hours at a stretch, and she could no long remember his face or the sound of his voice, only his characteristic – not unpleasant – smell, a little like fresh leather. But anyway, she acquired a boyfriend and her parents liked him very much, for he was very bright and great things were expected of him. What was more they liked *his* parents very much too, so much so, in fact, that they became close friends with them. Her boyfriend's father and hers, for instance, would go to rugby matches together. Her mother and his would go to art exhibitions. They assumed Justine would welcome this, and as far as she knew she did, though she couldn't help feeling a bit as if her parents had married her off before she'd even made that decision herself. They would talk quite openly about when she and her boyfriend would have children and where they might buy their first house, and how perhaps, in due course, the two of them and all the parents together might acquire a gîte on the Atlantic coast where, as it had amusingly turned out, both families had taken holidays regularly, visiting the very same beaches, quite possibly at the same time.

But during her second year at law school, Justine met a beautiful and dangerous American boy, a year or two younger than herself, who looked like a movie star. He was talking to some other young women outside the residential block where she lived in term time. Justine was walking past them, assuming that this little scene had nothing to do with her, when quite unexpectedly he left the other women and walked right up to her, giving her no choice but to stop.

'Hello, I'm Rico,' he told her. 'Can I ask you your name?'

So she told him Justine, most probably blushing slightly.

'And you live here, do you?'

'During term time.'

'Can I see your room from here?'

She pointed it out to him. It was on the fourth and top storey. He didn't ask the number. 'Well, Justine, it's good to meet you,' he said, and she assumed that would be the last she'd see of him, and wasn't seriously troubled by the fact that his very bold and candid gaze had unsettled her a little bit, because this had been in a harmless and quite pleasant way, as you might be unsettled by a handsome actor in a film about people leading lives rather bolder and more imaginative than your own. You walk out of the cinema feeling a little bolder and more imaginative yourself. It lasts perhaps an hour or even a day, but you don't do anything about it, and you certainly don't expect to meet or have any connection with the actor himself.

But a few days later, at a quarter past ten at night, when she was sitting at her desk making some notes for an essay, she was startled by a tapping at the window. It was actually rather frightening, for after all she was on the fourth floor, and she simply froze for a second or two until she heard Rico's muffled voice from behind the curtain – 'Justine! It's me. Let me in before I fall! My hands are freezing' – and she went to the window to draw back the curtain, giggling with excitement and nerves.

His eyes were oddly bright and intense, never seeming to come to rest on anything for any length of time, and he was talking very quickly and animatedly at double the normal speed about whatever came into his head, but he didn't seem to be drunk, and she didn't know enough at the time to recognize the influence of cocaine, so it just made him seem rather magical, and charismatic, like someone out of a story. He produced a small bottle of brandy which he'd carried in his pocket while climbing, without any kind of rope, those four storeys.

'You're mad!' she said several times. 'You could have killed yourself! You could have broken your neck.'

But she was very excited by the idea that he'd taken this risk purely to come and see her – her, Justine, whose piano playing was only proficient, whose pots were conventional and ordinary, and whose grades were adequate only because she worked so very hard with her files and her coloured pencils.

And they drank the brandy and he told her all kinds of things, which he himself frankly admitted were not necessarily true, and she let him undress her, in spite of having a boyfriend whose father was a friend of her father's and whose mother was a friend of her mother's. She'd never before felt touched as she was by Rico's fingers or the brushing of his lips against her skin, not because the way he did it was really so different to her boyfriend, but because it was *him*, it was this stranger with the ridiculously bright and intense gaze and the almost unbelievable stories which he admitted were only half-true, but who had nevertheless undoubtedly taken a quite considerable risk climbing a student accommodation block with little in the way of footholds, quite literally risking his life just for the opportunity to spend an evening with her. (Justine didn't know at the time that hers was the third room he'd tried, having been rebuffed by the less impressionable but perhaps more attractive inhabitants of two others. He only told her this later when the politics of their relationship made it necessary for him to hurt and humiliate her.)

They had sex many times and he talked and talked about space-flight, aliens, deserts, hermaphrodites, Incas, giant squids with hardly a pause for breath and laughed when she attempted to make her normal, conventional, conversational offerings such as asking him where he grew up, or what his parents did, did he have brothers or sisters, had he been to university and if so which? 'This isn't really you, Justine,' he said. Justine knew of no other version of herself, had nothing else inside her head that she knew how to turn into words, but she loved the idea that another her existed, a her that wouldn't have to ask conventional questions, or perform boringly competent piano pieces, or underline her beautifully handwritten notes with coloured pencils. She loved the thought that of all people this man, who seemed to her to have sprung out of some American movie, could see that other her, even if she couldn't, and had singled her out because of it.

'Listen,' he said, 'have you heard of the Submundo Delta? Do you know where that is? I want us to go there. And Justine, you *need* to go there.'

She rolled against him and kissed him. They were both completely naked at that point. 'I can't go with you anywhere, you silly boy. I'm halfway through my studies, and anyway—' She broke off.

'And anyway what?'

'Oh, nothing.'

'And anyway you have a boyfriend. Who is very nice, and his parents live in Paris like yours, and his dad is a friend of your dad's.'

'How did you know that?'

He laughed and rolled his eyes. 'I can read minds, Justine. I'm not like other people. No one on Earth is like me, and that's why I need to go to the Submundo, which is like nowhere else on Earth. And you need to go there to find the real you. You can't even see her but I can. She's like a bright colourful bird locked away inside a cage inside a dark room, inside a boring grey old house. Come to the Submundo with me, Justine. What have you got to lose?'

She had only barely heard of the Delta at that stage, if she'd even heard of it at all, which was odd, given that it was undoubtedly the strangest place on Earth, and much stranger than other places famous for their uniqueness, and particularly so given that, at the time, no actual permit was required to get there and you simply had to persuade a riverboat company that you were a serious traveller and would not cause problems on the way. But, as Justine was to discover, the world forgot the Delta, much as people in the Delta forgot the world. Encircled by its ring of oblivion, the Submundo skittered away from ordinary human consciousness, and no one thought about it at all unless actually brought up against the fact of its existence. Rico had a book, though, or a book of sorts. It was a mimeographed hippy publication, with a crudely drawn map which showed the Delta, and the Zona that surrounded it, and the Lethe and Nus and Amizad. They were just names to her back then, of course, but the book said the trees had purple-pink leaves, and the entire forest was only the surface of a dark and secret sea teeming with strange life from another world, while the human inhabitants spoke their own obscure dialect of nineteenth-century Portuguese with traces of Yoruba, and lived in little settlements, like the villages in fairy tales, surrounded by mystery and enchantment.

(10)

Rico taped up a handwritten sign in their little cabin: 'YES YOU DID GO ASHORE AT NUS, JUSTINE.' It was her paper, of course, her pencil, her sticky tape, for she had done all the organization for the trip, and had financed it for both of them from a sum of money recently left to her by a great-aunt in Bordeaux. It seemed a fair division of labour to Justine at the time, and even a kind of penance for the safe and bourgeois nature of her existence up until now: he had the brilliant idea because he was brilliant; she did the boring parts because, until that promised time when the Delta finally unlocked her, she was indeed boring and boring things were all she was good for.

That was not to say that she liked his sign, though. It stayed there throughout the slow, meandering journey through the Delta, and she pretended she saw it as a harmless tease, but she would have preferred to take it down. She was very troubled by the idea that, in that mysterious zone between the Delta and the outside world, she might have done something that she would normally regard as wrong, whether of her own free choice or because she had been talked into it, and she felt sure that she wouldn't have gone ashore at all, unless Rico had suggested it and she had felt unable to say no, just as she now felt unable to tell him she didn't like his sign. In fact, rather than say that, she tried very hard to like it and, each time she saw it, she told herself that her objections were silly, and that she should positively welcome it. For wasn't Rico just reminding her that she had come here in search of liberation?

Meanwhile, Rico cheerfully played his guitar on the cargo hatch, smoking cannabis and singing, sometimes renditions of American pop, and sometimes the songs he made up himself. He could only play block chords, of which he knew perhaps ten, didn't have a good enough ear to tune the instrument properly, and didn't seem to notice that all his songs sounded the same. But he wasn't troubled or embarrassed by his limited musical ability in the way that she had always been troubled by hers, even though she had passed all her piano exams up to the Troisième Cycle and, on the guitar which she'd taken up at university so as to be able to play music in her room for relaxation, she could play a number of fairly difficult pieces with reasonable competence. And this too made her feel inferior to him. She admired the way he was willing to play in his own way where the whole boat could hear him, and she felt ashamed of her own doubts and inhibitions. Rico told her that her family and her class had emphasized achievements of every kind except the one kind that really mattered, with the result that in that one vital sphere her growth had been criminally stunted. But very soon, he assured her, in the freedom of the Delta, that stunted inner self of hers would unfurl its wings and fly.

This wasn't hard to believe on a boat that was winding its way through the Submundo forest. The branches and flowers seemed to her to be coiled up like springs, full of mysterious and inhuman energy. And while the sinister bluebirds, the purple waterlilies and the harts that came out at night and watched them from the shadowy banks with the phosphorescence glinting on their jewel-like eyes were all disturbingly strange, at the same time they were still *there* and not *here*, reassuringly separate from her as she watched from the boat. They were very unsettling but still manageably so.

To begin with, Amizad seemed to offer the same sort of reassurance as the boat, since it too was surrounded by the forest but separate from it. At first sight she found it a charming, if slightly run-down pastiche of a small European town, such as you might find, she imagined, in Belgium or Luxembourg, with its novelty clock, and a patisserie, and several pleasant cafés, all of them very ordinary-looking and quite unlike the strange things she'd seen or glimpsed in the forest. She found herself and Rico a small apartment to rent, and set about financing their life by offering various services to the bright young researchers and their families who were beginning to come to the new institutes on the slopes above the town. She cleaned their floors and ironed their clothes, she offered them tuition in French and French literature – this was quite popular with bored spouses who were not themselves involved in research – and she began to make the little pots and figurines which would eventually become her main source of income.

Rico, meanwhile, continued her education with regular trips out into the forest in search of duendes, which he liked to encounter, if possible, while already under the influence of drugs.

Duende encounters terrified Justine right from the start. There was an immense store of self-doubt and self-hatred hovering round the edges of her mind, the product of a lifetime of anxious comparisons of herself with others, her family with other families, and her family *and* herself with those superstars of the bourgeoisie with their complex, ultra-intelligent and challengingly fearless faces who looked out from their chic living rooms and unusual gardens in the colour magazines – the brilliant opera singer, the fearless public intellectual, the rule-breaking entrepreneur, the maverick young scientist who would turn upside down the way we thought about the world itself – so that to be near a duende was to feel a hurricane-force gale of self-loathing blowing through her, flinging to the ground all her little attainments, and all the small differences between herself and others that she tried her best to think of as her personality, like so many houses of cards. 'You are worth nothing,' said the voices inside her head. 'You were a disappointment to your parents. Even to Rico, you are a disappointment. He allows you to be with him, but he doesn't love you, and if you had the slightest self-respect, you would leave him.'

Rico laughed when she asked him if he loved her. 'What do you *mean* by love?' he said, lying there naked on their scrumpled bed in their tiny and slightly damp bedroom (for nothing was ever quite dry in that humid air, unless you had air conditioning), while she began to get ready to meet a gloomy Irishwoman who wanted to practise her conversational French in order to stave off her boredom, and fear, and growing sense that the American physicist she had married was not really the man she should be spending her life with at all. 'What really is it but a fancy pink ribbon the bourgeoisie like to wrap around sex so as to make it safe and respectable like all their other possessions? You know I like fucking you because you know I can never get enough, and I know you like fucking me from the way you squeal. What more do we want, eh? What more do we need? I'm not going to be your dad and look after you, and you're not going to be my mum and look after me, but why would we want that anyway, when we've come all this way to get away from that crap?'

And as to the painful feelings the duendes stirred up in her: 'Let them happen, sweetheart, just let them happen,' he said, as he prowled a metre ahead of her through the forest at dusk, his eyes darting this way and that in search of the creepy frog-like creatures that so fascinated him. 'Let them do what they do. It's like peeling off scabs, you know? Peeling off layers and layers of them, until there's no more left and for the first time in your life you'll be able to move freely because you've finally reached the skin and are naked, really, really naked at last.' He turned towards her, licked his lips. 'I can hardly wait. In fact, why don't we lie down here right now?'

'Not now,' she said nervously. 'They might creep up on us.'

'They don't creep, Justine. They just arrive. And why should we mind that? They won't harm us. They just show us more of ourselves than we normally see.'

One time, they ran into some Mundino men out on a duende hunt, and Rico, gabbly with excitement, decided they should fall in with them. So she and Rico drank the men's brandy and ate their bread and meat, and Justine pretended to laugh like a good sport at ribald remarks directed at her which she couldn't understand but which Rico seemed to find hilarious, even though, like her, he spoke no Portuguese, let alone Mundino Creole. And when they finally found and killed a couple of duendes, Rico enthusiastically helped to decapitate them and string up the headless corpses in a tree.

'But I thought you liked duendes?' Justine said to him as they walked back to Amizad later that night. She was struggling with the dark, dirty elation she had felt at seeing the creatures squirming and thrashing at the ends of sharpened poles, and with the fact that, in spite of herself, she had reached out and briefly handled one of the severed heads with a shriek of appalled and excited laughter. Stupid things, she'd thought to herself as she did so, you thought you were so clever messing around with our minds, but all you showed us in the end was just how much we hated you and wanted you dead, and now look what's happened to you as a result!

'Sure I like duendes,' Rico said with a shrug, 'but there are plenty of them, aren't there? And that was a new experience we wouldn't otherwise have had.' He looked round at her and grinned.

But where would that end? Justine couldn't help herself from thinking, as she tried not to look around herself too much for fear of the creatures that were coming out of the pools. After all, it wasn't unknown for her to want to kill Rico, and he, much less inhibited, had told her out loud on at least three occasions that he felt like killing her. And that would be an experience too, wouldn't it? To want to kill someone and then just go right ahead and really do it, rather than allow yourself to be pulled back by other more cautious forces inside your mind, as the friends of a drunkard pull him away from a fight: that would be something pretty unique and unforgettable, wouldn't it? Just to do exactly what you felt like doing, in the moment the feeling came to you.

'This forest is the true democracy,' Rico said. 'It strips away all the crap. It doesn't care about certificates and trophies or any of that shit. It doesn't even care about right or wrong. And nor do I, Justine, that's what you need to understand. I don't give two fucks about any of that.'

His clarity was rather thrilling, and so was his ability not to be deflected by softer feelings such as pity or guilt, or even to feel them at all as far as she could tell. But it wasn't easy to be with a man like that. The two of them made friends with some of the scientists from the research stations. Even though very few of them were French, these people tended to come from backgrounds much like Justine's – the kind where you are rewarded from an early age for retreating from the world into a book, the kind where, even when you are very small, every expression of interest in knowledge or culture is rewarded by shining-eyed pride and delight – and most of them had had to work very hard and very conscientiously to get the jobs they had. And of course this meant that some of them, like Justine herself, were very much drawn to Rico's casual dismissal of everything they had been trained to think of as important, and everything they'd worked at for so long, for when you have been trained to do a thing, you have also have been trained *not* to do other things that you might otherwise have done with pleasure, so you are left with a sense of yourself as a kind of espaliered tree, like the ones pinned to the garden wall where Justine had grown up, that could otherwise have stood by themselves and spread out their branches whichever way they liked under the sun. To these people, Justine was just a rather unsuccessful version of themselves, but Rico appealed to the part of them that was buried or severed. He began to have affairs with some of the women, or more often just casual one-off fucks, and didn't bother to hide them from Justine, merely suggesting that if she felt jealous she should do the same.

'This is just me, Justine,' he told her. 'I don't do it to hurt you,' here he winked, 'or not usually anyway, not unless I'm mad at you at the time, but I've never concealed from you that my whole project is to break down the boundaries that contain me. No more walls. It's what I'm all about and if you don't like that, you don't have to be with me. I don't want you to go, mind, but don't imagine for one minute I'm going to try and stop you.'

There was one scientist who was different from the rest. She had *not* had to work hard to get the job she had, and didn't need to be conscientious to keep it, because she was so much more intelligent than the vast majority of human beings that she could achieve really impressive goals without even trying. Oh, how Justine's parents would have loved a daughter with that kind of talent, destined for Nobel Prizes, and TV appearances, and glittering academic posts all around the world! Indeed, as Justine discovered, this particular woman had actually been featured already in several colour magazines, with and without her former husband, including a piece in *Time* about the most promising faces among the rising new generation which included a whole excited page on her achievements, and a full-page portrait too. A scientific genius *and* a beautiful woman: Justine's mother and father would have wet themselves with excitement if only that could have been her. But colour magazines and prizes seemed to mean nothing to Jael. Like Rico, she held in contempt the tight, anal, snobbish and socially anxious culture of the bourgeoisie with its obsession with knowledge and achievement as the benchmarks of human worth. 'She's always hoping to a produce a perfect turd in the potty,' Jael once said sneeringly of her former colleague Mary Boldero, 'long and curled and precisely placed, and just the right shade of brown, so that all the world will stroke her hair and tell her what a good girl she's been.'

Jael might be like Rico in that respect, but she was much smarter than him, and in fact the relationship between the two of them was in some ways the mirror image of his relationship with Justine. Just as Rico had once told Justine that he saw something inside her that she couldn't see in herself, so Jael told him now that he was a great scientist, a scientist of an entirely new kind, a scientist for a whole new epoch of human understanding, in spite of his having (as he'd told Justine) dropped out of school at fifteen with no qualifications at all, and he seemed as amazed and flattered and swept away by this as Justine had been when he climbed up to her window. She couldn't help herself from wondering, when he was away with Jael, and she was lying by herself in their bed, whether Jael too had tapped at other windows and only settled on Rico because her previous choices had sensibly declined to open up and flutter out into her web.

And just as Rico had done with Justine, Jael made clear to Rico that her relationship with him would not be exclusive. It was for that reason, Justine supposed, that Rico maintained her for some time as a useful back-up, a place he could come to when Jael was otherwise engaged, a woman he could have sex with when his sexual obsession was having sex with someone else, and a woman he could take it out on when Jael had made him feel small and rebuffed. Rico had more than met his match in Jael, Justine realized with a combination of pity and guilty pleasure, and these powerful but contradictory feelings, taken together with her own insecurities, meant that she willingly continued to play the part of

Rico's girlfriend whenever that was possible, even when she was very clearly number two at best in his list of women, and he spent most of his nights with Jael.

Indeed sometimes, back in those days, all three of them would do things together, and these included several trips to Nus, for the way that the Zona vanished from memory as soon as you left it was utterly fascinating to Jael and Rico. Justine didn't feel the same way. She didn't know what happened there, of course, but she feared that she was subjected to humiliations of various kinds by the other two and that she willingly submitted to them. No light can escape a black hole, and nothing that happens inside it can ever be observed from outside, but that doesn't mean it has no *effect* on the rest of the world, and so it was with the Zona. When you emerged from it, your memories of the place were instantly blotted out, and even your emotional state reverted to exactly how it was at the moment you went in, the contents of your brain unchanged in every respect, but of course you knew you'd been there, and you knew *why* you'd been there. And that knowledge, since it originated outside the Zone of Forgetfulness, stayed with you. If you were excited by the idea of going to Nus, you'd reach the frontier of the Zona in a state of excitement, and would therefore also be in a state of excitement on crossing back out again (whether back into the Delta or on into the outside world), so that this excitement about something that itself was unknowable became vividly associated with the place, even though you remembered nothing about it, and the same was true if your feelings were more of dread. So the Zona was powerful, and Rico and Jael positively welcomed that power. 'You know what we need right now?' Jael would say. 'Another cold shower of nothingness to freshen us up.'

And in spite of all her fears, Justine would go along.

•

Later, Justine wished she could at least say that she had been the one who dropped those two, that she'd put her foot down, that she'd evicted Rico from the apartment she'd found and paid for, and told him to find his own place and earn his own money and conduct his own weird relationship with this other woman without involving her. But the truth was that they'd dropped her. The first stage was that Rico stopped asking her for sex, though he continued to return to the apartment several times a week. She had the impression that this wasn't just about her, but that his interest in sex itself was waning as the constant duende contact made him stranger and more distracted than he'd been before. 'I am descending below the engine,' he would sometimes say, helping himself to the beer she'd put in the fridge, or to the bread she'd bought that morning from the Italian baker, and then he'd giggle and prattle in that random way he had, with his mouth full of the food and drink he was gulping down before crawling off to sleep by himself, or rushing out again to find Jael. After a while, his visits to the apartment petered out altogether, and he moved in permanently with Jael. (Justine still saw her sometimes with other paramours, but it seemed she now felt able to take them home even when Rico was there.) Pretty soon Rico only barely acknowledged Justine if he saw her in the street, and then a time came when he didn't seem to notice her at all, any more than he would notice a stranger, though Jael continued to give her a curt nod. Jael had an income from the world outside which continued to flow even after she'd quarrelled with all her scientific colleagues and abandoned the research post that had brought her to Amizad, and so she was able to support them both. This was just as well for Rico. The way he was now, it was hard to imagine him finding any work at all, or even finding anyone else to live off as he'd lived off Justine, for all Jael's talk about him being a great scientist.

Without Rico and the project of liberation that he'd sold to her, Justine asked herself what she was doing in Amizad and whether she should go back to France. But she never did. She kept putting it off until it would have meant unravelling more than she could bear, and rejoining a race that started long ago, against competitors already well settled into their stride. Instead, she set up her pottery at the edge of town. The research establishments on the slope kept growing both in number and size, and those were well-paid people up there who needed Christmas presents and mementos and things to put on the mantelpieces in their rented houses and apartments on the Rock. She kept herself busy and avoided going into the forest or on to the Lethe, and the longer she avoided these things, the less she could face the idea of ever doing them again. Rico had insisted they confront the forest and the duendes, and though she'd hated that, she'd just about managed to do it. But now that there was no one to pressure her to embrace it, the forest grew in her mind from being something that she'd rather not face if she didn't have to, to being something she dreaded to the point where even the thought of it elicited a terror close to panic. She even became uncomfortable in the company of Mundinos because she couldn't bear the thought of their lives out in the forest, in little villages that sometimes had as few as a dozen adults, facing the prospect every night of duendes crawling up on to their jetties and over their roofs. And yet they endured somehow, this was what she didn't understand; they endured, and didn't give way to fear, and by all accounts made at least some sort of life for themselves with songs, and weddings, and festivals, with nothing to protect them except that horrible carved god Iya, looking down from her pedestal with her blank stone eyes.

So she didn't go back to the world outside, and nor did she go out into the Delta, but she decided that Amizad was enough. It was a little town such as you might find (or so she imagined) in a rural part of Luxembourg, but one that she could not leave, not even to go to another part of Luxembourg, yet she persuaded herself somehow that it was a reasonable canvas on which to paint a life. It was a pretty town, she told herself, or at least not entirely without charm, and, though it was small and uneventful, that, she decided, wasn't necessarily a bad thing. She made a few friends such as Nicky in the Bem-Vindo hotel, who admittedly preferred music and books that Justine found cheap and manipulative while at the same time being utterly scornful of the ones Justine loved, and who, it could not be denied, was prone to complain about her own lot at great length while showing almost no interest at all in what was happening for Justine, but she was company of a sort and always willing to meet up. There were also various regular social events that Justine took part in where she would help raise money for little comforts for the Mundinos in those remote villages where it was said that some people were barely aware even now that they were no longer alone in the Submundo Delta, or that there was a town on the Rock with a hospital and even a small supermarket, and boats going back and forth to the outside world.

It wasn't the life she had imagined before she met Rico, and it wasn't the life either that he'd seemed to offer when she agreed to accompany him – that wild and beautiful bird had never emerged from its cage – but it was a life of sorts. And when the news reached Amizad that, far away in Geneva, in that vague foggy half-

remembered place called the outside world, it had been decided
that duendes were 'persons' entitled to the protection of the law,
she thought to herself that this was a cause she could perhaps
make her own. It wasn't an original thought on her part. All the
outsiders in Amizad agreed with the decision, or said they did
anyway, all the scientists and administrators, and the sundry others
like Justine, just as all the Mundinos in Amizad regarded it with
contempt. Justine didn't like the creatures, it was true, but (as the
entire outsider community was telling itself in the two cafés, and
in the canteens of the research stations, and at the dinner tables of
one another's apartments, like bees or ants passing back and forth
the pheromones that keep the whole nest working together) the
duendes had been here in the Delta since long before the Mundinos
arrived, let alone the still more recent arrivals like themselves,
and some said the life of the Delta had been like this, not just for
thousands, or millions, but for hundreds of millions of year, so it
would be absurd and unjust to say that the duendes didn't belong
here, or blame them for making people feel uncomfortable, when
they hadn't asked people to come here in the first place.

Thinking she would do her bit, as the English said, for this new
cause, Justine worked hard to come up with an image of duendes
that was recognizable and at the same time *appealing*. This was
difficult for her, not only because it was the closest she'd ever come
to making something original, but because it meant suppressing
very powerful feelings. In truth, she was more terrified of duendes
now than she'd been when she first arrived, and more revolted
by them too, but she reminded herself as she worked that these
feelings were wrong and unjust, and her efforts were rewarded by
praise from people from the research stations who came into her
shop and bought the figurines and told her how wonderful it was

to see representations of duendes that conveyed their vulnerability, instead of, as usual, their inscrutability, their mysteriousness, their exotic and frightening otherness. There was even a piece about Justine on the front page of the little English-language weekly, *The Delta Times*, that circulated among the expatriate community of Amizad, with a large if blurry photograph of her posing a little shyly with three of her ceramic figures.

But really she knew that the lovable duende was a piece of nonsense, a sentimental lie, which was of course why the policeman with the stern face had thrown it in the harbour. She hated him for that. It wasn't so much his inconsiderateness she minded – he'd just returned from the forest, after all, and was clearly distracted – but, more than anything, the way he'd shown up the deep crack in the ground on which her life was built.

V. THE POLICEMAN

(11)

Hyacinth had an apartment in a blue-washed house close to the southern edge of the town, near Justine's pottery shop and Mrs Fantini's restaurant and store, and next to a similar house that for some reason had crumbled into ruin. When Ben called on her for the walk in the forest they'd arranged, she came down to the door to meet him, bringing a flask of coffee and her drawing things in a canvas satchel.

They walked round the lump of volcanic rock that marked the end of the town and on to the track which Ben had walked a few days previously.

'Apparently I made a faux pas the other day,' he told her. 'I insisted on looking inside a chief's hut for evidence.'

She winced. 'Oh Jesus, Ben. That was *not* a good idea. That will completely alienate the chiefs, and it's the chiefs you need on your side.'

'I understand that, but what else are we supposed to do? I did try to appeal to the old woman's sense of fairness.'

'Well, that won't hurt, unlike barging into her home, but, to be honest, I don't think it'll cut much ice. Their society works very differently to ours. Back in London or New York, you or I could spend whole days sharing the streets with thousands of people we don't know, so naturally we have a set of rules and principles that allow us to get by as autonomous individuals surrounded by anonymous strangers, but, in a village like that, people very seldom meet anyone who isn't connected to them in some way by blood or marriage. The idea of being autonomous private individuals with some kind of abstract obligation to people or creatures they have no connection with … well, it just isn't part of their repertoire. Right and wrong isn't about fairness for them, and it's not about freedom, it's about connection. That's one reason why Mundinos don't make good city dwellers.'

'*Are* there Mundino city dwellers?'

'Sure. There's a Mundino quarter in São Paulo. I spent several months there. It's a brutal, lawless place. Their culture doesn't equip them for dealing with people they don't know or care about, and of course there's no Iya there to watch over them when no one else can see them.'

'But Iya doesn't *really* watch over them here!'

'Doesn't she?'

Ben was momentarily bewildered. 'Well of course not, Hyacinth. She's a made-up character. She's a wooden carving with stones for eyes!'

'Who do you think made her up, then? Do you think a bunch of Mundinos sat down together one day and said, "Now we'll design a god"?'

'I suppose not, but—'

'She grew organically, Ben. She's a living thing. She just happens to live in human minds rather than in the material world. Much like the things *we* believe in.'

'That's not right. We're scientific. Science exists whether you believe it or not.'

'Our *values* aren't scientific, Ben. "Human rights", "democracy", "duende personhood", all that stuff: it has no more objective existence than Iya! We imagine that our values are scientific because a respect for science happens to be one of them. But look at Baron Valente. He was a *big* fan of science. In fact, he endowed whole laboratories and libraries and museums specifically so as to advance the cause of science: there's a Valente Institute in Lisbon, a Valente Library in Rio. As far as he was concerned, his outlook was entirely based on science but it was nothing at all like ours. It was all about hierarchy, and the right and duty of the advanced races to conquer and rule the backward ones. He'd read his Darwin, and that's what he took from it.'

They walked for a while in silence: the almost unbroken silence of the Delta forest. It was very soothing: the warm air, the dim light, the tempting oases of sunlight off through the trees. And Ben had to admit to himself that he also liked being with Hyacinth.

She had a mole, he noticed, a few inches down from the top of her left shoulder.

'One thing about Iya,' he said. 'It's only just occurred to me, but she looks a bit like a duende!'

Hyacinth laughed. 'Oh, I know. I've put that to Mundinos many times. They always hotly deny it and insist that she came with them into the Delta from the outside. But there were no gods like that outside the Delta in the 1860s. The religious beliefs the Mundinos brought with them would have been some combination of Christianity and African animism with maybe the odd Amerindian deity thrown in, and Iya's not like any of those. So you're right. She's a kind of duende.'

'But that's mad! They hate duendes!'

'Perhaps it would be more accurate to say they have a complicated relationship with duendes.'

'Oh come on, they kill them!'

She laughed. 'I know, I know, but people have layers,' she said, and Ben thought at once of the three notebooks lying unopened in that drawer in his hotel room.

Hyacinth patted her knapsack. 'Shall we drink this coffee? We could sit in the sun by that pool over there?'

They took off their shoes and dangled their feet in the water, sitting amongst the fleshy pink vegetation that grew round the pool while the great white sun shone down, its edges throwing out tiny shards of coloured light.

'I saw an old woman sitting like this last time I came this way,' he said. 'She was all on her own and completely naked, drinking milk from those white flowers you see everywhere.'

'I expect she was what they call a louco. You do see them occasionally. From what I can figure out, most of them are Zonitos, people from the Zona, who've strayed over the boundary into the Delta itself.'

'What happens to their minds, if their whole life has been lived in the Zona?'

'Basic motor functions seem to survive,' she said. 'They can walk. They can drink water. But everything else is lost: memories, language, knowledge, even their own names.'

'Dear God, how awful.'

'Yes, but my guess is that they do it on purpose. I've known quite a few people in my life who'd have been more than happy to have swept the whole slate clean. And the Delta looks after loucos in its way. Honey-milk provides them with nourishment, the Mundinos leave them alone, and the forest fills up all that empty space in their heads with itself.'

'So they're a kind of zombie, almost?'

'I wouldn't say that. I've watched them a number of times. I think they're conscious. I think they savour being alive. I even envy them in a way. I sat and watched an old man once, picking a single flower, drinking off the honey-milk from it, and then just very slowly examining it, testing it with his fingers, stroking it against his cheek. It was actually very peaceful. Nus is full of evil, I think. If you were once a child prostitute there, or a slave kept chained in a basement for tourists to act out their sadistic fantasies, I imagine the life of a louco is pretty much like heaven.'

Ben was suddenly very agitated, as if the ground he was standing on had become a thin and brittle crust over a chasm. What was in the chasm he didn't know, but he knew he'd chosen to get off the boat at Nus and he knew that, back in that drawer in his hotel room, were three unopened notebooks that might well tell him.

'But some loucos are Mundinos, yes?' he said.

She looked round at him. She looked a little quizzical, as if she'd noticed how anxious he was to move the conversation on from Nus.

'Maybe even people from the world outside?' Ben added, to fill what seemed to him an uncomfortably lengthy silence. He wondered if Hyacinth knew he'd got off the boat at Nus, or had some idea what he'd been like during those days inside the Zona. She might have kept a diary herself, after all. Keeping notes on how people behaved in Nus: wasn't that exactly the kind of thing an anthropologist would do? And for a moment he had an impulse to blurt out all of it: Nus, the notebook, his fears about his own secret self.

'Oh, for sure,' she said. There was something a little offhand about her tone as if part of her was still wondering about his unease. 'It would take longer to reach that sort of state, obviously, if you weren't a Zonito, because you can't just wipe away your memories all at once. But if you let the duendes open up your mind … well, I don't know, obviously, what it's like to stay in the presence of duendes for any length of time, but I think maybe it's like a kind of drowning: frightening at first, but then rather peaceful when your lungs are full of water and the struggle is over. And unlike drowning, it isn't fatal. You'd reach that peaceful state and then just stay there. You can see the appeal of that, can't you?'

In that moment he could. To be free of all the worry and guilt that came from having a past and a future! But Ben just shrugged. 'I suppose that's why Mundino villagers think the duendes are a threat to them. They reckon they'd all be loucos by now if they hadn't kept the duendes at bay.'

'Exactly.'

'It's pretty much what Mama Elena said, in fact.'

'Well, Ben,' she said, quite gently and kindly, 'the Mundinos *have* been living in the forest a lot longer than anyone else. They do know *something* about it.'

She poured coffee into cups and passed one to him.

'I feel you think I'm rather slow and literal-minded,' he said with an uncomfortable laugh. He was no longer over the chasm, and no longer felt the slightest impulse to talk to her about himself and Nus. The relief of that was huge.

'Slow and literal-minded?' she exclaimed. 'That's not true at all! Anyone can see you're very smart.' She studied his face for a second or two. 'I think the difference between you and me is that you're much more linear. You want there to be an answer. You want there to be a right and a wrong, so you can know how to act. But me, well, I just can't stop myself from seeing everything as linked together, so-called good things and so-called bad ones, all joined up in one single complicated dance.'

'I think that's what I meant. Or something like that. You make me feel a little naïve.'

'Focused, let's say. You're focused. It isn't a bad thing. Specially if you want to make something happen. I may make you feel naïve but people like you make me feel rather detached and irresponsible. You do stuff. I just watch, and maybe make the odd picture of what I see.'

He sighed. 'Well, making something happen is turning out to be rather challenging here. I spoke to a biologist – Mary Boldero, she was called – who said the only solution to the duende killings was to move all the Mundinos out of the Delta completely.'

Hyacinth clicked her tongue in distaste. 'Arrogant cow.'

'You know her?'

'Not really,' she admitted, 'except by sight. But I know the type. You get the old Amizad hands like Katherine Tiler, the old sixties Marxists who came out here identifying with the Mundinos as the victims of imperialism. And then you get the new types, the bright college-educated young things who basically despise the Mundinos for their ignorance and superstition. They don't like duendes any more than anyone else does, of course, but defending the duendes allows them to feel they occupy the moral high ground in relation to the Mundinos.'

'Harsh!'

She chuckled. 'And probably unfair. Maybe we could have a swim when we've finished the coffee?'

'That would be good,' he said, wondering a little uneasily in his British way what exactly they were going to wear. 'Oh, by the way, I saw Mary yesterday with this oilman who's been staying in the hotel.' He sipped at the strong black coffee she'd brought for them. 'I wonder if he would like the Mundinos moved out as well, so he can exploit the Delta in peace.'

'You mean this new guy Tim Dolby? I think that's quite possible. He wouldn't have to deal with the Legislative Council then, or draw up contracts with a hundred different chiefs. The only people he'd have to worry about would be a few dozy old bureaucrats in Geneva who've never even been here, and are hoping to pick up some consultancy work when they retire.' She lay back on the ground, let herself be cradled by the pink vegetation, its spring-like coils vibrating with every movement she made. 'It would be a truly shitty thing if that happened. The Mundinos might not have wanted to come here in the first place, but they've made the best of it. They've built a truly unique society.'

'Unique? Really? Aren't there societies a bit like theirs all over the world?'

She turned towards him in her soft pink bed, her hands behind her head. 'Feel the pull of this forest, Ben! Just stop and notice how it's tugging at you right now at this moment, never mind how it is when duendes are around. And think of all the sad little nobodies in Amizad who don't even dare step off the Rock. And then consider the fact that most Mundinos never step *on to* it. That is a pretty unique cultural adaptation they've managed to make.'

'The forest doesn't seem to trouble *you*,' he said, and as he spoke, he felt an old memory being activated, one of those trivial fragments of the past that drift into consciousness for no obvious reason. It was only half-formed, a feel, a kind of shape, like the shape of a name you're trying to remember but can't quite reach, but it seemed to have something to do with the Scout hut, and that patch of waste ground opposite it that Hyacinth called her wood. The smell of diesel fumes was in there, and the way the collar of his Scout uniform chafed on a hot day, and an uncomfortable emotion: a feeling of being exposed, made to look foolish, shown to be afraid…

'I love being out in the forest,' she said, and he felt his half-retrieved memory sliding back into whatever place it was that unattended memories lay waiting for activation. 'But I'm only here a month or six weeks at a time, and most of that in Amizad. I expose myself to the Delta in modest doses, and I only rarely run into duendes. I get the impression you like the forest too?'

Whatever it was, the fragment of memory had gone. 'I guess I do,' he said. 'It seems to kind of ... I don't know ... unlock me.'

He was surprised to hear himself say that. Even the fact that he'd spoken such a thought aloud at all was almost evidence that it was true. She moved her right hand from behind her head to touch him lightly on the arm. 'I can see it doing that to you, Ben. I could see it already on the boat. And it's a lovely thing to watch. It feels like you needed something like this.'

He thought perhaps she was right about that. He was feeling happy, in fact, and it was a feeling he hadn't experienced for a long time. But it wasn't just the forest that had made him so, it was the realization that Hyacinth liked him in much the same way that he liked her. Who would have thought it? But it was true. It suddenly struck him that they were only a short distance away from a kiss.

For a moment that seemed delightful, and then it became something else entirely and he recoiled from her in his mind. Did he even like her, he asked himself, this woman who chose to stand outside of life, observing and not taking part? Wasn't that selfish, and immature, and even a bit creepy? And anyway, did he *ever* really like what seemed to be happening between them? Not just with Hyacinth, but with women in general? Pheromones. Shiny eyes. Giggly excitement. Ugh! What a desperate business it all was. How repulsive even. Damp mucus membranes. Bags of bones and skin and guts, pressing clumsily together in search of – what? What could one sack of guts, half-filled with shit, hope to find in another, except more guts, more shit? Yes, shit and guts, that was about it. And anyway, if she really knew him, she wouldn't like him at all. This whole attraction thing was just a trick played by nature to get you to do what it wanted.

Hyancinth sat up abruptly. 'Ah, there they are,' she said tautly, pointing across the pool.

Guts – and – shit, guts – and – shit, the words were running round and round in his mind to the tune of 'Three Blind Mice'. 'What do you mean?' he said, and then he spotted them too. Two smooth grey heads were poking up from the water underneath the opposite bank, their small black eyes fixed on the two human beings.

He felt the pit beneath him, and the chambers where he couldn't bear to look. He seemed to glimpse a dim room where he sat all alone at a long table, eating a meal that tasted of nothing at all. Good boy. Good boy. Good little lonely bag of guts and shit. And then just for a moment he sensed a bright blade in brilliant sunlight, an exultant burst of pure red blood …

The two of them stood up. Hyacinth grabbed her knapsack. Without saying anything to one another, without even meeting each other's eyes, they walked quickly back to the path.

(12)

As Katherine Tiler had promised, there was another, larger, meeting in that brown airless room in the Town Hall. It was a meeting specifically about how to stop duende killings and everyone present felt obliged at least to present themselves as being concerned about the problem.

Tiler herself, for instance, opened with a solemn statement on how she and her staff were completely committed to protecting what she even managed to call the 'indigenous population of the Submundo'. She was not a very accomplished performer, speaking her lines doggedly like a farmer reluctantly roped into a village theatrical, and Da Ponte who spoke after her was even more wooden, but no one laughed and no one said to them, 'You're only performing a part,' because the rule of society was to take what is being said at face value, or at least to pretend to take it that way.

You wanted to believe people, that was the thing. It was something that Ben had had to struggle to overcome at the beginning of his police career, because he found that once he started not believing people, it made him doubt everything to the point that all the words he said, and even the thoughts inside his head, had started to seem like performances. There was a reason for people being predisposed to accept things at face value. It kept you away from sinking into that deep well, that pit, each layer cancelling the last, descending downwards into meaninglessness.

Among the new people there was a Mundino man in his mid-sixties called Branco Muti who was the chair of the Legislative Council. Ruggedly handsome, with a crinkled, leathery face, and wearing a three-piece suit and a cravat, he was utterly charming, insisting on everyone using his first name, speaking excellent British English and even wanting to know what part of London Ben came from. 'Walthamstow? Know it well! Lived just down the road from there myself.' He'd worked in London for several years, apparently, and then in Rio, before coming back to the Delta. His performance was much more accomplished than Tiler's or Da Ponte's but it was almost camp: his protestations of concern about duende killings were fulsome, and he insisted earnestly that the

Legislative Council was 'one hundred and fifty per cent on board', but he kind of twinkled as he spoke, almost openly acknowledging that everyone present was playing a game.

Another new participant was a small, grey, watery-eyed man in his sixties with a clerical collar and broken veins in his cheeks, who was introduced as Father Hibbert, the parish priest not only to the entire Submundo Delta but also to the Zona that surrounded it. His approach was one that Ben had often seen used by vicars: he played the role of the priest in a slightly deprecating way, undermining himself professionally in order to bolster his credentials as a fellow human being: 'I'm afraid the theologians haven't quite got round to deciding whether duendes have a soul or not, ha ha, but let's take a stab in the dark and say that, since they are indubitably God's creatures, they are deserving of our protection.'

Ben was temporarily distracted by fractal patterns inside his head, unfolding steadily and at great speed. He pushed them aside, as Tim Dolby took his turn to speak.

'I know companies like mine aren't exactly famous for concern about these matters, but here's a chance to make a new start.' He was apparently present because of his company's willingness to bankroll initiatives to safeguard the precious life of the Delta. As he spoke, the oilman positively glowed with the sincerity of his desire to make the world a better place, and he was so charming, so disarming, so willing to acknowledge that others present might, perfectly understandably, be sceptical about what he had to say, that he persuaded everyone there, including himself, that he really did care passionately about the well-being of the duendes.

'I want us to demonstrate that we are a different kind of organization that really takes seriously its relationship with the world around it,' he said. 'I genuinely believe there is a commitment to this in the company, and one thing I can tell you absolutely for certain is that I wouldn't be here myself if I didn't believe that.'

For a moment, the image came into Ben's mind, very vividly, of a single purple leaf, coiled and springlike, somewhere out there in the forest where no one could see it.

'This is nineteen ninety,' Mary Boldero said. For she was there too, representing the Association of Delta Scientists of which it seemed she was the secretary. 'Not eighteen ninety. And we really shouldn't even be having to discuss this.' She spoke about the uniqueness of the duendes, how science had barely even started the work of understanding them, how they built structures of such intricacy that the design went right down to the microscopic level. 'To allow them to be endangered,' she said, 'just because we're afraid of challenging the very recently evolved customs of a very small and very poorly educated community, would just be … well, there are no words … an act of such utter crass stupidity that … that …'

Here would have come tears, it seemed, if she hadn't stopped and accepted a glass of water from Dolby. Tears, of course, always seem a pretty good sign of genuine feeling, but in his police work Ben had often seen people weep who'd later been proved, without any doubt, to have been lying. Their tears had been real enough, and therefore, presumably, so were the emotions that generated them, but emotions didn't necessarily come from where they seemed to come from.

Dolby picked up the baton from Mary. 'I agree one hundred per cent,' he said. 'I'm a businessman, and I tend to think of myself as pretty hard headed, but I have to say I am blown away by this place. I am completely and utterly …' And, oh wow, here he too choked up a little, not as much as Mary obviously – that would have looked like imitation – but enough to necessitate a tiny hesitation. None of this was faked, Ben was sure, but all the same Dolby was making tactical choices. Various pathways were offering themselves to him, including even the path to tears, and he was deciding which one was best to go down in order to achieve his objectives. 'I am completely and utterly blown away,' he repeated.

And now, with Mary's willing acquiescence, he took over from her as the principal advocate of the duendes in this meeting, questioning Ben in a very respectful and even humble way, always acknowledging Ben's professional expertise and his own ignorance of policing matters, but insisting all the same, as a good advocate should, that Ben give him answers he could understand. What were Ben's impressions so far? How, based on his policing experience, did one eradicate a behaviour in a community which the vast majority within that community regarded as justified and even necessary, particularly when … and he paused here to make clear that he meant no disrespect to Branco or Da Ponte, the former responding with a wonderfully elegant gesture to assure him that no offence was taken … particularly when the police force itself was inevitably and quite rightly staffed by people from the community in question? And did Ben not think, given the unique nature of the victims, and the ubiquity of the crime, and the fact that the perpetrators themselves had only quite recent roots in this area, that perhaps this meeting needed to consider a Plan B – only to be instigated, obviously, in the event that all other methods failed – of carefully managed relocation of the Mundino community elsewhere, or perhaps simply on to the rock of Amizad, which he understood duendes seldom visited, in a way that preserved their identity and allowed them to maintain their existing community networks? 'Or am I jumping the gun here?' he said. 'Am I simply not getting it? I mean, feel free to tell me to shut up if I'm talking crap, but sometimes an outsider view can help.'

It was a lot of questions to deal with but Ben felt oddly relaxed. Everyone else, it seemed to him, had their own complicated agendas, but his position was much more straightforward. His entire job was to stop the duendes being killed.

'It is now a crime within the jurisdiction of the Special Protectorate to kill duendes,' he said, brushing aside the lingering confusion in his head – the fractals, the spiral leaves – that duendes themselves had created. 'That's non-negotiable. But I've never heard of a situation in which it was necessary to evacuate an entire community to prevent a crime. Our job is to educate the locals about the new reality, and find ways of detecting and prosecuting offenders, the same as we would do with any other serious crime in any other community.'

As he spoke, he felt his own authority growing. He felt he was quite successfully standing up to the charismatic Tim Dolby, and earning the respect of everyone else. He remembered why he liked his job, and his increasing sense of purpose helped to drive away the lingering vertigo of the duende encounter. And, at least while he was speaking, he was persuading himself of something. He was persuading himself that this duende killing thing was a problem he could actually do something about.

That night, Ben opened the left-hand drawer of his desk, where his torch lay, along with a pack of playing cards, a paperback novel, the brittle white spiral from that duende structure outside Espiritu, and those three unopened notebooks, sealed by their elastic bands. He took the torch and, after a moment of hesitation in the disturbing yet fascinating presence of a forgotten self, separated from him only by those elastic bands, he pushed the drawer firmly closed again and walked over to the southern end of town. He thought perhaps he'd go and see Hyacinth. The torch was in case she wanted to go and have a look at the forest.

Hyacinth wasn't in, though, so he continued past her apartment and Mrs Fantini's little restaurant-cum-grocer's shop, thinking he'd visit the forest by himself. It was dark now and he was very daunted by the idea of being out there at night on his own, with the pools glowing and the silent creatures among the trees, but it was an intensely exciting prospect all the same.

The light was on in Justine's pottery shop towards the end of the road, and there was some kind of largish object fastened on to the window. As soon as he noticed it, he felt the now-familiar disorientation, the disintegration of his sense of self into random and contradictory thoughts, and realized that the object was a duende. It was spreadeagled over the window, fastened there with its suckered hands and feet, its face pressed tightly up against the glass, looking in. He wanted to turn away from it but he forced himself forward until he was standing right behind the creature. Inside the shop, Justine was cowering in a foetal ball at the base of the counter, her eyes covered by her hands, but peering out at the duende between her fingers and giving low hoots of terror. From her shelves, rows of cutely appealing ceramic figures dumbly watched the scene.

'Get off there!' Ben yelled at the duende. It ignored him completely, just wriggling very slightly as if to get itself into a more secure or comfortable position.

He approached close enough to touch it. He wasn't Ben Ronson by then. He barely knew whether he was the man standing behind the duende or the woman cowering in the shop, or whether both of those people were just ghosts and there was really nothing more in existence than the rapidly unfolding fractal patterns that were filling up his mind. But some automatic part of himself reached out and shoved at the creature. Its flesh was smooth and boneless to the touch. He was terrified that it would turn its head and look right into his eyes, but it just dropped to the ground, sprang away like a frog, and bounded off up the track in a series of hops and skips.

He went into the shop, the cool sensation of touching the duende's skin seeming to spread over his body as he did so, as if his own skin was being enveloped by something cool and taut that he couldn't push away. Justine's face was blotchy with terror, and he was terrified himself. Those fractal patterns were still unfolding inside his head, incredibly intricate and entirely meaningless, and once again he had a powerful sense of countless dark chambers all around him, packed with things that he couldn't name and didn't want to see, crouching there in their cages, oozing with rage and longing and despair. Justine clung to him, she pulled him back into the little pottery behind the shop, pressed him against the bare plaster wall, groping at his groin and pressing lips on to his that were slimy with snot and tears. A small node of pleasure formed amidst the fear, drawing the fear into itself to assemble a structure so old that it went back to the days under the sea. There were two constituent parts of it, one with flesh that folded inwards, one with flesh that folded out, but it was difficult to remember which was him and which was her until that particular behavioural system completed its allotted task, and the brief stream of pleasure was abruptly withdrawn.

He pulled away from her. She reached for a piece of rag to wipe herself.

'I'm not sure what's just happened here,' he began, 'but …'

'It was nothing. You don't even like me, and I certainly don't like you and the way you judge me. But don't go yet, please. Oh God, I hate those creatures, I hate this place, I hate the forest.'

'Leave then, for Christ's sake! I can't understand why people don't leave this place when they say they hate it.'

She shook her head. 'It's what Nicky said. I've left it far too late.'

When she said she was ready to be alone again, he continued along the road, rounding the rocky outcrop and stepping back on to the forest track, with a feeling of intense excitement. A full moon was rising, making faint shadows of interlocking spirals with its dim grey light. The pools and the creeks glowed. There were plops and splashes, as creatures climbed out of the pools and crept off through the trees. A flat, ribbon-like creature, three metres long, emerged from a channel in front of him and flowed across the forest floor, while ghost rays, white and seemingly headless, dived and flapped between the spiral branches. One of them flopped against a tree, with a sound like a deflated football thrown against a wall, and clung on there, but he couldn't see it well enough to make out what it was doing.

He was about to turn on his torch when he heard a voice ahead of him, a male human voice, laughing and singing, and the twang, twang, twang of a badly tuned guitar. He found Rico sitting on the far side of a lake with his feet dangling in the water. Ben could just make him out in the phosphorescent glow, and see that there were duendes with him, three of them, pawing at him with their long, sucker-tipped fingers.

'It's all alive,' Rico was singing as if it was some kind of nursery rhyme. 'We're all alive. It's all alive.'

Ben stood watching him from across the water. His mind was already full of nightmarishly intricate and meaningless patterns and he had no desire to go any nearer.

'You're out late, Inspector,' said a voice just next to him. He started and flipped on his torch. Jael was sitting with her back to a tree, watching her boyfriend's performance.

'What are these patterns you get inside your head when duendes are near?' Ben asked her.

She held her hands up to shield her face. 'For Christ's sake, turn off that torch if you're going to stand there. You're blinding me, and you're distracting him from his work.'

He flipped the switch. As his eyes adjusted to the dim phosphorescence, he saw the secret sea extending underneath the forest floor beyond the banks of the lake, the submerged sea-trunks like the columns of some gigantic cathedral.

'People live way up on the surface most of the time,' Jael said, now more of a shadow than a real person. 'That's why everything seems so vivid and deep when you first come here. But that apparent depth is nothing really. Rico goes *way* down. He goes so far down that all those layers of memories and associations are left far away above him. Part way down, there's an engine. It's surprisingly simple. It's made up of maybe a dozen drivers at most, but every single aspect of human behaviour and human society is generated by the interaction between them. It's like clockwork, really: all those gears spinning this way and that, but at the centre of it all, just a simple spring.'

'Is that what people mean by the subconscious?'

'I don't know what people mean by that. Anything inside themselves they can't see, I suppose, or anything they choose not to look at. Like a book that lies there unopened.'

He felt her watching him from the shadow of her face. Perhaps she knew about the three notebooks in his hotel room? She was there on the boat after all. She was there in Nus.

Then her boyfriend shouted out from across the lake. 'It's all alive! We're all alive,' he yelled excitedly, banging away at his out-of-tune guitar. And he gave a little shriek of laughter, as if he were a child and the duendes were grown-ups tickling him.

'He's incredible,' Jael said. 'No one else has ever dared to go where he goes. No one. He's like Neil Armstrong and Einstein and Buddha all rolled into one. He goes down there and tells me everything he finds. He's the one that should get the fucking Nobel Prize.'

'He goes right down to what … to this … er … engine, you mean?'

She laughed. 'Oh, Christ no! That's *trivial*. He goes *way* deeper than that. The engine is just the beginning, Inspector. Evolution, survival, instincts, yada yada, yawn yawn yawn. And underneath that chemistry and physics and cosmology and mathematics, yawn yawn yawn. It's only when you're past all that stuff that things start to get interesting. Because what's beneath physics?'

It took a second or two to realize this was a question she actually wanted him to answer. 'I don't know,' he muttered. 'The Big Bang, do you mean? Subatomic particles? I'm not sure I—'

'Everything is alive,' Rico yelled out. 'Ha ha! Everything is alive.'

'Everything is alive,' Jael repeated. 'That's where he's got to. Which means he's going back in a way to the beginning of history, because people saw spirits in everything once. Ignorant and untutored people still do, of course: spirits in animals, spirits in plants, spirits in the stones and the sky. That's how the Mundinos see things, and that's what you'd hear if you talked to some uncontacted tribe in New Guinea and asked them how the world worked. But you don't hear it, do you, from smart, educated people like you and me? No, for people like us, the boundary of the animate has been shrinking steadily backwards for centuries. First step was, instead of little gods all around us in everything, there were a few gods in the sky. Then there was just one god, with the material universe as a kind of machine that God made, so science began dismantling animals to see how they worked, as you'd take apart a watch. Then we got rid of God completely. And then finally we realized we couldn't make an exception of ourselves. If there was no spirit anywhere else, there was no spirit inside us either. *We* were just automatons as well. So you can hear supposedly quite smart people these days saying to one another that "consciousness is an illusion". Ha! Me and Rico often have a laugh about that.'

Twang, twang, twang went the cheap guitar. 'Everything's alive!' her boyfriend shrieked from across the water. The duendes pawed him. Dark spirals hung over the glowing water. The Submundo scent filled the air, sweet and bitter but with something else in it that had no name. Ben's brain pitched and yawed. The fractal kaleidoscope unfolded inside his head, patterns inside patterns inside patterns inside patterns, on and on. The ditties were there too if he chose to notice them, the ditties and the puns and the shadowy chambers with memories in them, and the dim silhouettes of his desires.

'That's where our civilization has come to,' Jael said. 'Conscious-ness is an illusion! We're so alienated from our own natures that we deny the reality of the one and only thing that we can know for certain definitely exists, while insisting on the reality of constructs like, for instance, so-called quarks whose supposedly objective existence can only be demonstrated by a long chain of abstract reasoning that ninety-nine per cent of human beings are unable to follow. Talk about fucking alienation!' She gave a contemptuous snort of laughter. 'I mean, Jesus, no one would accuse the Mundinos of being great philosophers, but even *they* could see the nonsense in that! So could a fucking tribeswoman on the New Guinea Highlands who prays to aeroplanes! I mean, think about it. Consciousness is "just an illusion" but quarks are real! *Really?* Come *on*! Oh, and wait a minute, what are quarks made of?'

'What?' Ben was startled by the question. It was as if the presenter of a radio programme he'd had on in the background had suddenly addressed him by name. 'Quarks? How would I know?'

'Well, take it from me, they're not the bottom. I'll tell you what makes the shadows on the wall of the cave. More shadows. On and fucking on. No end to it. There's always something else.'

'Alive alive-oh!' sang Rico across the lake. 'Alive alive-oh!' One of the duendes had its hand splayed out over his face. Another was stroking his shoulder. A new duende was climbing out of the water in front of him.

'But we're not outsiders in this universe,' Jael said. 'That's the thing. Our minds are made of the same stuff as everything else. Take that on board, and we're back at the beginning, right? Do you follow? We're back at everything being spirit. It's just a tiny twist, from nothing being spirit to everything being spirit again, do you see, because either way it's all one stuff? It's all *this* stuff. This weird fertile nothingness that can know itself and can never cease to exist. You can't explain it. How could you? How could you explain the ground of everything, when there's nothing beyond to relate it to? But you can *know* it. And when you know it, you also know that it just has to be. It's just what being is. There's really no question to be answered. And that's what Rico's getting right now.'

Jael sniffed. 'Anyway, Inspector, you smell of sex. Who've you been fucking this evening?'

'Who is Rico?' Ben asked her. 'Where did you meet him? How did you make him become your experimental subject?'

'Ever the cop, I see.' She passed a hand over her face, looking out across the water to her boyfriend and his strange companions. 'I didn't make him do *anything*, Inspector. I found a man who liked nothing better than getting off his head, and I offered to look after him while he did it, as thoroughly and as often as he liked, without even needing to take drugs.'

She sniffed again. 'You could use a wash, you know, Inspector. Why don't you dive in and have a swim?'

He liked the idea as soon as she suggested it, but there was no way he was going to do anything like that in her cold and controlling presence, let alone in front of Rico and his duende familiars. 'I'm going to walk on,' he said.

Jael shrugged. 'He's *not* my experimental subject,' she said. She'd taken out a cigarette and lit up so that Ben briefly saw her intense, agitated face in the flare of the match as she turned away from him and back towards Rico across the lake. '*He's* the primary researcher. *His* subject is everything. *I'm* the assistant who writes things down for him.'

Ben found his own pool about a mile away, an almost perfectly round one perhaps thirty yards across, surrounded by dark silent trees. He stripped and dived in. The water was cool and suffused with soft light. He swam across it and back again four or five times, very quickly, full as he was of coiled-up energy. He only stopped then because he noticed something he hadn't spotted before: the mat of roots that surrounded the pool didn't reach down quite to the surface of the water. There was a gap between them of perhaps five inches, with the root mass forming a low roof, from which small fibrous rootlets dangled down into the water.

He dived underneath. When he surfaced five or six yards in, the top of his head touched the forest floor, but he found that if he tipped his head back a bit and grabbed hold of handfuls of the rooty fibres, he could hang there comfortably and breathe the cool, smoky-smelling air in a kind of secret cave below the forest. It was almost completely dark but he could still see the glow from the pool, and the silhouettes of thousands of tiny rootlets in between the pool and himself and, though he couldn't see it, he could *hear* the space extending into the distance in the other direction. The creaking of the woody ceiling was louder and more echoey here, like the space beneath the floorboards of some enormous house, and from everywhere came the sound of dripping water, each drip-drip-drip with its own slightly different rhythm, its slightly different pitch. It was rainwater, he supposed, that had percolated slowly down through the forest floor until the base of the rooty mass became so saturated that it dripped into the hidden sea. The sound of his own breathing was louder here too, and sometimes there was a splash, nearby or in the distance, or a series of splashes, as of some living thing breaking the surface. Duendes could find him here, he knew, and this time he was in their realm. But he was defiant. If they came, they came.

His head was full of energy, from the duendes, from the forest, from everything that had happened that night, but also from the conversation with Jael for, much as he disliked her, she'd spoken of things that fascinated him. Even when he was a very small child as young as four or five, he'd struggled in his head with the mystery of matter and mind. (He'd been quite the philosopher, in fact, back then. Perhaps all children are, as they grapple with the still novel experience of having come into being.) He'd felt he could understand how matter might form itself into more and more complicated mechanisms – even into mechanisms capable of analysing information and responding to it – but it had seemed to him an entirely different matter to explain how those mechanisms could become subjectively aware of themselves. As a teenager and a student he was still interested in this, and had read many attempts to explain it, but he'd discovered there was always a sleight of hand involved: in order to make the question into something even vaguely answerable, the authors would invariably define 'awareness' or 'consciousness' in a way that made these words mean something other than the really fundamental thing he wanted to understand, and while these other things might in themselves be fairly interesting they were nevertheless trivial by comparison to the mystery that obsessed him. Sometimes the authors he read would go as far as to dismiss altogether the question he wanted answered: it wasn't even a question, they'd say, it didn't really have any meaning. This had always angered him. How mean, how small-minded, to deny the reality of something just because it made you feel ignorant and small and without answers!

And Jael was quite right, he thought: this thing he wanted to explain, this thing that all those authorities sidestepped or dismissed as not really being a thing at all, was actually the one and only thing he could really be sure existed at all. He'd known that since he was four years old, perhaps even earlier. True, he could not point to that thing and name it in a way that he could be sure others would recognize, because he himself had direct experience of only a single instance of it, and that single instance was something that no one else could see. Naming it unambiguously would be like trying to describe the colour purple without being able to refer to examples, or talk about wavelengths, or speak of other colours from which it could be derived, but purely and simply in terms of his own subjective experience of what the colour purple actually looked like. It simply couldn't be done. But that didn't make the thing trivial or meaningless. Purple had no point without it.

And if no one could make the leap from matter to this thing he wanted to understand, if no one could show how one caused the other, if it was really impossible to bridge that gap between the world we saw and the secret awakeness which, inside each of us, was the ground of everything, perhaps that was because of a misunderstanding of the nature of the relationship. Perhaps, just as Jael said, this wasn't a question of mind and matter, but of something else that encompassed both. He'd heard it called mind-stuff, though, then again, as soon as you tried to name a thing like that, the words skittered away from their intended meaning like a bar of soap on a wet floor.

And it seemed to him, though he knew he was on less firm ground now, that it was just about possible to imagine that a completely different form of life might not only have a different chemistry and different anatomy, but might even involve the mind-stuff itself being configured in some manner unfamiliar to human beings, so that things that seemed impossible to humans, or at least to modern scientific humans, came to that life form quite naturally. Mama Elena had been right to mock him. Science had knocked in vain on the impenetrable wall of the duendes' ability to influence human minds, trying but failing to find some mechanism consistent with what it already knew: some kind of electromagnetic signal? A chemical released into the wind? A form of hypnosis? These had all been theories, but no one could get any of them to work.

Another splash, perhaps a hundred yards away, brought him back to where he actually was, and he was suddenly struck by the absurdity of his situation: a middle-ranking policeman from London, up to his chin in water and in pitch darkness, was hanging beneath the roots of a forest, and, all by himself, debating the nature of mind and matter. He laughed out loud, but the closeness of his laughter was unexpectedly disturbing in that wooden cave, as if even his own self was an intruder on his solitude, and he stopped abruptly, only for the absurdity to strike him once more and set him off again. Well, why not? he told himself. He was so far away from anyone that nothing mattered. He could have a heart attack down there and die, and no one would ever find him or know what had happened to him.

After a while he let go of the fibrous mass above him and swam slowly back towards the glow, small roots brushing softly against his hair. Almost at the edge of the pool, he noticed that rows of small elongated objects were hanging down like bats in a cave, and as he swam closer he realized that they were bluebirds, hundreds of them, their eyes wide open but somehow completely blank: the only creature that normally came out in the day, resting down here at night while the other creatures played among the trees. But they didn't wriggle and stir as sleeping bats do. Their curled mouths, sinister and mocking in the daylight, were so still as to seem without any particular significance at all. They were like toys put away in a cupboard.

It was only as he emerged from under the root mass that he thought, for the first time since he'd stepped into the forest, about what had happened with Justine. How strange. Only a couple of hours ago he'd had sex with a virtual stranger against a wall, and he hadn't even come back to it in his mind. He climbed out of the water, feeling the mild night air on his wet skin. For a moment, he thought of Hyacinth, and felt uneasy. Could you be unfaithful to a relationship that hadn't even started, he wondered, as he pulled on his clothes?

Two harts were climbing out of a smaller pool nearby. He switched on his torch. Their eyes glittered in its beam, but they didn't run. They had no ears, and no horns, and their white skin was smooth as a seal's.

(13)

'Hi, Ben, may I join you?' The oilman was carrying his breakfast on a tray. Ben had already eaten his and was just finishing his coffee. 'I've been having a look round this amazing Delta and I'd love to share impressions with you.'

Dolby dug into his grapefruit, and began to enthuse about what he'd seen. The bluebirds. The harts. The ghost rays. The amazing dance performed for him by Mundino villagers and the rhythms of their homemade guitars. Wow, just wow! But then his tone changed, and became serious and concerned, one man of the world to another, speaking frankly and confidentially about troubling things they'd both seen, but which tact and due respect to local sensitivities had made it difficult to discuss up to now.

'The killings aren't going to stop, are they? Not while things are like this. I mean, a handful of cops, who probably agree with the killing themselves, are not going to stop it happening in the communities they themselves come from. It'd be like expecting cops in fifties Alabama to prosecute a lynch mob in their own hometown. It just ain't going to happen. Least of all under the watch of that dozy Katherine Tiler. I mean, you're the expert here obviously, and correct me if I'm wrong, but I'm assuming this is what you'll be saying in your report?'

Ben had learnt as a detective to keep a poker face. Behind this mask, though, he was, at first, amused. Part of him was still in that woody cave under the forest and from that perspective, the business of the world did seem rather funny. In fact, he had to prevent himself from laughing at the absurd intensity with which people like Dolby schemed and schmoozed in pursuit of their peculiar and arbitrary goals.

'I'd discuss it with you if I could,' he said, 'but I think it's best not to say what's going to be in my report until I've actually written it.'

There was a momentary flash of irritation in Dolby's face, but in a fraction of a second he'd caught and swallowed it. 'Oh sure, sure, I understand.' He cut the top off his soft-boiled egg. 'One thing that really got to me was the sheer wretchedness of the Mundino people. I mean, history really has dealt them a truly shitty hand, hasn't it? Cut off from the modern world in this weird place, which apparently even their own folk tales say is cursed.'

'So there's oil under the Delta, is there?'

Ben saw the businessman notice the abruptness of his change of subject, and consider for a fraction of a second the possible reasons for it.

'Almost certainly,' Dolby said. 'But you know what, Ben –you're okay if I call you Ben, right? – I describe myself as an oilman because I kind of enjoy the effect that has, but my company has interests that go way wider than oil, and I'm not really involved in the oil side of things at all. Basically, what we do is turn naturally occurring organic compounds, of which oil is only one, into forms that people can use. And we think the real potential here in the Submundo is the stuff *above* the ground. There's plenty of oil, after all, all around the world, but there's only one Submundo Delta, and it's rightly protected against any kind of extraction, just like Antarctica. Even an evil oilman can see the sense in that.'

Ben could almost see the engine inside the man, with its simple imperatives: food, sex, status, control, group membership ... It really was comical once you'd noticed it and realized that, for all his cunning, all his charm and subtlety, all the many layers of complex motivations which he understood to be himself, the entity called Tim Dolby was really just a clockwork toy.

'Above the ground?' Ben asked, stifling a laugh.

Dolby glanced at his eyes with a trace of unease. He sensed that the policeman wasn't taking him seriously but couldn't work out why. 'Sure. Basically this place is a treasure house of organic chemistry, but I'm not talking about stuff we'd have to mine or drill for, I'm talking about stuff in the trees and the animals which could be harvested with absolutely minimal environmental impact. I'm very excited about the possibilities. We could be looking at vaccines against cancer. We could be looking at solutions to world hunger ... I mean, have you checked out the nutritional content of that yellow milk those flowers produce? Mind blowing! And then, of course, there's the way the duendes can unsettle people's minds, or the fact that you can't get here without losing a slice of your memory, and once we figure out how all of *that* works, there've got to be all kinds of amazing applications. I just can't believe how much untapped potential there is here, and I don't just mean potential for profit, I really don't, though of course that's important if you're going to raise the capital you'd need. No, the potential I'm talking about is the benefit to humanity. There are a number of things we need to be very very sensitive about, of course, but you know, the possible prizes are huge!'

Ben liked Dolby. True, the oilman was skilled at making people like him, but even allowing for that, Ben liked him. He had energy, he had optimism, he enjoyed making things happen, and these, after all, were all attractive qualities, qualities that distinguished human beings from, say, fungi, which simply insinuated themselves under the ground, absorbed nutrients, and didn't really *act* at all. And Ben had always admired people who acted. It was one reason he'd become a policeman and not, as had several times been suggested to him, pursued his studies to a higher level and moved into some kind of academic life.

And this thought raised a question in his mind which he had been avoiding. He had been here over a week now, but what had he *done*? What was his plan? What was he going to be able to say at the end of all this to the people who'd employed him? How was he going to write a report, as he'd been asked to do, of perhaps thirty thousand words? Because the truth was that, apart from a couple of fairly unproductive meetings, and one entirely unproductive trip to Espiritu, he'd done nothing at all about the matter that he'd been brought in specifically to address. There was even an office set aside for him in the Town Hall, he suddenly remembered with a feeling almost of panic, as if this vital fact had somehow slipped his mind. There was a room in there somewhere with a desk and a filing cabinet, and a pile of papers which he himself had requested be found for him. Yet he'd never been to the room, didn't even know where it was. And if he didn't go there soon, he'd surely have to abandon the idea of going there altogether, so unthinkable would it have become to ask to be taken to it.

But the thought of going there, forcing himself through those papers and trying to make sense of typed reports and tables of statistics which were supposedly to some extent a representation of what went on out there in the magenta forest, with its pools and channels, its iridescent birds, its remote little villages on the water's edge huddled round their blackened statues of their duende god, made him feel sick: actually physically sick. And this was the case even though the idea of continuing *not* to do anything, just letting things drift, just wandering out in the forest, and hiding in the water, and having random sex with freaked-out owners of gift shops, and talking to defrocked biologists and hippy Neil Armstrongs of inner space, and daydreaming, and losing himself and forgetting almost completely who he was, until one day the world found out about his incompetence, his irresponsibility, his complete abdication of the trust that had been put in him … even though all of that too was terrifying, panic-inducing, like some kind of slide or chute that he was already on, already slipping down at a rapid and constantly accelerating rate as it became steeper and steeper and more and more impossible to get off with every day that passed.

'Are you okay, Ben?' the oilman asked.

'Oh. Yes. Sure. My apologies. This place, eh? It kind of gets into you, don't you find?'

Dolby seemed unimpressed by this idea. 'I guess. A bit. I'm not noticing it as much as I thought I would. It does affect some more than others I gather from those medics up there on the ridge.'

His eyes very slightly narrowed as he said this and Ben realized that the oilman was reappraising him. He no doubt knew, as Ben did, that the effects of the forest were generally stronger with people who were in some way troubled or insecure, as if the internal boundaries and walls of such people were rather more flimsy than those of folk more at home and comfortable inside themselves. Someone like Rico, for instance, had probably done half the forest's work before he even set foot in the Delta.

But then Dolby laughed, shifting the conversation away from Ben in a way that seemed to be motivated by kindness, and which therefore involved a kind of demotion. In the oilman's mind, it seemed to Ben, he was gradually becoming a less and less significant player, though Dolby was a decent man, and would continue to treat Ben with respect. He means well, Ben told himself, swallowing a sudden powerful desire to punch the businessman in the face.

'Mind you,' Dolby said, 'it clearly does *have* an effect. I notice all those research guys base themselves up there on the hill, as far away from the forest as they can get. And at the other end of the spectrum, those poor Mundinos, who have to live right out there among those weird spiralling trees, apparently have a rate of mental illness that's maybe four or five times the norm. They came here against their will, that's what I keep reminding myself. They were tricked into coming here by this guy Valente, and they wouldn't have stayed if they thought they had a choice, or knew that they were still on planet Earth. You can kind of understand why they'd take it out in the duendes, can't you? I mean, they weren't scientists. How could they know what kind of thing these creatures were?'

Did he really think his agenda wasn't visible? Ben wondered. It was staringly obvious that Dolby wanted those Mundinos moved to make things easier for his company. And the very fact that he wanted this made Ben want to resist, not so much on the Mundinos' behalf, but because what Dolby was really telling him was that Ben's own presence here was pointless and irrelevant, just a bit part in one of those little theatrical performances that kept the political windbags happy while the serious people got on with the work of the world. What was more, unless Ben could come up with some new way of meaningfully reducing duende killings, Dolby would be proved right and have his way. And Ben was out of his depth, he had no ideas, he didn't know where to start, he didn't even know what outcome he wanted to reach. It was true that Dolby was also out of his depth, but he had the huge advantage of not realizing it.

'Are you a family man?' Ben asked.

His intention had just been to change the subject and gain time, but the question proved more powerful than he had expected it to be because, for a second or two, Dolby had difficulty bringing his own personal circumstances to mind and was unable to answer. 'Uh, well, I'm …' he began, and then stumbled. This was one of the known effects of the Delta. Apart from the actual loss of memory that occurred on the way in, there was also a distancing effect that made your life outside, not completely out of reach, in the way that the Zona was, but blurred and hazy, as if it were remote not only in terms of miles and the difficulty of the journey, but in time.

'Uh, sure,' Dolby said, having remembered who he shared his life with. 'Screwed up one marriage, I'm sorry to say, but the second one is going great. And one beautiful little boy. How about you?'

'One screwed-up marriage. No kids,' Ben told him, amazed at the power of the sudden flood of grief.

He made himself go to the Town Hall. He explained who he was to the receptionist and asked to be taken to his office. 'I've been working in my hotel up to now,' he explained to her, anticipating her judgement, though the receptionist seemed entirely uninterested either way. 'It just seemed easier for the preliminary work.'

To reach his allotted office, he had to pass through a hall where six or seven women were banging away on large old-fashioned typewriters under a slowly revolving fan. With no external window of its own, his room had an internal window, now propped open, at the top of the partition wall, through which filtered a small amount of the hall's brownish light and a little of its soupy brown air. The desk was nearly covered with stacks of papers, files and lever-arch boxes.

One of the typists knocked on his door as he was trying to settle himself behind the desk. She explained that her name was Sandra and that she'd been instructed to prioritize his work if he needed anything done.

'That's great, Sandra,' he told her, standing up to shake her hand. 'I've been working in the hotel up to now. The Bem-Vindo. Seemed to make sense. Very comfortable there. Nice desk. And I had plenty to get on with.'

It would have been good to have some kind of acknowledgement from her of the reasonableness of his choice, and ideally a statement to the effect that of course the hotel was preferable, nothing could be more natural, and that she was, if anything, surprised he'd come in to the Town Hall at all. But, like the receptionist, she didn't comment or give any indication, one way or the other, of what she thought of his explanation for his absence from the office that had been prepared for him, or his failure to do anything with the papers that, most probably, she herself had been detailed to search out. She simply waited for him to finish what he was saying so she could go back to her work.

'But good to finally be here,' he told her, 'and thanks so much for, you know, getting everything ready.'

She closed the door. He picked things up, put them down again. He'd asked for the same kinds of information that he'd have asked for in a London borough if carrying out an investigation into a particular problem in a particular community – recorded crime rates, local services, health statistics, economic indicators, that sort of thing –

and to his surprise a considerable amount of such data had indeed been collected together, even though this was the Delta, and even though, in the villages he had visited, there'd been no discernible sign of the Protectorate authorities having played any part at all, positive or negative, in the community's life. But though he could read the words and the numbers, they stubbornly refused to yield up anything resembling usable information. And meanwhile there was a smell in the building of old paper, and mould, and school ink, and stale oniony breath, which he tried to put out of his mind, but kept on nagging at him until he found it almost impossible to bear. And so, after three pointless and interminable hours, leafing back and forth through the material in front of him and taking nothing in, he left, muttering something to Sandra about stuff he needed to check up on back in the hotel, though he knew he'd never come back, and she seemed indifferent either way.

He walked to Hyacinth's flat, but she wasn't there. So then he walked a little further to Justine's shop, but it had a sign hanging on the door saying 'Closed until Further Notice'. There were no cute duendes left on her shelves. Mrs Fantini's place was open, and finding himself very hungry, he went in there and ordered some of her fried pork for an early lunch. He was the only customer, and Mrs Fantini herself came to stand by his table and talk.

'Still trying to stop us killing duendes?' she asked.

'I am,' he said, spearing some pork and a bit of sweet potato.

'I don't know why you bother. They walk upright and have arms and legs like we do, but they're animals, not people.'

'They're not human,' he conceded, 'but they're certainly not like what we call animals. Think of the structures they build! Think of what they can do to our minds! They're incredibly sophisticated creatures.'

But she was impervious to the arguments that had convinced the committee in Geneva to redefine duendes as persons. 'They're just animals, no different from that pig you're tucking into.'

Ben looked down at the white flesh on his plate, and remembered reading somewhere that cooked human flesh looked and tasted much like pork. Mrs Fantini had a point, he had to admit. A pig at least had eyes you could look into and see feelings you could recognize: fear, affection, excitement ... It might not be able to talk. It might not be able to build cities, or explore the structure of matter, or cultivate fields, but in its essentials it was constructed in much the same way as a human being. Whereas duendes ... well ... nothing about them was comprehensible. There was no evidence they had language. If they had emotions, they were impossible to discern. Their motives were completely inscrutable. They were even said to be the children of trees. But 'just animals'? No. Surely you only had to meet a duende to realize this wasn't so?

'So how come you Mundino folk are so afraid of duendes, then, if animals are all they are?'

'We're not afraid of them, but they're always scheming to get us, and we—'

Ben laughed. 'Scheming? Hang on! I thought these were just animals!'

'They are.' Her jaw set warningly against his anticipated charge of inconsistency.

'But if they're so smart, then—' He broke off, dismissing his own point with a wave of his hand.

'I'll tell you something, Mr Policeman,' Mrs Fantini said in a rather complacent tone, as if Ben had just conceded he was in the wrong. 'If the duendes left us alone we'd let them be. But they don't, do they? They creep into our villages. They cling on to our boats. They follow us in the forest. What do they expect?' And then she laughed. 'And you people from outside, you're such hypocrites! You tell us the duendes are harmless but you live here on the Rock, don't you? Most of you live on the slopes and work on top of the ridge, as far from the forest as you can get.'

She shook her head. 'Not that I blame you for being afraid. How could you not be, when you're all alone in your heads, with no Iya to guide you or watch over you?'

Outside, rain had begun to fall, heavy rain that seemed to come down in bucketfuls rather than drops, streaming from the roofs, pouring along the gutters. As he reached the harbour, great boulders of thunder began to roll around above the sky, while sheet lightning from beyond the far shore of the Lethe made giant daubs and brushstrokes of whiteness emerge momentarily from the uniform grey to reveal vast caves and canyons made of cloud. Standing by himself at the waterfront, he was drenched through, his clothes so heavy with water that they were almost falling off. And the rain kept coming, the surface of the river pocked with the impact craters of the constant bombardment, while pulses of even heavier rain came and went in sudden frantic drum rolls, bombarding the decks and roofs of the boats along the quay: a police motorboat, the oilman's launch, Mary's submersible with its name in big blue letters.

'So what now?' Ben asked himself. And the boulder rolled about again on the bare uneven floor of the heavens, and the canyons flashed into being and disappeared. He didn't know where to go. He couldn't bear the idea of his hotel room, or of having to be pleasant to lonely, desperate Mrs Martin, but still less could he bear the idea of riffling back and forth through papers in the shameful futility of that brown, onion-smelling room in the Town Hall.

A small boat appeared at the entrance to the harbour, with a boatman and a single passenger. The boatman was stripped to the waist so that the rain could simply stream over him, while the passenger was wearing a hooded yellow waterproof. A grey head appeared above the harbour wall and seemed to watch it, or Ben, or the whole town of Amizad, as the boat crossed the harbour and came up alongside the quay almost immediately below him. A second grey head followed as the first duende climbed right up on to the top of the concrete barrier and Ben felt a sudden loneliness so intense that it almost physically hurt, a well of loneliness that descended from far above him at the very beginning of time all the way down to this small and insignificant moment in which Ben Ronson briefly existed.

As the boatman fastened a rope to a ring of black metal set into the side of the quay, the passenger looked up and Ben realized it was Hyacinth. Back from a field trip presumably, she was very obviously tired, and soaked through, and looking forward to a towel and a hot drink and a change of clothes, but here he was in front of her, standing in the storm like a crazy thing, with his sagging clothes hanging from him.

VI. THE ANTHROPOLOGIST

(14)

Hyacinth was not someone who readily showed her feelings. She had actually felt quite drawn to Ben on the boat, and on their walk even more so. He combined self-reliance and vulnerability, worldliness and naïvety in a way that for some reason she found very attractive. She'd even been willing to forgive him the arrogance of his behaviour in Espiritu, barging into the hut of Mama Elena. But when she and Ben encountered those duendes in the pool, all these feelings had suddenly felt silly and childish.

She had encountered duendes on each of her six previous field trips, often several times, and she knew that, while the forest opened her up and made her less wary and more open to emotions in general, duende contact exposed the childish neediness which lay behind so many of them, leaving her with a sense of herself as clumsy and blundering and unformed. She felt ashamed and embarrassed about what now seemed a crush of a rather immature kind. She was annoyed with herself, and in her need to distance herself from Ben, she had begun to find him a bit creepy in a narrow, blinkered, bottled-up way. Knowing that this new negative feeling was most likely as much of a projection as the old positive one, she did her best to be polite to him for the rest of the walk back to Amizad, but she found it hard to speak to him, let alone look him in the eye.

She was too old for that kind of game, she told herself afterwards. Of course life could be lonely, and of course it was exciting to reach out towards another person and experience again that moment when the possibility seemed to open up of crossing the void and being with another spirit – there were a million songs to tell you that, a million movies – but she should know by now, without need-ing duendes to remind her, that those exciting and ridiculously hopeful feelings were basically a trick played by biology, which saw an opportunity for reproduction looming, and duly turned on a tap to flood your bloodstream with a drug not unrelated to heroin to dampen down your critical faculties and accomplish the formation of a couple. As soon as you reached that longed-for peak, the descent began almost at once, not necessarily to some sort of hell, obviously, but back to a place where, as before, you were essentially alone again, except that, if you'd not been careful, you were now shackled to another person – not a 'soulmate', and not your missing 'other half', but simply another person – whose needs you were now required to take into account every single day unless and until you could summon up the courage and energy to disentangle yourself. And disentangling yourself was incredibly hard. As a member of a couple, so she'd discovered from personal experience, she quickly became so habituated to her companion that nothing remained of the original glow, and yet for some reason the relationship was nevertheless so excruciatingly painful to give up that it involved many unsuccessful attempts before she could finally bring herself to go through the entire miserable process. It was like smoking, which she also now avoided. That habit had given only the most trivial of pleasures, but letting go of it had been one of the hardest things she'd done.

Of course, she knew that this was a jaundiced view which didn't necessarily reflect everyone else's experience, and she knew there were reasons for her being the way she was, though she tried to avoid spending too much time examining them. That kind of inquiry seemed to her a rather boring way of spending your life, however popular it might be with people with her sort of background, for whom an exquisitely cultivated self-awareness was an important social attribute. She felt more comfortable with folk like the Mundinos for whom self-analysis was simply not a thing, and who saw themselves as ranged as a group against external forces, rather than as distinct and complex individuals who needed the help of others to battle small demons inside themselves.

Or that at least was what she told herself, but in moments of scepticism about her own story, she had to admit that, although she enjoyed her encounters with Mundino villagers, it wouldn't really be true to say that she was at home with them, or was like them in any way. In fact, she enjoyed being around them precisely because she wasn't like them. When she was in a Mundino village, she was inevitably an outsider looking in, and, since that was the position she naturally gravitated to in any environment, it was pleasant to be accepted, welcomed, and even honoured in that role.

All her life, she'd resisted joining teams or taking sides. When a friend invited her to express indignation towards some other group of people (for instance, people whose political views the friend disapproved of) she always wanted to say, 'Well, I don't suppose *they* see themselves as the bad guys. I imagine they see their actions and their views as being every bit as normal and justified as we imagine ours to be.' It seemed to her that the same basic architecture was present in every human and group of humans, so that the differences between individuals and groups were presumably the result of different circumstances and different histories rather than of some people just stubbornly or wilfully being *wrong*. And so the popular pastime of making judgements about the moral shortcomings of other groups of people had always bored her. Such judgements, in her experience, were rituals whereby tribes defined and differentiated themselves and established their credentials as, so to speak, the Chosen People, even if they had no God to choose them. As for the business of trying to work out how to make things better in the world, that just exhausted her, since she could see drawbacks in everything. But she found life interesting, and on the whole she liked people, and liked especially the way that human beings gamely juggled the blatant contradictions of their existence and came up with personalities and cultures and societies that actually did work more or less, even if on paper they were the most ramshackle of improvisations, like the little community of humans and animals and plants that had managed to co-exist in her childhood in the ruins of Diski Row.

But it just didn't suit her to pick one person, or one group of people, and attach herself to them and say, 'These are my own people, this is my own special person.' And while obviously what nearly happened between herself and Ben would have been a very long way from any sort of serious or permanent attachment, still, in her experience, such attachments did rather rapidly become the expectation once you started kissing people in forests, unless you were with the kind of person – and she'd found a few – with whom you could have a very clear understanding from the start that this was not the way it was going to go. Ben *wasn't* that kind of person. He was too conventional, and too little aware of his own needs and limitations. He was nice to look at, no doubt about that, and a good man quite probably, and perhaps not *really* creepy, and certainly thoughtful and intelligent, but he would be such hard work, as people always were when they were too contained and bottled up to really know themselves.

She was unsettled by the whole business, though. She couldn't deny that. And while her usual habit was to chill out in Amizad for a week or two when she arrived back in the Delta, acclimatizing herself before beginning the fieldwork itself, catching up on a bit of reading and enjoying the odd ambiance of that funny marooned little town, this time she felt the need to get out straight away into the forest and the Mundino villages.

There was a man called Horga who she regularly hired for her field trips, a sensible middle-aged man with a reliable motorboat who knew his way round the countless channels that branched and divided across the Delta, and (a particularly important qualification in Hyacinth's case) didn't feel the need to chatter all the time. Seeing his boat in the harbour, she packed some things and went to find him, and soon they were swinging out on to the wide smooth waters of the Lethe, with the purple fringe of the forest stretching along the far bank half a mile away. She felt herself relaxing already as Horga turned left and northwards towards the mouth of a large northerly tributary of the Lethe known as the Corrente.

Boa Sorte was the only village on a side channel of a side channel of the Corrente, and was one of the most remote and northerly human settlements in the whole forest, only a couple of miles away from the formidable black escarpment of the Montanhas de Vidro that sealed off the Submundo Delta from the north. As usual, a row of cabins extended over the water, propped up by poles, but there was no one there to see or hear the boat arrive because the whole village was occupied. Hyacinth could hear guitars and singing from the central square behind the cabins, and see the smoke of a fire. What was going on, as she and Horga both knew, was a Cabeça party, an impromptu celebration of a fresh crop of duende heads.

Horga watched her face with a degree of anxiety as he turned the boat towards the jetty. He himself had been born in a neighbouring village but he lived in Amizad now, and she knew he'd know about the decision of the committee in Geneva, and the arrival of the British policeman, and even about Hyacinth's own friendship with the British policeman, for the two of them would have been observed talking on the quay and walking together in the forest, the latter being, in traditional Mundino society, tantamount to a commitment to marry. And she knew that all of this would have been talked about by now across much of the Delta, for the Mundinos kept a very close watch on the outsiders who had arrived half a century ago to establish the Protectorate. What they were being protected *from* was rather unclear, as several Amizad Mundinos had sourly observed to Hyacinth, particularly now that the outsider community seemed to have taken the side of their traditional enemies from beneath the forest floor.

'Don't worry, Horga,' Hyacinth said, 'I've no intention of getting involved in this. They sound like they're winding down. Why don't you take the boat back up the channel a bit and we'll wait?'

They moored beneath some trees round a bend in the channel. Horga rolled home-grown tobacco into a fat cigarette and, as he smoked, strolled about collecting a handful of nectar flowers. He offered one of them to Hyacinth, but she didn't feel hungry, so he tossed back the honey-milk himself. Then they waited, her on her back in the soft waterside vegetation, him with his bare feet dangling in the water, picking his teeth and listening to the music. Cabeça parties, as they both knew, didn't usually last more than an hour or two, unless there'd been a really bumper crop. The singing carried on while the heads were smoked to preserve them but, once that had been accomplished, people usually returned to their normal activities.

'They say there's a jaguar in these parts,' Horga said after a while. She was half asleep by then, and his deep voice broke through into thoughts and images that were just beginning to seal themselves off from the outer world and become dreams. She opened her eyes. He was sitting on the bank with his back to her, framed by purple spirals, and was opening his tobacco pouch to make another cigarette. Water from the escarpment's many streams flowed through these northern channels into the wide sea of the Delta and they were somewhat faster flowing and more stream-like themselves than were the sleepy overgrown waterways you found in the forest nearer the Rock. She could hear the silvery trickling of the water as it riffled softly through the roots and fibres beneath her head. In the background the singing continued. It took the form of a single voice, sometimes male, sometimes female, alternating with a deep chorused response. Back and forth it went, call and response, each cycle finishing with a comforting descent back to the key note, as if to say, it's all right, here we are, still alive, still getting by.

'A jaguar? Should we be worried?'

She wasn't an anxious person in that kind of way, and didn't really *feel* worried at all, but she'd collected several stories about jaguar attacks in the Delta, usually in the upriver villages close to the boundary of the Zone of Forgetfulness. It wasn't hard to imagine how terrifying it would be for such a creature to wander out of the Zona and find itself in a completely unfamiliar place with no idea how it got there. If it had spent its previous life in the forests of the Zona, it might be left with no memories at all.

'No, nothing to worry about,' Horga told her. 'It's kind and harms no one.'

'Ah, like the gentle jaguar that walked and slept alongside the first Mundinos?' This was a story she'd heard in many forms, right across the Delta.

He lit the cigarette, which popped and crackled like a miniature bonfire. 'It's still here now, apparently,' he said. 'People meet it sometimes.'

'Oh really? What does it do?'

He shrugged. 'Often it's sleeping when they find it, from what I've heard, or drinking honey-milk from the flowers. Apparently, it fascinates the duendes. They're often around it, and sometimes the bluebirds too, but they all leave it alone to do what it wants. Ha. They know better than to tangle with a creature like that. '

Well, it was possible, Hyacinth thought (while in the background the guitars pounded away and the single voice was answered by the chorus). It was always difficult with Mundinos to establish whether or not a story was literally true because its literalness or otherwise was not so self-evidently important to them as it was to outsiders, but creatures from outside did undoubtedly sometimes find their way into the forest, like that green lizard she and Ben had seen from the boat, or the poor, lost-looking, injured pigeon she'd noticed a few days afterwards near the Amizad clock tower, soon to be torn to pieces, no doubt, by a flock of bluebirds. So there was no real reason to think that jaguars couldn't find their way here from time to time. She could imagine, too, that, when the forest had worked on them, they might seem gentle, just like the human loucos. But she had always thought that the tenacity of the gentle jaguar story wasn't so much an indicator of the frequency with which jaguars wandered into the Submundo, as a reflection of the deep emotional appeal to the original Mundinos of having as an ally a powerful creature from their old familiar world.

Horga glanced round at her. 'So you don't mind people killing duendes, then?'

It was a good question. Hyacinth sat and thought for several seconds before answering, unsure herself as to why she felt so indifferent about an issue which stirred up such strong feelings among the younger outsiders on the Rock. 'No, I don't think I do mind it all that much,' she finally said. 'Not really. I suppose it just seems part of life round here.'

'Ha! Exactly!'

'But now let me ask *you* a question. If it was possible to kill all the duendes, every one, so there were none of them left in the Delta, would you want that?'

He frowned and drew deeply on his cigarette, holding the rich syrupy smoke in his lungs for several seconds before exhaling. 'We wouldn't kill them if they left us alone,' he finally said, his face temporarily hidden from her by smoke. It was an interestingly evasive answer. 'And anyway,' he added, 'we couldn't kill them all, even if we wanted to. People have been killing them all my life, and there are still just as many as ever. They breed down there in their villages under the forest. They don't really need to come up here at all.'

After a while she took out her pad and pencils. She did a quick sketch of Horga's profile looking out at the water, stoical and actually very Amerindian-looking from that particular angle. And then she tried to draw the waterway itself, with the big purple leaves and helical white bell-flowers dangling down over it. She thought briefly about the duendes. The fashionable new theory was that they were one and the same species as the trees that hosted their larvae, but why stop there, she wondered? Why assume that Delta life was divided into species at all? Or even, for that matter, into individuals?

But pretty soon she forgot all that and became engrossed in the way that the water formed little V-shaped waves around the leaves and flowers that touched the surface, and how these waves complicated the reflections on the surface of the glass-clear water, and diffracted the shapes of the dark columns, just barely visible below, that were the gateways to the hidden sea. How best could she represent all that, given that she couldn't possibly draw every single leaf, or every single shadow and highlight, and even if she could, such a literal image still wouldn't convey the sense of being here, breathing in this warm and strangely scented air, in this immense and powerful silence?

For she and Horga were up to their shoulders in silence now, real deep silence, broken only by the occasional creaking of the trees, and the very soft tinkling of the water below them. It was a little while before it struck her that this silence was actually new, and meant that the singing had stopped and the Cabeça at Boa Sorte had finished.

The village was a welcoming place. Horga dropped her off there, with the understanding that he'd return the next day. She had several long sessions with the affable chief, Mama Susanna – who was a large cheerful woman in her middle fifties – along with a cast of other villagers who came and went. Beneath the statue of Iya and in front of the customary mural of the corpse servants, Hyacinth recorded on to cassettes their explanations of the complicated cosmology of the Delta, and how Iya helped the human beings protect themselves and their animals against the duendes, whose chief, Boca, with her many arms and eyes that pointed in every direction, waited at the bottom of the world and fed on souls, but Boca wasn't *all* bad, for it was also Boca who caused the trees to grow and filled the flowers with milk, a substance that would be dangerous except that Iya purified it for her human followers, just so long as the right words were spoken to her in one of the many Mundino rituals of cleansing and placation that also included leaving a baby chicken out in the forest four times every year for the bluebirds, who would kill the chick but would never eat it, as anyone could see for themselves who went back to look for it, showing that the bluebirds too were the servants of Boca and therefore not after the chick's flesh but its spirit, which they carried down to their many-armed chief deep down at the bottom of the water …

On and on. In all kinds of ways the stories contradicted the stories told elsewhere on the Delta, and even themselves, and yet, as Hyacinth saw it, they wove out of a seemingly haphazard mishmash of fears, longings, observations, politics, memories, dreams, history and pure and reckless invention, an intricate if chaotic fabric which served both to contain the village of Boa Sorte and to connect it imaginatively with all the strange things out there in the world beyond it, even the stars and moon, so as to make life feel simultaneously more exciting and more manageable than it would otherwise be if there were no stories but only the bare facts of everyday life, unexplored and unadorned. And what more could you ask? she thought.

Well, okay, actually, there were a *lot* more things you could ask for, she immediately corrected herself, for Hyacinth constantly policed her own sentimentality. Boa Sorte was a place where even the most important person in the village lived in an unlit and unplumbed single-roomed hut, decorated with dried duende heads, and was far poorer in a material sense than pretty much anyone who had any kind of a home at all in America or Europe, even the very poorest. Children dying was a routine event, and all kinds of rules and taboos and social pressures placed the lives of every individual villager minutely under the control of others. And, if all that wasn't hard enough, there were the duendes to contend with too, creeping up from beneath the forest to fill up heads with forbidden thoughts, constantly reminding people of lusts and enmities that they would otherwise have managed to ignore, and which could so easily become a threat to the stability and harmony of the whole community. Boa Sorte was certainly no utopia. And yet it wasn't obvious to her – it never had been obvious to her – that life there was necessarily less rich in interesting and fulfilling experiences, or less likely to yield up moments of contentment, than life anywhere else.

Hyacinth asked Mama Susanna about the jaguar, and the chief not only confirmed Horga's story but produced as evidence a single black claw found in the forest nearby, which certainly looked to Hyacinth as if it came from a large cat. The creature had been seen on many occasions, Mama Susanna told her, by people gathering rushes or firewood, or harvesting honey-milk. She even brought in witnesses from the village who all confirmed that the creature really was gentle and wise, and one of whom insisted she had heard it speak in a soft, deep voice, almost too low to hear, giving her comforting messages from her dead baby son in the spirit world.

If this had been Borneo or Papua, Hyacinth might have proposed a search for the animal the next day, for there'd have been hunters willing to lead her to it if she made it worth their while. But she knew from experience that the Mundinos were useless as trackers, not because they were stupid or unskilled, but because this wasn't a skill they had ever needed to develop. (They were gatherers, certainly, but they weren't hunters: there was no creature in the forest that was good to eat, and they lived perfectly well on honey-milk, supplemented by the produce of their vegetable plots and domestic animals.) In any case, she was still not entirely convinced that there was an actual physical jaguar out there to be found. The claw looked authentic, it was true, but she couldn't tell its age and for all she knew it had been lying in the forest for years. It was even possible that someone had brought it into the Submundo as a keepsake or talisman when the Mundinos first arrived back in the nineteenth century, for she'd discovered that every village had its own collection of such things: a Victorian fob watch with no hands, a mother-of-pearl button, an old coin, a little guitar made from the shell of an armadillo.

They made a big fire in the middle of the village that night, an exotic visitor like her being a treat for all of them, and they fed her honey-milk, both fresh and fermented, and pork, and eggs, and cabbage and sweet potatoes. She didn't sleep very deeply, what with the energy of the forest pouring through her head, but she dreamt constantly, lying there by herself in a hut vacated for her by the chief's daughter, and listening to the trickling sounds beneath the village, and the creaking and groaning of the forest adjusting its great mass to fluctuations of pressure in the air and water that surrounded it.

'Did you have a good time?' Horga asked her when he came to pick her up the next day.

She told him she'd had a great time, absolutely the best, and he was pleased and laughed. But as they headed back down the channel towards the slightly larger channel it joined on to, and then along this larger channel towards the even larger Corrente, passing thousands of magenta trees, a couple of Mundino villages, and one crashed biplane encrusted in glistening white spirals, a certain melancholy set in. Why, she asked herself, did she so much enjoy the company of people who were so different from her in the way they saw the world and the rules they lived by, that any real intimacy, any sort of shared understanding, was entirely impossible, meaning that she and they were really a sort of novelty show for one another? Or to put it another way, why did she enjoy the company of people who she would never seriously think of living among for anything other than a short time? As she'd told Ben, privacy and freedom meant little to the Mundinos compared to connectedness, and though in theory she admired that, in fact she was their exact opposite, valuing privacy and freedom more than almost anyone she knew, and distrusting any kind of lasting connection as a potential trap.

Perhaps it was lucky for her mood that rain began to fall, building up rapidly to a downpour which pockmarked the entire surface of the Corrente channel and reduced the banks, less than thirty yards away, to a greyish-purple blur, screened from her and Horga by countless rods of water. Thunder rolled again and again and the strobe effect of lightning flashes turned the scene briefly into a flat glassy plain covered all over with vertical shards of glass. Horga had stripped to the waist soon after Hyacinth pulled on her yellow plastic waterproofs. She glanced across at him, wondering if she should be concerned, out here on the water, about being struck by lightning, but he just smiled and waved as he sat by his outboard motor, so she turned forward again and allowed the storm to draw her into a kind of trance in which there was no real boundary between the inside of her head and the water in front of her and all around. It lasted all the way back to Amizad.

When at last they swung into the harbour she noticed the solitary figure standing on the quay, more or less at the point where Horga always moored, but paid no attention to it until Horga had tied up the boat and she'd reached up to one of the ladders set into the side of the quay. And of course then she saw that it was Ben the policeman. He was soaked through, his clothes so heavy that they were just dangling from him, and his hair plastered down on his head. She couldn't imagine what he was doing there in the storm without even a coat, but she was tired now – she'd emerged from her trance and was back inside a body that was short of sleep, bored of being soaking wet and stiff from several hours in a jolting motorboat – and this seemed in any case to be a ridiculously over-dramatic way of meeting again after their last somewhat awkward parting (what a vast amount of time seemed to have passed since then). And she was also uncomfortably aware of Horga's gaze and of him no doubt wondering what she was going to say to this policeman who was supposed to stop duende killings when she herself had very definitely witnessed the aftermath of such a killing just the previous day. Hyacinth was pretty comfortable as a rule with moving between different worlds and adjusting her outlook accordingly, but it was one of those processes you didn't want people to actually watch. Most of all, though, she just didn't want the bother of a human interaction with someone who might make some sort of claim on her attention.

But still, she couldn't just ignore him.

'Hello, Ben! What are you doing out here in all this?'

It was obvious to her, just to look at him, that the forest had got to Ben as it did to many people, but, thank God, he put a brave face on it so she didn't have to deal with it.

'Christ knows!' he said. 'I suppose I got so wet, I thought I might as well stay out in it.' She could tell he'd noticed she wanted to get home, and she appreciated that, and so she relented from her initial thought that she'd just say hi and nothing more, and suggested to him that they arrange to meet quite soon. Then she touched him on the arm and told him he should go to his hotel and dry off, before slinging her bag over her shoulder and heading back to her little rented apartment, to close the door, strip off her clothes and get warm and dry all by herself with no one to trouble her at all.

VII. THE POLICEMAN

(15)

The boatman who'd brought Hyacinth had emptied the last of a jerrycan of fuel into its motor, and was pulling a tarpaulin over the boat when he noticed, seemingly for the first time, the two duendes watching from the harbour wall. Instantly tensing, he stared at them for a few seconds and then looked up uneasily at Ben. Ben wondered whether, if he hadn't been there, the boatman would have gone for the creatures with a boathook or a machete. But the man shrugged, finished tying down the tarpaulin and then slowly climbed the ladder, encumbered by the empty jerrycan and a bundle of wet clothing. He nodded to Ben, and, after one last uneasy glance at the duendes, headed off in the opposite direction to Hyacinth, the rain running down over his bare back. So now it was just Ben and the two duendes left.

Or so he thought, until he noticed that another figure had arrived at the end of the quay. Rico, thin and wasted, was sitting there in just a pair of shorts with his feet dangling over the edge, gazing out across the water towards the duendes. Ben looked around at once for Jael, who he'd come to think of as Rico's minder, or even almost his owner in the sense that one owns a pet or a performing animal, but this time Rico seemed to be alone.

He walked over to him. 'Hello, do you remember me? I'm Ben from the boat. I saw you in the forest the other day.'

'She thinks I'm her diver,' Rico said. 'She sends me down, and waits for me to come back up again.' He was no longer looking in Ben's direction by the time he'd finished speaking, his eyes drawn back to the duendes on the harbour wall with their small black eyes and their identical, meaningless smiles. They were staring straight at the two humans.

'*That's it, that's it,*' Rico whispered, '*that's the way.*'

Ben squatted down in front of him in the hope of catching his attention. 'Are you talking to the duendes?'

But Rico didn't look at him, just grinned to himself in response to some inner thought. 'They can't hear you, dude,' he said absently, tossing a morsel to the policeman while at his core he concentrated on something else entirely. 'They've got no ears.'

'No, but I wondered if you had some other way of communicating with them.'

Rico didn't respond to this, just watched the duendes, oblivious to the rain streaming down his face and dripping from his nose and his chin. Ben saw him mutter something, but it was much too quiet to hear beneath the downpour beating down on the concrete and the water, and the booming of thunder rolling about above the forest on the far side of the Lethe.

'Can you talk to them in your mind?'

'They can't talk,' he said, still without looking at Ben, and still smiling to himself. He muttered something else that Ben couldn't hear and which didn't seem to be intended for him.

One of the duendes dropped off the harbour wall and disappeared beneath the ravaged surface of the harbour itself. The other followed straight away.

'Dear God! Have you called them over somehow?'

Rico wouldn't answer. Even his smile had faded. It was as if he was no longer aware of Ben's presence. But Ben remembered how Rico had been in the forest and how the duendes had crawled all over him, and realized that, if he stood here much longer, something like that was going to be happening right here in front of him, with those duendes as close to him as Rico was now.

'She thinks I'm *her* diver,' Rico said, speaking very much to himself and not to Ben at all, 'but one day I won't come up again.'

Ben walked quickly away from him towards the town square, and didn't look back. He just couldn't bear the thought of seeing the creatures pulling themselves up on to the quay with their suckered fingers.

(16)

The hotel lobby, which doubled as a bar and lounge, was unusually lively. There was a feeling of energy and even excitement, as if the onslaught of rain outside the windows had created a sort of wartime camaraderie and sense of purpose. Several men and women were sitting at the bar, the barman was busy, and three or four separate groups were at tables around the room, including a group centred on Dolby the oilman, whose two tables were pushed together under a painting of the clock tower in a gold frame. Mary Boldero was there, and several bearded young men, their heads leaning forward as they talked intently. There were papers on the table in front of them, and coffees and glasses of water. Dolby glanced over, recognized Ben and waved, no longer very interested in him as a useful contact but acknowledging him as a human being. 'Jesus, Ben,' he called over, 'you look like you've got about half the Lethe soaked up into those clothes.'

Everyone in the room looked across at Ben. At another table Nicky Martin sat talking to a friend with short fair hair. 'My lord, Mr Ronson. You're soaked through. Can we get you anything?'

'I'll be fine, thanks.' As he spoke, Ben realized that the friend was once again Justine the potter. He hadn't recognized her because she'd cut off her hair, which made her look more grown up and a little tougher.

Justine looked at him uneasily, as if uncertain whether to acknowledge she knew him. 'Hi,' they said awkwardly to each other, and Ben squelched and dripped off up the stairs.

After he'd showered, he felt in a better mood than he'd done all day. In a clean white shirt, white linen trousers, and a pair of white slippers provided by the hotel, he made himself a cup of mint tea and carried it to one of the two armchairs on either side of the window, each of which had a small round table beside it with a pad of hotel notepaper, and a white pencil on which was stamped the image of the clock tower that, right now, was being pummelled by rain just outside the window. He took up the pad and wrote at the top of the page, 'Duende killings. Options.'

1. Prosecutions. Increase the size of the police force with recruits from outside of the Delta. Criminalize not only duende killings but the keeping of duende heads and body parts. Rigorously enforce the law, with random searches of entire villages as well as searches every time bodies are found or killings are reported by informers. Arrest and imprison offenders.

2. Fences. Address the reason for the killing, which is the upset to villagers caused by duendes coming among them. Surround the villages and their gardens with duende-proof chain-link fences topped with razor wire, and lockable gates. This would involve moving villages back from the waterfront.
3. Relocation. Do what Dolby wants and move all the Mundinos out of the forest.

He looked down at what he'd written. These, or some combination of these, really were all the possibilities, given that the Mundinos were unlikely simply to be persuaded to stop something which to them seemed natural and necessary. And here was the root of his problem. It wasn't actually that he was indecisive, or lazy, or any of the things he'd been accusing himself of ever since those grim few hours in the Town Hall. It was simply that none of these options appealed to him, or struck him as something he could recommend. The fence option, for instance, would not only change Mundino villages into ugly besieged fortresses but would actually prevent the duendes themselves from doing something they seemed to want to do. For after all, if duendes really were intelligent creatures, they must know by now the dangers of going near the Mundinos and yet, with a vast expanse of empty forest at their disposal, they continued to do it very persistently.

He could resign, he thought. He could write a letter setting out why this wasn't really a policing problem. Even just considering this possibility felt like lifting a heavy burden from his shoulders. But there was no hurry. He lay down the pad and stretched out. He'd sleep on it. He'd allow himself a little more time before he made a decision. His tea was cool enough to drink now, and he took a sip. He really was in no hurry to leave this place.

•

There was a tap on the door. It was Justine. 'I thought that probably we should speak,' she said. 'You know, after what happened.'

'Yes. Good idea. Of course,' Ben said, though he didn't really see the need, and invited her to sit in the other chair on the far side of the window. She was wearing jeans and ankle boots. Cutting her hair short had greatly changed the way she looked.

'I wanted to say ...' she began.

'Please,' he said. 'It feels like you're going to apologize for something but, whether or not it was a good idea, what happened was something that we both chose at the time.'

'In a way, I suppose. But I'm conscious that I grabbed hold of you, and if something like that had happened the other way round, I know I would have experienced it as an assault.'

'Well, I didn't see it that way. Not in the circumstances. Our brains were scrambled by the duende being so near. '

She frowned. Without the long plait and girlish clothes she'd worn before, this tall, angular woman, a few years older than himself, had a slightly austere appearance. It seemed she'd finally given up on the fruitless project of trying to be young. 'I wanted to take control of something,' she said. 'You had rescued me. I'd given way to terror, and you'd managed not to, and so you drove the duende away and released me. And of course, I ought to be very—'

'I was scared too,' Ben assured her, 'but it was easier for me. I saw the duende in the distance. I had a chance to prepare myself. I didn't have to feel cornered.'

She brushed this aside with a wave of her hand. 'You rescued me, and I should have been grateful. Well, I *was* grateful in a way, of course I was, but I was also angry. I couldn't bear the idea of being the helpless little princess that the knight in armour had to come and save.'

'Well, as I said, I didn't—'

She wouldn't let him finish. 'Because, you see, I've been there before. Rico climbed up to my tower like I was Rapunzel, and I was so grateful to him that I was willing to give him anything. I was grateful to him like a little child is grateful to a kind grown-up, and I didn't notice for a long time that actually *I* was the grown-up. He'd made *me* into the grown-up almost at once so he could just relax and be a child with no responsibilities. I organized everything, I paid for everything, he sucked at my breasts. But at the same time he still wanted to be the big man, so at regular intervals he would punish me for being the thing he'd more or less made me be. He'd punish me and frighten me so as to make me feel small and turn me back again into a little child and then, when he'd done with that, he'd expect me to look after him again. So I could be a defenceless child or I could be a gentle mother, and both of those were wrong in his eyes, yet he wouldn't allow me to be anything else.'

'Are we talking about Rico who goes around with Jael?'

'Oh, I'm sorry. This is such a small world, and we all know one another's histories. One forgets that people from outside don't know everything from the moment they arrive. Yes, I am talking about that Rico.' She laughed. 'Though I'm not sure why, to be honest. It's really not your problem at all, is it? I do apologize!'

'Rico was down on the quayside an hour ago. I tried to talk to him. He seemed to be communicating in some way with two duendes on the harbour wall.'

'Really?' She thought about this for a few seconds. 'I don't know how he can bear to be near them. They always expose me to a sort of icy wind of scorn, telling me I'm dull, and ordinary, and—' She broke off, dismissing what she was about to say with a small sweeping movement of her hand. 'But they never bothered

Rico in that way. His mind's constructed in a different way. More
… more chaotic, I think. He never even pretended to be a balanced
human being. And now, well, I'm afraid he's barely human at all
any more. Jael uses him as a tool, an instrument. She doesn't care
what happens to him, as long as he helps her learn whatever it is the
duendes know that we don't.'

'I had the feeling just now that Rico was growing tired of being
a tool.'

She studied Ben's face as she weighed up what he'd said. 'Do
you think so?' she said. 'Knowing Rico, I wonder if it's just that
the duendes are beginning to have more power over him than Jael
does. He doesn't really have a will of his own. He's like a cuckoo, but
instead of laying eggs in other birds' nests, he hitches rides on the
will of others.'

'Well, I hardly know him at all, of course, so—'

'I was walking behind you, you know, that time you threw my
little figurine into the harbour.'

'You were behind me? I'm so sorry, I had no idea. It wasn't that I
didn't like it exactly, it was just that I'd met some real ones not long
previously, and—'

She laughed. 'You didn't like it. Don't pretend otherwise. You
disliked it so much that you couldn't bear the idea of carrying it
even as far as this room. I can't say I blame you. Those figurines
were dishonest. They were me denying everything I really feel
about the duendes and sticking this false image over the top, like
… I don't know … like a Mickey Mouse sticking-plaster over a
festering wound. Everyone praised me for making those things, but
that's only because they wanted a sticking-plaster too. They can't
deal with the fact that the duendes are powerful, so they liked it
when I reduced them to something cute they could pity.'

Justine had been looking down at her hands, but now she glanced up at Ben. He felt a momentary stab of desire. She was only a few years old than him, but it was just enough of an age difference to be noticeable in the lines on her forehead and round her eyes. Rico was not the only man who was attracted by the idea of a mother, he thought. But in any case, the body remembered where it had been, and where it had found pleasure.

'I threw all the rest of them into the harbour too,' she said. 'The whole lot. And the cute Mundinos as well. Because Mundinos are scary too, don't you think? They face something that the rest of us can't face. I feel that very much. Every time I meet a Mundino who still lives out in the forest, I feel reproached. I think most outsiders feel that, no matter how much they cluck their tongues about Mundino superstitions and duende killings and all of that. In fact, I sometimes think that's *why* we criticize the Mundinos. To make them seem smaller, and help us feel bigger.'

'I've not met so many Mundinos. I like Mrs Fantini in the place up the road.'

'Oh yes, Mrs Fantini. She has a house here in Amizad, but she says she has to keep going back to the forest regularly to get back that feeling of being alive. There's a lot more duende in the Mundinos than they know, I think.' She laughed. 'It's a funny thing about this place – probably you've already noticed it yourself? – you see things in other people all the time that they can't see themselves at all.'

'Mrs Fantini sees us outsiders as lonely creatures, hidden away inside our own heads, with no Iya to watch over us and connect us together.'

She nodded distractedly, no longer really listening. 'I was a little too harsh on Rico just then. I mean, it was hard to know the truth of anything he said, but from what I gathered, I believe his own mother didn't care for him at all. She had him put in care, and he wasn't treated well there either. So it's not surprising, when you think about it, that he both wanted me to be a mother for him and wanted to punish me when I *was* a mother.'

Ben pulled a face. 'Well, that's a psychological explanation. I suppose it makes a *sort* of sense, but, when you're a police officer, you get pretty sick of that sort of thing. If you ask me, whatever happened to him, it doesn't make it fair for him to treat you like that.'

'No, but look at him, look what he's done to *himself*! And, after all, he's not the first person to get the people around him confused in his mind with the ghosts inside his head. I do it too. All the time, I feel the whole world watching and judging me and deciding that I'm dull and disappointing.' She glanced at Ben again, eyes narrowed suspiciously.

It was still raining outside. Gusts of wind threw bucketfuls of water against the window. Ben imagined the whole Submundo Delta filling up with run-off from the mountains around it, and the Valente Falls over to the west roaring and smoking with the extra volume but yet still not keeping up with it, so that the hidden sea rose beneath the forest. It would fill that wooden cave, he thought, and seep up through the mat of roots above it to meet the rain soaking down from above.

'Another thing about Rico,' Justine said. 'I should give him credit for making me face the forest. In that way at least, he performed an adult role. To be honest, ever since he left me for Jael, I've given way to fear. You saw the result of that the other night, I'm afraid. It's crazy, really, that I've let it get to that. The one thing about living in the Delta that makes it unique is the very thing I hide from, and all I'm left with is life in a dull little town, cut off from all the other towns and cities in the world.'

She frowned. 'But I don't want to leave this place,' she said quickly and firmly, as if Ben had already suggested it. 'This is me, you know? The Delta is where I live. I don't belong to France any more. I don't belong to the world outside. I just need to embrace the place where I am.'

She stood up, and he stood politely too. 'Anyway,' she said, 'you've assured me that an apology isn't needed for what happened, so I won't apologize. But I didn't thank you properly and I should do. Not just for driving that duende away, but for making me think about what I've allowed myself to become. I'm grateful for that.'

He bowed his head slightly. 'Well, my pleasure.'

She laughed, a surprisingly full and throaty laugh from someone who had struck him as so timid and fragile on first meeting, and she opened her arms to him, inviting an embrace. 'Come on, Mr Englishman, you and I were fucking each other against a wall not long ago. Don't you think we could run the risk of being just a little less formal now?'

'Sure,' he said. 'Of course. Very British of me.' And he stepped into her embrace and let her hold him against her. He smelt her warm fresh skin. He saw the lines and wrinkles on her neck. She was older than him. He found that very exciting. But he wished this wasn't happening all the same.

'I'm full of agitation,' she whispered. 'It eats me up. I could call it fear. Or I could call it a form of energy which it just so happens I've got no idea what to do with, but …' She hesitated. He could tell she wasn't at home with the way she was talking. 'But I could call it desire,' she said.

They kissed. It just seemed easier than not doing so. And soon they lay down together on the hotel bed.

'You're rather a success with women here in Amizad,' she said when she was pulling on her clothes again.

'Why would you say that?'

'Everyone says you're close to Hyacinth, who I think is very interesting and attractive and nice. And then there's—'

'*Do* they?' Ben interrupted. 'Close to Hyacinth? *Why*? We were on the boat together. We've met a couple of times. I certainly like her, but ... close? I don't see why anyone else would think they know that.'

She shrugged. 'And then there's my friend Nicky downstairs.'

'Oh now, come on! That really is ridiculous. There is literally *nothing* there at all. Who could possibly think otherwise?'

'She's taken a real shine to you. And she seems to think that you're not completely immune to—'

'Oh, for goodness' sake!'

'It's this place,' Justine said. 'Even if we avoid the forest, it touches us, and we notice things on the edges of our field of vision that normally we'd not see at all.'

'I really don't like her,' Ben said.

Justine laughed. 'Nor do I, now you mention it. And yet she's quite possibly my best friend here in Amizad. What do you make of that?'

He went to the window after she'd gone. Rain was still falling as hard as ever, and a part of the square was flooded between the Hotel Bristol opposite and the Town Hall to his right.

He saw Justine, in a green plastic raincoat and carrying a yellow umbrella stamped with pictures of owls, emerge, turn right and hurry off towards the upper part of the town, away from the harbour.

He realized he hadn't asked where she lived. Shortly after she'd disappeared from view, the three-wheeled van of a greengrocer's shop –'Fruteiro de Michael'– crossed the flooded area, sending up a great fan of water as it headed off down the main street. He thought at first that, now that Justine and the van had gone, the square was empty, but then he noticed Rico. He was squatting at the foot of the clock tower, with his arms wrapped round his bare knees, staring at the downstairs window below Ben's room, where the people were gathered in the bar.

And as Ben looked down at him, beautiful wasted Rico sitting out there in the rain in his shorts, something happened which Amizad people had assured him just never happened at all. Two duendes appeared, half a mile from the harbour and right in the middle of the town. One leading, the other a couple of yards behind, they hopped and skipped across the square and settled down beside Rico, one on each side, their little black eyes following his gaze towards the window below Ben's.

Ben hated the idea of them looking up and noticing him so he withdrew into his room. He felt besieged. He didn't want to go downstairs to the room that Rico and the duendes were apparently watching for some reason, and he certainly wasn't willing to go out into the square while they were still there. So what was he going to do? He had already written down his few options for the management of duende killings, and had already concluded, to his own immense relief, that he'd gone as far as he could go with that. He had a couple of novels with him, but his present circumstances were far too strange for an invented story to have any sort of appeal. On the other hand, there was no chance of his getting any rest if he just lay down on his bed. He sat at the fake Louis XIV desk and pulled out the drawers, wondering what else he could fill the time with. He seemed to remember bringing some playing cards and, if so, he could perhaps play a game of patience. But what caught his attention were the three notebooks, his notes from oblivion, each one held closed by thick elastic bands, one blue, one purple and one red. He took them out and turned them over in his hands. He could remember writing the words on the cover of the blue one, 'Journey to Nus', and he had a pretty good recollection of what he'd written in it for the first three days or so, but he knew there were two more days when he was inside the Zona but hadn't yet reached Nus, which he couldn't remember anything about. He had no recollection of writing the second, purple, diary at all, of course, or the red third one that had been on his knee when he first emerged from the Zona.

He hesitated. He knew he didn't want to look at the purple or the red notebooks, but he thought perhaps the blue one wouldn't be so bad. He already knew what he'd written at the beginning, after all, and towards the end, though he would by then have crossed into the Zona, he would still have been on the boat, so that whatever happened couldn't really have been so very different from what had happened before.

So, taking care not to look out of the window, he carried the blue notebook over to the armchair, removed the bands from the cover and began to read. He could remember writing the opening pages and could recall the scenes they described, but even they exuded a certain mystery. A past self, even a remembered past self, was still a different person from the one sitting here now, even if only separated from him by five or six weeks. For instance, as a London boy whose previous travels had all been confined to Europe, that former self was quite excited by the exoticism of the green tropical vegetation he was passing through – the monkeys, the parrots, the constant din of insects – and he reacted to them in a completely different way from how he would react to them now, having encountered magenta trees and bluebirds with teeth, and the strange, white, headless rays. But of course this previous self was still recognizably him. From the brief mentions of Hyacinth, for instance, Ben could see that his usual rather pathetic anxieties about how he appeared to women were niggling at him back then in a way that was still entirely familiar. Yet even there his perspective felt different now from what it had been at the beginning of the journey.

But then a past self is always mysterious, he thought. Even the Ben Ronson that just a few minutes ago had been rummaging through the drawers of that ridiculously ornate desk already felt quite remote and distinct from the Ben that was sitting here now in this fancy armchair with the blue diary on his lap. No one had seen that former self standing there – he hadn't even seen himself – and there was now no evidence for his existence outside of Ben's memory. He was already a kind of ghost, as this self too would be in just a few minutes' time.

Ben turned the pages of a diary which excitedly described a tapir glimpsed on the bank, a fisherman in a canoe, a place where an enormous forest tree had fallen across the river and blocked half of it with a mass of green foliage, necessitating several hours' delay while the crew attacked it with a chainsaw, and he remembered all these things, though it was as if they came from long ago.

He also remembered writing the entry from the 3rd of July:

I'm sitting on deck writing this under the electric light on the starboard side. Hyacinth is sitting under the light on the other side of the deck reading a book which, appropriately enough, is

called *The Other Side*. Hundreds of moths and other insects are
whirling round the light and from time to time a bat swoops in
out of the darkness and grabs one. Mrs de Groot had one of her
migraines after dinner, so is down in her cabin being attended by
Mr de Groot. The engine chugs and smokes away, and from both
banks comes a constant din of insects. We can see the nearby
trees in the light from the boat, but behind them the forest is just
a silhouette. Occasionally a fish leaps out of the water, or a bird
flaps across from one side of the river to the other.

Korzeniowski reminded us at dinner that the boundaries
of the Zona are unstable, shifting back and forth by several
miles. 'We may have passed the outer boundary,' he told us
with a shrug, 'or it may still be ahead of us. You can't tell at the
time, of course, because it doesn't feel any different.' It's only
when you're out of the Zona again and look back, he said, that
you can know when it was that you crossed into it, because the
moment of crossing is the point beyond which you no longer
have any recollection of the journey. He suggested, for example,
that if we discovered later on that we could recall the main
course of the meal, but nothing whatever about the dessert,
then we could probably conclude that the crossing occurred
between the two courses. And here he made one of his jokes,
which are always difficult to spot because he doesn't smile or
change his tone of voice. 'Though it could mean, of course,'
he said, looking down without enthusiasm at the canned fruit
salad we had in front of us, 'that the dessert simply wasn't
worth remembering.'

It's leaving the Zona that is the really disorientating bit,
apparently, not the going in, because, assuming you're awake,
you know when it happens. Korzeniowski says that, even

now, after all his years on the Lethe, it's a big jolt for him, that moment when he suddenly realizes that he doesn't remember the previous second, or the previous hour, or the previous two or three days. He knows roughly where he is, of course, because he knows which way he was headed before he entered the Zona, but without referring to his records, he doesn't even know who's on board (for people get on and off at Nus) or what cargo he's now carrying. 'Luckily, I'm on a boat when it happens,' he said, with a grim, humourless chuckle, 'and I'm travelling at about eight knots in the middle of a river. As you know, it's not so great for aircraft pilots.'

Myself, I find the idea of entering the Zona to be a pretty big deal as well, even if you can't know exactly when it occurs. The fact is that, whether or not we're in the Zona now, we'll definitely be inside it tomorrow morning. And so, dear future self outside of the Zona, you may or may not be able to recall this evening or remember writing this, but you definitely won't recall anything about tomorrow. And all being well, the next thing you'll be able to remember is something that may be stranger still, because by the time you've passed through the Zona, you'll be in the Delta itself.

He hesitated for some seconds before turning to the entry for July 4th:

We're definitely inside the Zona. I don't feel any different, and I can still remember perfectly well what happened yesterday and the day before, and my life back in England. But (apparently!) in a few days' time, there'll be a me that won't remember today at all.

And that's weird. Knowing that this me, the one who's sitting here writing this, as usual, under the starboard light on the deck, will leave no trace in your mind, future self reading this diary, and whatever thoughts or feelings I have over the next three days will simply disappear as if I'd never had them at all.

And whatever I *do*, for that matter. As long as I don't do something the consequences of which will still be obvious after we emerge from the Zona. Like, I don't know, a *murder,* say. And even then, as long I cover my tracks carefully, and there are no witnesses (other than people who are themselves leaving the Zona, of course!), I will emerge from the Zona completely unaware of what I've done. I wonder how justice works in Nus. If a suspected criminal manages to leave the Zona, he himself can't know if he committed the crime he's accused of and won't be able to defend himself in court. And police officers from Nus can't follow him unless they're prepared to forget everything they know.

But never mind that. I'm sure what most intrigues people about the place isn't the difficulty of enforcing the law. It's the possibility of escaping your own conscience that really grabs the imagination, isn't it? It certainly grabs mine. July 4th. It's very exciting. It's Independence Day in more ways than one. From now until I cross out of the Zona again, dear future self, you'll only know what I choose to tell you. And even then, how will you know I'm telling the truth?

He looked up from the notebook. This wasn't easy to read. It wasn't pleasant to hear inside his head the voice of a man who was supposedly himself, with the same body, the same memories of life in London, who nevertheless knew perfectly well that this Ben could know nothing of him other than what he chose to tell. And there was a streak of sadism in the way his past self taunted him with this fact. Knowing that what he did wouldn't be remembered seemed to have broken the tie of loyalty that normally exists between a person and their own future self.

Ben turned the page. July 5th. It was the last entry in the book, the last before the purple notebook of which he remembered nothing at all. But he couldn't bring himself to read it. After all, he told himself, the power of that arch and teasing ghost relied entirely on Ben's being interested in him. Without that, the ghost was impotent, he was no one, he was nothing at all.

At some point the rain had stopped completely. He stood up and looked out of the window. As he expected, Rico and the duendes were no longer there – they were creatures of water, after all – and a few people had come out into the square. There were even a couple of folk already sitting outside the Bluebird, the larger of the cafés. The priest, Father Hibbert, was at a table by himself with a small glass of something clear. The cloud cover was breaking up. Behind the Town Hall the huge glittering Delta sun was descending towards the ridge at the top of the island, the silhouettes of the research stations picked out sharply against the evening sky.

VIII. THE OILMAN

(17)

Tim Dolby first decided to go to the Delta over a meal in London with his old college friend Ziggy Stamford. They were both headlining at an event on 'Progressive Entrepreneurs as Agents of Social Change'. It hadn't quite lived up to their expectations and, when they'd delivered their contributions, they weren't keen on hanging around with the windbags and professional conference-goers. So they picked up a bottle of wine and went to a tiny little place in Chinatown which Ziggy insisted did the best Peking duck in London.

'You hear much of Jael lately?' Ziggy asked after they'd had a glass or two.

'Funnily enough, yes,' Dolby told him. 'After a long gap, I did hear something recently. She's moved to this place called the Submundo Delta. You heard of it at all?'

'Um … yes, I think so. Weird biology, yeah? Some kind of weird field around it that scrambles radio signals or something? Or did I dream that?'

'No, you didn't. I had to look it up myself, but yes, that's about it. Odd that it's not better known, isn't it?'

'It is weird, actually, now you come to mention it.'

Even weirder was the fact that they almost wandered straight off the subject again, though the research people in Amizad had since told Dolby that the Submundo was like that: straight lines of intention just sort of wandered off and petered out. Dolby took a sip of wine, glanced across at the couple at the next table who were having some sort of muffled row, and was about to speak about something completely different when with a sort of grunt of effort, Ziggy asked him a follow-up question.

'So … uh … what's she doing down there, then?'

'Well, I'm not sure, but you know her big thing has always been this whole mind-matter question, so I guess it's something to—' He broke off. 'You know what, Ziggy, why the fuck *don't* we know more about that place? In fact, more to the point, why the fuck don't *I* know more about it? My business is organic chemistry, and the Submundo has life forms that are completely different to anything else on Earth. I mean, for Christ's sake, the potential must be *huge*!'

Ziggy laughed. 'Well, go there then, Tim!'

'You know what, I damn well will!' Dolby said, and he dragged his organizer out of his pocket and made a note right then in big letters. 'GO TO SUBMUNDO DELTA!'

Ziggy laughed. 'You think you might forget otherwise?'

Dolby shrugged. He had no idea why he'd felt it necessary to make the note, but as he looked down at the words on the page, he felt reinforced by them. He felt he'd prevented the idea from just skittering away out of his reach.

'Mind you,' he said, 'it's hard to get there, from what I gather. Planes can't fly there.'

'Seaplanes, surely?'

'It's not the lack of landing strips, it's some weird memory thing. There's a moment when you suddenly lose your memory of the last twenty miles or something, and it kind of freaks people out, and they crash. Only way you can get there is by boat.'

Ziggy's passion was flying. He had several planes of his own and was a skilled stunt pilot. He was also in the process of acquiring an airline. 'Oh for fuck's sake, Tim, that *must* be crap! Okay, I accept that a sudden loss of memory might be disorientating if it was completely unexpected, but why on Earth shouldn't a properly prepared pilot be able to carry on flying in a straight line? I mean, everyone sometimes realizes they've travelled some distance without remembering it. It's a completely ordinary experience, and it doesn't make you crash! In fact, I'll tell you what, let me know when you go down there, and I'll fly in myself to prove it.'

Dolby laughed. 'Okay, you're on.'

They chinked glasses. Dolby was distracted for a moment by the couple on the next table: he was telling her she'd changed and she was insisting that, no, *he* had. He glanced across at them, and then back at Ziggy, who'd also been distracted by the conversation. They smiled. And then for a moment he couldn't remember what they'd been talking about, until he saw the words he'd written in his still-open organizer. Oddly, they felt like instructions from someone else.

'I don't know, Zig,' he said. 'It's Jael's stamping ground now, apparently. Maybe I should leave her be?'

They'd been quite a couple, Jael and Tim, back in the early days. They'd met in college in LA, and they were pretty much the smartest, the coolest, the most ambitious and also quite possibly the *best-looking* pair in the whole school: Jael and Tim, the Pre-Raphaelite beauty and the Greek god. Everyone liked them, everyone wanted to be with them, and the best part was that what the rest of the world saw in them they saw in each other too. Tim thought Jael was amazing, she thought he was, and as a pair they felt themselves to be unstoppable. They had their hands in everything, they got amazing grades, they excelled in sports – him in ice hockey, her in soccer – they took part in political debates, experimented with interesting drugs, and still found time to screw like rabbits, but way, way more inventively. Either one of them alone, they knew, was going to achieve more in life than 99 per cent of their peers, but both together ... well ... wow! Together they'd achieved critical mass.

So they got married. Of course, he knew that she was smarter than him. As he used to say, if the average person scored 5 on a scale of 0 to 10 and pretty smart people scored 6 or 7, then he was maybe an 8, but Jael was off the scale. That was okay, though, because, as she acknowledged herself, her smartness was a kind of specialist skill, like being able to play a piano concerto after a single hearing, or figure out a checkmate twenty moves ahead. In other spheres they were equals, and both agreed that he definitely had the edge when it came to managing people. This was basically because he enjoyed people more than she did. He had the skill of always being able to find something in other people that he could like, and it was a very useful one, because people liked to be liked, and while to Jael the dumbness of other people was simply an intolerable irritation, to him human obtuseness was itself an interesting challenge, a particular property of the raw material that he had to work with. If you wanted to synthesize a new polymer from mineral oil, you didn't blame the oil if you couldn't make it work, after all, you went back to the drawing board and tried to figure out another way. The way he saw things, it was just the same with people, although he had a certain respect for the purity of Jael's approach, which was basically, keep up with me or fuck off.

They were both equally ambitious. By common consent, she was headed for Nobel Prizes and multi-million-dollar research projects, but, while he had the makings of a pretty decent scientist himself, he knew he was never going to be the best, so he went into the oil industry instead and became a businessman. He was *very* good at that, and he saw something that very few people in the industry could see back then. He saw that oil wasn't always going to have the same central role in the world economy. New developments were already on the horizon: alternative sources of power, new ways of synthesizing the chemical compounds that were needed for modern life. (A lot of people didn't know, for instance, that it was perfectly possible to synthesize a form of gasoline from air and water alone.) Most of these options, as practical propositions, were still far off, but he knew that the ones who started heading in their direction would be the ones who got there first.

And he loved his work. He loved to do stuff. He loved to make things happen. And, being human, he especially loved to make things happen that he could count, or point to, or touch, and say to himself and to others, 'That thing there is only there because of me, it's only there because I put it there.'

But now a crack appeared between him and Jael. They were both doing incredibly well. They had a big house which people came from the glossy magazines to photograph, and everyone seemed to want to know what they had to say, and what they were going to do next. This was fine with Tim because he liked to be the centre of attention, but Jael very quickly grew bored of it. She didn't care any more about these markers of success. What had the décor of their kitchen got to do with anything, she'd ask, and even, what difference would a Nobel Prize make? She'd still be the same person, and the world would be the same world. The point wasn't to accumulate cups in the trophy cabinet. The point was to understand the world, to see it whole. Everything else was trivial.

And increasingly she'd tell him that he'd sold out and that all his company did was cheapen and bastardize science by using it, not to learn about the world, but (as she put it) 'to make stupid dumb things to sell to stupid dumb people in order to make other stupid dumb people rich'. And she couldn't understand why he wanted anything to do with it, unless, deep down, Tim Dolby was just as dumb and shallow as all the rest of them.

So they fought a lot, and both of them started seeing other people: both of them, but her especially. She was burning up with surplus energy and rage against the stupidity of everything. She needed somewhere to take all that or she'd explode. And since no one else was apparently smart enough to really *be* with her, she worked her way through one man after another, or sometimes two or three at a time, using them and discarding them with the ruthlessness of an industrial process. Yet still, for a while, she and Tim continued to share that beautiful house, and limp on as a sort of couple. Everyone had told them they were made for each other and that was hard to let go of. And, of course, even ferocious fighting is a kind of energy that isn't very far away from sex.

Meanwhile, their careers continued to blossom. She had a reputation by now of being awful to work with, but she was also known for helping every institution she joined to achieve all those stupid targets that she herself so despised, like publications in prestige journals, and research grants, and coverage in the media, so they were all still falling over each other to persuade her to work for them. But increasingly, whatever they offered her wasn't good enough. Her colleagues weren't smart enough, the institutions didn't give her the freedom she needed and, in fact, never mind the institutions and the failings of her colleagues, even *science itself* wasn't good enough, for at least in the form that the modern world had come to understand it, it was dumb and trivial and beside the point. 'It's just fucking stamp-collecting, Tim,' she said. 'Don't you get that? It's an infinite paperchase, which impresses the stupid, but really leads nowhere at all.'

'You've changed completely,' hissed the woman at the next table. 'Everyone can see it but you.'

'Well, she can't expect to have the whole place to herself, can she?' Ziggy pointed out, manoeuvring duck towards his mouth. 'I mean, if she wants to flush her career down the toilet, that's up to her, but that's no reason why you shouldn't pursue whatever you want to pursue.'

Dolby looked down at the message in his organizer. 'No, of course not, but … you know … I don't want to stir all that up again.'

'So what's she actually doing down there?'

'She went out to join a research project, fell out with everybody as usual and, from what I gathered, has ended up working on her own in a way that other scientists don't recognize as work or science at all: no publications, no peer review … nothing.'

'What a waste of a talent.'

'I know. Apparently some of the people down there think she's actually gone nuts. You can kind of imagine that, can't you? That merciless, laser-like gaze she directs at the world finally rebounding on her. But anyway, nuts or not, she'll always being able to support herself, so she really doesn't need anyone at all.'

'She's got a bunch of patents, yes?'

'Yeah, she's got a guaranteed income for the foreseeable future. So she doesn't need employers, she doesn't need grants, and of course prizes and honours don't mean anything to her. Nor do possessions, actually. So she can do whatever she damn well likes, and define "work" and "science" in whatever way she chooses.'

'Well, I still don't think the fact that she chose that place to commit career suicide means that you shouldn't be allowed to go there.'

Dolby dabbed his mouth with a napkin. 'No, I guess you're right.'

Tim had married again, to a normal dumb human being like himself, and they had a little boy. It wasn't the best marriage in the world – his need to work all the time probably precluded that – but it was nice that they didn't have to be up till five in the morning on a regular basis to scream abuse at one another, and he hoped that the houses and cooks and maids went some way to compensate for the absence of himself. He particularly appreciated not constantly being told that everything he did was trivial and worthless. Was there *any* criterion of success that wasn't in the end arbitrary? he asked himself. Wasn't it Jael who was really on an infinite paperchase?

'In fact, you know what, you're *absolutely* right,' he now told Ziggy. 'Damn it to hell, I am going there!'

'Brilliant! Let's drink to it!' Ziggy said, glancing down at what Dolby had written in his organizer, as if he needed reminding what exactly they were drinking *to*. Dolby took out his pen again, put a circle around the words 'GO TO SUBMUNDO DELTA!' and underlined them heavily several times.

They raised their glasses.

'Yeah,' said Ziggy, 'and don't forget to tell me when you go. I really mean it about taking a plane down there.'

•

When Dolby looked into how things worked in the Delta, he came across the usual array of what Jael would have seen as maddening hurdles and stupid, stubborn people, but Jael herself, as far as he could tell, wasn't going to be a problem. She seemed to have dropped out completely and he was told she was hanging out in the forest with some hippy she'd picked up. His own take on hippies was that they were basically adults who didn't want to grow up. The drugs, the freaky music, the bright colours, the elves and wizards, the search for easy, lazy, wow experiences: all of it, as he saw it, was about trying to live in fairy-tale world and not face the challenges and hard work of the real one. And of course you could understand why fairy-tale chasers would be drawn to the Delta, but it was disappointing to think that Jael might now be one of them, because fairy-tale chasing was the opposite of science, it was trying make mysteries rather than unravel them.

Take Nus, for instance. He knew that no one could explain that weird strip around the Delta which you couldn't pass through without forgetting what happened inside it, but he knew precisely what was there. Nus was built on the same plan as Amizad. It had the same architecture and layout – a clock tower in the main square, a town hall, a couple of hotels, and so forth – but it was much more run down. There were a lot of guns there – people carried them openly – and there were several brothels and a dog-fighting pit, as well as freely available drugs more or less on every street corner and all kinds of smaller niche businesses catering to various vices. There were also a number of well-guarded warehouses along the river where latex from the forest was stored for export.

He knew all this because, firstly, he kept notes and took pictures when he was there, and secondly he looked at other people's accounts and pictures. It wasn't that difficult and, as he discovered, the boat captains who traded there had figured it all out long ago. They made careful notes of every conversation they had with their Nus trading partners, and they took and kept lots of pictures. That way, when you moored on the quayside at Nus, even if you didn't actually remember the hundred other times you'd been there, and even if you wouldn't remember the particular transaction you were engaged in after leaving the Zona, the people who came to meet you would be people you recognized, knew something about and were expecting to see. The man who piloted Dolby to Amizad – he was a former Russian naval officer called Strugatsky – had showed him a much-thumbed album that he always carried with him on every trip to the Zona, along with his Polaroid camera. He had photos of all the main streets in Nus in that album, photos of the quay and what the place looked like when you approached it from the west or the east, and photos of all the people he dealt with, along with their families and their employees, all surrounded by scribbled notes in tiny Cyrillic characters, crossed out and revised as he learnt new facts or changes to how things had been before. And Strugatsky insisted that he *did* remember Nus. In fact, he told Dolby that he remembered it more clearly and in more detail than many other places he'd been, simply because he'd had the self-discipline to develop a way of doing so.

Dolby admired him for that. Some people loved a mystery, and preferred a romantic mist to a bright clear view, but that wasn't him at all. If there was an unsolved problem, he didn't want to sit around saying wow, he wanted to start the process of finding answers. And the thing that struck him about this whole river journey thing, pretty much as soon as he heard about it, was that it was crazy. It really was completely mad that, at the end of the twentieth century, what could very possibly turn out to be the world's most important biochemical resource was unreachable by phone and could only be accessed by travelling for a month each way in an uncomfortable boat, with days lost from memory in both directions. This was a ridiculously big ask for busy, ambitious professionals, and particularly so when you remembered there was only so long they could stay in the Delta before their performance tailed off and they needed to get outside again for a break.

There had to be a way round this nonsense. Roads weren't practical, obviously, and planes frequently crashed when they crossed the Zona, though no one seemed to know exactly why. His friend Ziggy had insisted that this didn't have to be the case, but even supposing that planes really couldn't safely cross the Zona, Dolby was sure there must be some other way. And by the time he met Mary and the others in the hotel, he had a solution which he was pretty certain was viable. There would be a lot of politics to sort out, and it wouldn't be cheap, but he told them he was confident that, with their backing, and the backing of the institutions that funded them, he could make it happen.

'We can build a monorail!' he said. 'We can start it just on the outside of the Zona with an airport right next to the rail terminal, and extend it over the forest all the way to Amizad.'

He'd done some rough sums, he told them, and he figured you could end up with a journey time of maybe fifteen or twenty hours all the way from New York or LA to the Delta, which would include three to five hours of train travel to cover the same distance that now took a whole month by river.

'It would finally nail this myth of the Delta as some sort of mysterious inaccessible place,' he told them, as they sat round their two tables in the Hotel Bem-Vindo with the rain outside the window.

They'd had a couple of slightly odd interruptions to start with – first poor Ben, who was so drenched he looked like he'd fallen into the Lethe, and then some guy with staring eyes and nothing on but a pair of shorts, who looked straight across at Dolby before the hotel staff ushered him out again – but now he was getting into his stride.

'The Zona itself would only take about twenty minutes to cross,' he said, perhaps exaggerating a little, 'and, let's face it, who hasn't lost twenty minutes at some point on a journey?'

They laughed at that. One of the men said, 'I've driven from Queens to Westchester before now and arrived without any memory of going through the Bronx.'

'Exactly,' Dolby exclaimed. 'Which kind of demystifies the whole business, doesn't it? The only thing that's different about this is that it always happens in the same place. Oh and by the way, if we're worried about train drivers getting disorientated by memory loss, as seems to happen with pilots, then we can automate the train, so it would cross in and out of the Zona without any possibility of human error. That wouldn't even be hard to do: an automated train, with a track going all the way to Amizad from outside of the Zona in a straight line right over the top of the forest. It would be pretty expensive to put in, of course, over some very difficult terrain, but it would be entirely doable, and actually not as difficult as many successful engineering projects we could all think of in other parts of the world.'

They were all very keen on it. They were ambitious, focused people like himself and, while one boat trip might be fun, regular trips were a major irritation for Delta scientists, and a massive waste of their valuable time.

'It should have happened already,' Mary said.

He banged his hand on the table. 'Of course it should. I shouldn't be meeting you in this little colonial hotel from the nineteen forties. I should be in a smart air-conditioned conference facility reachable in a day from any major city on Earth. And that facility should be right in the heart of the modern bio-tech city of Amizad.'

'What about the psy effects, though?' a man called Charles asked. 'The forest, the duendes, the Zona?'

'Well, they'd continue to be interesting, of course,' Dolby told him, 'but they wouldn't create the kinds of problems they do now, would they, if folk could enter or leave the Submundo Delta in a few hours? It would be perfectly feasible, for instance, to work here during the week, and then go outside for the weekends.'

'God, wouldn't that be great?' Charles said. 'I manage to get maybe three months' work done here by staying up on the ridge as much as possible, but by the end of that, I have to get out and recalibrate, or I start to get kind of dreamy and my work loses its edge. And the whole river journey rigmarole drives me nuts. You can't even get any serious work done on those tubs.'

'And what about the Mundinos and the duende killings?' Mary asked.

'Well, to a large extent that problem would solve itself,' Dolby said. 'If they're next to a growing and prosperous hi-tech city with excellent transport links to the rest of the world, an awful lot of Mundinos are going to vote with their feet and leave the forest, either to come to work in the city, as their equivalents have done all over the world, or to leave the Submundo Delta altogether.'

'That would take some time, though,' Charles said, 'and meanwhile they'd be slaughtering duendes.'

Dolby nodded. 'I know, and you're right. They may well need to be actively incentivized to move. Well, that's entirely doable. It seems to me that there's been a lot of muddled thinking about those guys with people like Katherine Tiler seeming to think of them as their babies to protect. But the Mundinos aren't babies, they're human beings living a very hard life in a difficult situation they didn't choose. I mean, all this talk about "unique culture": okay, sure, they have their own dialect, their own songs and dances and so forth – I've seen some of them, as I'm sure you have too, and very enjoyable they were – but we need to get that in proportion, don't we?'

Of course he knew they already agreed with him on this, but he also knew that people very much liked hearing their own convictions rehearsed in front of them as if newly minted, so they got the chance once more to agree vehemently with themselves. Wasn't that 80 per cent of the conversation at an average dinner party?

'It's not like these people are some sort of indigenous population that has been here for thousands of years,' he said. 'They're the descendants of landless peasants and freed slaves who were basically dumped here in the mid eighteen sixties. The indigenous inhabitants of the Delta are the *duendes*. And of course, they *have* been here pretty much for ever, and they're the ones who the Mundinos have been killing on an industrial scale. I don't want to screw those people over, and I'm sure none of you do either, but there are perfectly good options which are surely better than the life they lead now. They could move to Amizad and be given decent houses or they could be helped to move back to Brazil. If they wanted, they could be rehoused together in villages where their songs and language and so forth could be preserved. What is *not* an option, though, as far as I'm concerned, is for them to continue living out on the Delta and murdering the locals.'

They were all in full agreement with that. 'Absolutely!' 'Some of us have been saying this for years.' 'If the duendes were human, it would have been a completely different story.'

'So,' Dolby said, 'we'd end up with a prosperous city on the Rock, properly connected with the outside world, with a thriving scientific community, and a Delta forest restored to its pristine state and valued for what it is. There'd be *no* losers. The duendes would be protected, the Delta would be responsibly managed for the benefit of humankind, and the Mundino people would be given an opportunity to join the rest of us in the modern world, and not have to stay stuck in the forest which – and we really need to regularly remind ourselves of this – their *own stories* describe as a place of banishment.'

He looked round at their faces. They were the chosen representatives of the entire research community on the Rock, and it was obvious that they were all on his side.

He laughed. 'Okay, well, that's my rant over. Except to say that I do need you guys' support. If we can get the politics right, I can get the money, but I need your backing with the politics. To be frank with you, I'm not going to get any real help from Katherine Tiler.' There were groans and rolled eyes at this point, and the odd ironic cheer. 'Maybe she's been affected by the length of time that she's been here, I don't know, but, whatever the reason, she seems pretty dedicated to doing nothing and leaving the Mundinos to their fate, even though she's notionally their protector. I guess she sees herself as their protector against *everything*, even progress and prosperity.'

They laughed at that, and a couple of them clapped, which made people in the rest of the room glance round to see what was happening. The rain was still falling outside, and Dolby suddenly had an odd feeling, a sense of a kind of gap inside him, a hole in his usual optimism. He found himself wondering if Jael had been right all along. Maybe his goals *were* fatuous? Maybe he really *was* madly running along a road that led nowhere at all? It was a strange feeling and it wasn't something he'd ever experienced when talking to a receptive audience about an idea that excited him. But he mentally shook himself and pressed on, which was what he always did, though usually the process was pretty much automatic.

'I had high hopes of the British cop,' he said. 'You know him, I guess? The poor guy that came in a while back looking like a drowned rat? I read up on him, as maybe some of you did, and I gathered he'd done some really excellent work in London on culturally sanctioned crimes in immigrant communities. In fact, I was so impressed that I actually timed my visit on purpose to coincide with his. It would have been an amazing weapon in our armoury if he'd been willing to give his backing to what we all know has to be done. But, between you and me, either his CV was a little exaggerated or the forest has gotten to him even more quickly than usual. He just isn't letting me reach out to him at all, and as far as I can tell he's basically done nothing the whole time he's been here. All of which means that my one really important local ally here is you people in the research community, and hopefully the institutions you represent.'

'Well, we're completely with you,' Charles said.

'That's good to hear.' He was still struggling with that unfamiliar feeling of doubt. Were all his achievements, all the money he'd made, all the buildings that stood because of him, all the holes on the ground, all the oil and minerals and the things they were made into, all the people sitting in offices looking at screens because of ideas he'd had and business plans he'd driven through basically just there to bury his own smallness, his own dullness, his own failure to see what kind of thing the world really was?

He could see the faces of Mary and the others just beginning to register that there was something going on inside him that they should perhaps be worried about. But he knew that, though their subconscious antennae had already picked it up, they weren't yet aware that they'd noticed it. There was always a few seconds' grace, he knew, because of that default position humans had of accepting the surface of what was presented to them. He pulled himself together.

'I'm really pleased that you're on board,' he said. 'I guess a cynic would say that of course you'd support me, because what I'm basically proposing is to hand the Delta over to people like you. But I don't think this is just a matter of self-interest. It's about the future. People like us are the rising class. We're the ones who the world's going to look to in the twenty-first century: the smart, liberal, secular technocrats who come out of the world's best schools and want to do stuff, and make stuff and find stuff out. And, I'll tell you what, it's right that they should look to us, because we actually *are* the good guys.'

They laughed at that, and again a couple of them briefly clapped.

'No, I mean it,' he said, all the time wondering if he really did, like a man on a tightrope suddenly sickeningly aware of the huge drop below him. 'We're the ones who stand against bigotry and prejudice, aren't we? And we're the ones who are building what's needed for a happier, more prosperous, more connected world.' It sounded strangely thin and tinny in Dolby's ears but he pressed on anyway: he'd said this sort of thing so many times before that he could do it on automatic pilot. 'You know what,' he said, 'I'm imagining it now, those smart, creative people flying into the terminal outside the Zona and transferring to the monorail that will rush them straight to the cool, high-tech city of Amizad, over the purple trees, over all those winding channels and streams, over the remains of Mundino villages crumbling back into the forest where people should never have been made to live in the first place. That's the future. It's not just how things *should* be, it's how, in the end, they're *going* to be. How could the future *not* belong to the people who are most willing to learn, most able to adapt, most driven by the desire to make things new?'

He felt slightly nauseous, his words like big soft turds flopping out of his mouth to thud down on the table. He needed to get himself away from there before it became obvious to the rest of them that he wasn't really behind what he was saying. 'Listen, guys, I'm not feeling so great, so I'm going to leave you. But thanks for your support, and let's talk again about a bigger meeting, maybe up in one of your lecture theatres.'

Mary stood up. 'Are you okay, Tim? Do you need any help?'

'No, I'm fine. I guess it's something I've eaten. I'll see you guys very soon.'

He had only a minute or two left to get out of there, before they would see through him, see how empty he was, how shallow, how insecure.

IX. THE POLICEMAN

(18)

Ben ate in the hotel that night and was already seated at a table under the yellow light of the dining room's old-fashioned chandeliers, when Dolby showed up. The oilman looked uncharacteristically subdued, and asked Ben almost humbly if he could join him.

'I guess I've finally experienced for myself the power of the Delta,' Dolby said, as they waited for their soup. 'It happened just like that! Bam! One minute I'm having a meeting, I'm doing something I've done a hundred times before, and then suddenly my head is full of all kinds of doubts and questions, in this weird, very vivid way that I've never experienced before.'

'Those doubts and contradictions are always there, is what people seem to think, but most of the time we barely notice them.'

Dolby shrugged. 'I guess so. I've never given houseroom to nagging doubts. What's the point? Keep moving forward. On to the next thing. If you've made the wrong decision, go back and deal with it. But if you never act until you're certain, you never act at all.'

But it was obvious that this account of his approach to life felt much less satisfying to him now than it normally would have done. The duende effect lingered, after all, and it seemed to Ben that

Dolby's words sounded tired and a bit desperate, not just to him but to Dolby himself.

The oilman fiddled with his spoon. 'The odd part was that it was in this hotel, just through there in the bar. Nowhere near the forest and no duendes in sight.'

'There were two duendes right outside the hotel,' Ben said, 'while you were having your meeting.'

'You're kidding?' Dolby was visibly shaken.

'They were looking in through the window where you were sitting, and with them was a guy ... I don't suppose you know him ... a guy called Rico, who's kind of halfway to being a duende himself.'

'Rico? Jesus!'

'You *do* know him?'

'I've never met him, but he's the guy who hangs out with Jael, right?'

'You know Jael, then?'

'You could say that. I was married to her. She was one of the reasons I came out here.'

Married to Jael? It took Ben right back to his detective days: the ways things slowly connected together, like isolated spikes sticking up out of a lake that revealed themselves to be the branches of a single enormous tree, when the water was drained away.

'I happened to hear that Jael had come here,' Dolby said, 'and I kind of looked into this place a bit and it got me thinking. I knew the Submundo would appeal to her because it was life in a completely novel form, and would open up the possibility of rethinking our ideas about the relationship between life and consciousness and the universe in general. I don't know how far she's got with that but, you know, good luck to her. What struck me when I read about it was that a place like this had huge potential for *my* kind of science, the kind that generates useful stuff that can be used in everyday life: fuels, medicines, plastics, heat-proof coatings—'

He broke off. Nicky Martin had arrived with the soup and wanted to know what kind of day the two men had had and what they'd thought of the rain. It must have been obvious to her that they were in the middle of something, and were impatient to get back to it, but that didn't stop her from talking about the rain for some time. In fact, Ben was pretty sure that it was precisely *because* he and Dolby were obviously deep into something, that she felt such a need to interrupt them.

When she finally left, Dolby crumbled bread into his soup. 'If I'm honest,' he said, 'there was probably also a part of me that just wanted to bug Jael. I like to think I've finished fighting those old battles, but I probably haven't. Obviously that in itself wouldn't be a good reason to come here but, like a friend of mine pointed out, the presence of mixed motives wasn't a reason for not coming here to do the job I'm paid to do.'

He scooped up soup, took a slug of red wine, grimaced at its poor quality. 'I wonder what was going on this afternoon, though? I guess Jael doesn't exactly welcome my presence, but it's not really possible, is it, that she could have gotten her boyfriend to bring along some duendes to bug me? I mean, they aren't biddable in that way, are they? Everyone keeps telling me you can't communicate with them at all.'

'No, but maybe Rico has—'

'I mean, Jesus, where *were* they, anyway?'

'At the foot of the clock tower, looking towards the window.'

'You didn't think to come and tell me?'

'Well, why would I? You and I agree, don't we, that duendes are the locals round here, and there's no evidence that they're harmful.'

'No. Fair point.' He looked down glumly at his soup. 'But for fuck's sake, how did he get them to come with him?'

'Maybe that's the wrong question. Maybe we should ask how they got him to lead them to you?'

He had his spoon halfway between the soup plate and his mouth. 'Wait a minute! What are you saying here, Ben? The duendes wanted to find me! That's crazy. Why would they be interested in me? How would they have any idea of who or what I am?'

'I don't know, but that's really the core of our problem here, isn't it? No one knows what duendes are, or what they know, or how they see human beings. And no one knows what, if anything, they want. People like you and me come blundering in, but we really have no clue what we're dealing with. And we assume that old hands like Katherine Tiler have been addled in some way by the forest, and we never consider the possibility that they might know something that we don't, or have some kind of relationship with the forest that we don't understand.'

Dolby took another gulp of wine as he considered what Ben had said, and then he laughed. 'I'm sorry, Ben, but you're really not making any sense. I mean, come on, it's *Katherine Tiler* we're talking about! I don't want to be rude, but I've met her type before. She's a timeserver, isn't she? A colourless nonentity. All she wants is to get through the remainder of her working life with the very minimum of hassle. If we weren't here in Amizad she'd probably be building towers out of paperclips all day, waiting for the clock to get round to going-home time.'

'Possibly. But how do we know that isn't the best course of action in the circumstances? I mean, in a situation which you don't understand at all, isn't any action just as likely to make things worse as make things better?'

Dolby had been twiddling his wineglass between his fingers while sitting at an angle to Ben and studying his face intently from the corners of his eyes. Now he plonked it down irritably on the table. 'Oh for fuck's sake, Ben, that's crap! No, of course we don't understand it, but that's why we need to work on understanding! We need to step up the science. We need to improve access so the best scientists will come here. I was saying this afternoon we should put in a monorail over the forest, and dispense with this whole ridiculous nineteenth-century nonsense with the boats. I mean, for Christ's sake, that belongs to the days of pith helmets! We need to get smart minds on the job here and give them the resources they need until they figure it all out.'

Ben laid down his soup spoon, took a sip of wine. 'Figure out what, though? What happens if, at the core of all this, there isn't anything to be done in the way that people like you and I like to imagine?'

In the space of a single day he had gone from being amused by Dolby's need to do things, to being shamed and almost panicked by it, and back to finding it ridiculous.

Nicky came and collected their soup plates. 'You chaps are looking very serious.' She could tell something intense was going on from which she was excluded, and it made her jealous. She longed to be included, really included, in a group of people, but didn't know how, for her jealousy itself got in the way, her fear of losing the spotlight of attention, even for a short time, to someone other than herself. And now her attempts to suppress both her longing and her jealousy were what made her voice unnaturally cheerful and bright. You noticed these things so easily in Amizad.

'Oh, just doing a bit of business,' Dolby told her, summoning one of the more routine versions of his affable smile.

'So you're obviously keen to move the Mundinos out,' Ben said when she was out of earshot.

'It sounds terrible when you put it like that! I'm just—'

'I'm curious as to who knows about your views on that. Would Jael know, for instance?'

He laughed. 'Okay, Sherlock Holmes, so what crime are you investigating here exactly?'

'I'm just trying to understand what happened this afternoon: two duendes and a human being of sorts coming into the square.'

Nicky returned with two plates: steak for Dolby, chicken curry for Ben.

'We were just talking about the duendes in the square this afternoon,' Ben told her, suddenly curious to know what she'd make of it.

She laughed. 'In the square? Who told you that? That's nonsense! There's no way it would happen. Once in a blue moon they come up on the quay, or into the streets at the edge of town, but never this far in, not in the whole time I've been here. And thank God for that.'

'Maybe you were mistaken,' Dolby said when she'd gone. It was noticeable that this time she hadn't tried to prolong the conversation.

'No. They were certainly there with Rico. I saw them by the clock tower, and I saw them earlier in the harbour too, also with Rico, or at least if not actually with him, then definitely connecting with him in some way. It's interesting that Nicky says it's unprecedented, don't you think? Duendes in the centre of town. I would guess that duendes acting in concert with a human being would have surprised her even more.'

'I've never met Rico. Would he by any chance be the barefoot guy with crazy eyes, wearing nothing but shorts, who came into the bar shortly after you and stared right at me?'

'Ah! That's interesting. Yes, that's him. So that supports my view that they were focusing particularly on you.'

'Well, I guess he might be curious, or maybe even jealous, about his girlfriend's former husband being here in Amizad.'

'From what I've heard and seen of him, he's well beyond feelings like that. I saw him out in the forest once. He had duendes all over him, but he just played his guitar and giggled.'

'Jesus.'

'Jael was watching him from a distance. It's how they operate, apparently.'

Dolby looked at Ben sharply, frowning and clearly frightened, and then occupied himself for a while with cutting his steak into little cubes in the American way.

'You haven't answered my question yet,' Ben said. 'Would Jael know about your plans for the Delta?'

'I haven't spoken to her for years, but I guess she knows how I see things. And of course Tiler knows, and so do several other locals, so I guess she could have heard from one of them.' He speared a piece of steak, munched on it. 'So what are you saying here, Ben? That Jael told Rico, and Rico somehow – what? – told the duendes? A bit far-fetched, isn't it? And even if that were possible, why would it be a problem for the duendes if the Mundinos left the Delta? You'd think they'd be pleased.'

'Well, obviously I've got no more idea than you do what the duendes want. But you're a powerful man. You could change the Delta completely, and that's obviously what you intend to do, seeing as you've given up a couple of months of your busy life just to be here.'

Dolby chewed on his steak. 'So what are you saying?'

'I'm saying that if duendes can think at all, and if their

understanding is mediated by Rico in some way, I can just about imagine them having some sense of you as being a threat.'

'*Me* a threat!' Dolby exclaimed so loudly and indignantly that a couple on a neighbouring table turned to look at him. He lowered his voice. 'I mean, Jesus, Ben, how about the Mundinos? They're slaughtering the duendes every day. I'm proposing to *stop* that!'

He seemed to have forgotten that stopping duende killings was supposed to be Ben's job, but Ben let that pass. 'Yes,' he said, 'but that's not *all* you're proposing.'

'No. I want to open this forest up to science, to shine a light on this amazing place and all its possibilities, to celebrate it even! And above all, for fuck's sake, to *protect* it! Why would they mind any of that?'

Ben took a sip of wine. 'But think about the Zona, and the way the forest slows people down and makes them dreamy, and the way that most of the world keeps forgetting that the Delta is here at all. Not to mention the plane crashes, and the block on radio signals. Does all of that add up in your mind to a place that wants a light shone on it?'

Oddly, he was suddenly very bored. There was something dull and poky about the whole tenor of the conversation. Who cared about all this? Who really cared? This was the kind of talk a machine could have: dealing with the world as a series of puzzles to be solved according to logical rules. He longed to return to the forest and just be still. And as soon as he realized this was what he really wanted, he also realized there was nothing to stop him. He could go back there right now, just as soon as he got away from Dolby and his tiresome need to solve things, and fix things, and build things. The thought filled him with the same almost heart-stopping sense of anticipation as he'd felt that first time he'd stepped off the Rock and on to the creaky wooden floor of the forest.

'Okay,' Dolby said, 'but still, I don't want to kill them, and I don't want to damage their forest. Christ, I know what people think about oil companies, but really and truly, Ben, I don't want to do anything to harm the duendes or the bluebirds or any of these creatures and I wouldn't be here if I thought that was going to happen!'

Ben laughed. 'I believe you. But why are you telling *me* this? I can't speak to the duendes, and I don't know what they want. For all I know they don't want *anything*. Maybe they just exist, like trees. They're supposed to be the offspring of trees, after all.'

'But you seemed to be suggesting that they were trying to punish me, or warn me off or something. And I'm just saying, for fuck's sake, *why*? I mean, if they want to protect themselves, why don't they go after the Mundinos?'

Ben laid down his fork. He had eaten all he wanted of his curry, drunk all he wanted of his wine, and listened to all he wanted of what Dolby had to say. Having once thought about returning to the forest tonight, he had no other appetite that interested him.

'Well, they *do* go after the Mundinos!' he said. 'They won't leave them alone. They creep into their villages, and over their huts. That's why the Mundinos keep killing them.'

Dolby considered this in his fair-minded way. 'I must admit, I understand their feelings a little better now,' he said.

Ben tossed his napkin on to the table and stood up. 'I need to go now, Tim. I'll see you soon.'

But the oilman looked so dismayed at the prospect of being abandoned that he didn't walk straight out. Dolby was basically a kind man, Ben reminded himself. He was kind and enthusiastic and he wanted others to share his enthusiasm. And perhaps more to the point, it did feel good to be in a position of power over him. 'Maybe it's a mistake to think of the duendes "going after" anyone,' Ben suggested. 'We don't know why they do things. We don't even know if they mind being killed.'

Tim Dolby gave an incredulous snort. 'Well, of course they mind! Every living thing wants to live!'

Was that necessarily true? Ben wondered. There had been a number of times in his life when he'd asked himself what exactly the benefit was of being alive. After Cynthia left him, for example. After she told him what a cold fish he was and how cruel and punitive. ('Do you even like women?' she said to him once. 'I suggest you sit down one day and give that some thought. Do you like women? Do you like human beings at all, for that matter?') But still, whatever his glum thoughts at the time, he had eaten, he had breathed, he had looked right and left before crossing the road, and here he was, still eating, still breathing. It was surely true that any sort of living thing that was indifferent to its own survival would soon cease to exist, wasn't it? And surely that must apply even to life as strange as the creatures of the Submundo Delta?

But still, duendes were not like human beings. An unexpected image came into Ben's mind. 'Suppose you wanted some information about your DNA and I suggested taking a spatula and scraping a few cells from the inside of your cheek. Do you think the cells would mind?'

'So you're suggesting that—'

Ben laughed. 'I'm not suggesting anything, Tim, because I don't know. No one knows. That's the point.'

•

The square was full of puddles that reflected the streetlamps and the illuminated signs of the two cafés: the blue of the larger and better-lit Bluebird Café, and the purple of the smaller Café Lisboa with its flickering letter O. The air was warm and a few people were already sitting at the outside tables. There was a smell of earth, mingled with the strange bitter smell of the forest. Hyacinth was at the Lisboa, sitting by herself with a glass of something white and cloudy, and a book. She looked up and saw Ben and, though he really didn't want to talk to her when Dolby had already delayed him, he felt he couldn't just ignore her, so he walked over to say hello.

'Hello, Ben. Where were you off to in such a hurry?'

He considered inventing some imaginary appointment that he couldn't be late for, but he couldn't think of a plausible one at this time of the evening. 'I was just going to have a walk in the forest.'

She frowned. 'Okay. Well, sit with me for a minute. Let me buy you a drink.' She turned and looked for the waiter, a young Mundino boy wearing an eyepatch. Having caught his attention, she turned back to Ben. 'Going to the forest at night? All by yourself? In a big hurry? You should be careful, Ben. That place can take control of people. Like a drug.'

Ben had met a good many addicts of one kind or another in the course of his police career, and he knew what she meant. There was a difference between wanting something and being controlled by it, and if he was to be honest with himself, the pull towards the forest came without doubt into the second category. The way he longed for it was more like the way a stalker was drawn, trembling and with pounding heart, to a particular lighted bedroom window, than it was like, say, the way that a hill-walking enthusiast anticipated a week in the fells. Deferral of gratification, even for a short time, felt unbearable. Eating, drinking, talking for a few minutes to someone he knew and liked: all seemed intolerable distractions. But, though Ben was capable of this insight, it had almost no force at all. Who cared what sort of longing this was, it was still a longing, it was still something he wanted badly! Why should he deny himself? Why should he stay up here, clicking and whirring on the surface, in the head of this little clockwork policeman, when there were all those thousands of fathoms beneath him, waiting to be explored?

'Remember that Dutch woman?' Hyacinth asked. 'Mrs de Groot? She's in the hospital now, under heavy sedation, while they try to settle her down sufficiently to be able to take the boat out of the Delta. And even so, she still tries to escape.'

'But I'm here to do a job, and if I don't understand this place, I won't know what to do.'

'You *won't* understand.' The waiter came over and asked Ben what he'd have to drink, and he reluctantly acceded, at her suggestion, to a glass of sweet Madeira wine. 'You won't understand in the way you mean.' Hyacinth laughed. 'Oh come on, Ben, you must know that! That's just about the weakest excuse I've ever heard! You must know you won't learn anything you need for your job by going out and mooning about in the forest. You *must* know that's not your real reason for wanting to go there!'

He had no answer to that, but suddenly a white-hot ember of adolescent rage appeared in his mind, as if flung out from some furnace beyond his view. What right did she have to tell him where he could go? Did she have any idea what a hard thing it was to have to forego something, not because you didn't really want it, but because you wanted it so much that however much of it you had, it would only leave you wanting it even more? 'You always do this to me!' he felt like yelling at her. 'You never let me just be myself!' But of course he knew this wasn't true.

Hyacinth was watching his face with concern. She could obviously see the struggle that was going on in his mind, but she seemed to think the point was settled nevertheless, because she changed the subject, her tone becoming humbler and more tentative. 'Listen, Ben, we should perhaps speak about that time we walked into the forest together.'

'Oh, no need, no need,' he told her hastily. 'We were both a bit confused by the duendes.'

'I think so.' There was a finality in her voice which he found painful: a door being gently but firmly closed. In fact, the sadness it stirred up was temporarily powerful enough to take precedence over even his desire to return to the forest. It reminded him acutely of an old unhappy dance in which women seemed briefly to offer him something he longed for, but then couldn't or wouldn't give it to him, or stopped giving it to him, or perhaps even gave it to him, only for him to discover he was unable to receive it, like some nutrient his body needed but his gut could not absorb.

'Ha. They really do mess with your head, don't they?' he said with an attempt at a laugh. The pain was sharp and raw, but when the waiter brought the wine, he was somewhat soothed by the alcohol entering his blood, and his thoughts turned back to the forest. The forest didn't ask anything of him, after all, it didn't hold itself back, and he had no difficulty letting it in.

'What are they trying to do, do you think?' he asked.

'What is who trying to do?'

'The forest, the duendes. The effect they have on our—' He broke off abruptly. 'Oh, by the way, did you know there were duendes right here in the square this afternoon? They were with Rico, and they were looking through the window over there at Tim Dolby.'

'Really? Are you sure?'

'I saw it myself. Dolby didn't see them, but he sure as hell felt the effect of them. He's really upset about it, because he sees himself as their protector. I told him I'm not sure they care about being protected in his kind of way.'

She laughed. 'Like the Mundinos don't care for the Protectorate.'

'I suppose so.'

She sipped her cloudy white drink. 'All the biologists here are hung up on a model of evolution that involves individuals competing against each other to survive, but I'd say the Delta makes better sense if you see it as more or less a single entity. I mean, what do I know? But if I had to guess I'd say the trees and the harts and the duendes and so on aren't competing against each other, and aren't fighting to survive as individuals, any more than our blood cells are competing against our bone cells.'

Ben laughed. 'Funnily enough, I just said more or less the same thing to Dolby in the hotel.'

'Really?' She smiled. They were both pleased that they'd come to the same conclusion. 'But the biologists won't have that,' she said. 'They say it doesn't work. Game theory, all of that. Some organism is bound to cheat. But what if the Submundo Delta as a whole has been powerful enough hitherto to either neutralize or co-opt any life form that threatens it?'

'How about the Mundinos?'

'Well, again, I wonder if perhaps from the Delta's point of view they *have* been co-opted. They'd deny it, of course, but they have a love-hate relationship with the Delta: as Iya they worship it, as Boca they battle against it. And maybe that in itself suits the Delta: to have humans who are semi-detached from it, as a kind of specialist sense organ that sees things in a different way. '

Ben knocked back the rest of his wine and before he could stop her, she called the waiter for another.

'People like Dolby want things to be neat,' she said. 'They want them resolved. They want this forest to become just another thing that clever people study and have interesting conferences about, and … I don't know … "sustainably manage". They want to integrate it into the way they already understand the world and make it knowable and safe. It never occurs to them that—'

She broke off, leant forward, put her hand over his. 'Don't go back to the forest, Ben. Not now, not by yourself late at night. It takes people different ways. Some can't stand to go into it at all. Some can take it in moderation like social drinkers. But some have a few sips and can't leave it alone. I think maybe you're that last kind, aren't you? Like Rico. Like Mrs de Groot.'

'Me? Come on!' Ben was offended. His clothes were smart and well-chosen, his hair was neatly combed, he was a successful police officer, with a distinguished career, a strong work ethic, an MA from a top university, a personal trainer, an exemplary fitness regime … How could anyone possibly compare him with manifestly disturbed and damaged people like mad Rico or crazy Mrs de Groot?

A new voice spoke. 'Hi. You two on a date? I'll tell you what, Hyacinth, you want to watch this guy.' Jael had appeared. She was wearing green dungarees over bare shoulders. She pulled back the chair between Ben and Hyacinth, reversed it and straddled it, leaning her elbows on its back. There were rings of various shapes and sizes on all of her fingers and thumbs. 'Have either of you guys seen Rico? He went out first thing and I've not seen him since.'

'He's been hanging out with duendes, apparently,' Hyacinth told her, her manner stiff and cool. 'And hassling your ex.'

Jael grimaced. 'Oh fuck. It happens so damn quickly these days.'

'What happens so quickly?' Ben asked.

She turned towards him and examined his face carefully for a few seconds with her disturbingly bright and always slightly narrowed eyes. 'Him running off with the duendes,' she said. 'It's so annoying. We're just beginning to get somewhere, and then this happens, and we have to go back to Nus to recalibrate. Time was we'd get two or three weeks of useful work in first, but now it's a matter of days.' She sucked on her lower lip and drummed her fingers on the back of the chair as she considered her next move. Then she shrugged. 'I guess I haven't got much choice but to go home and wait for him. It's a big forest out there. It's not like I could just walk out into it and expect to find him.'

Hyacinth cleared her throat. 'Do you not think that maybe you need to stop pushing him out there so much? I mean, it sounds like the duendes are having a progressively more powerful effect on him.'

Jael looked away from her towards the Bluebird Café, as if checking out whether there was someone there who'd be less likely to subject her to such tiresome questions. 'Well, we *wanted* them to have a progressively more powerful effect. That was the whole point. We wanted to go down deeper into his mind. And, just in case you wondered, he wanted it even more than I did.' She sighed. 'But I guess no experiment ever takes place in perfect conditions. There's always a snag, and in this case the snag is that the duendes have some sort of agenda of their own.' She turned back to Hyacinth. 'They were hassling Tim, you said?'

'I didn't see it, Ben did.'

Ben told her what he'd observed. Jael watched his face intently, like a falcon in the sky watching the movements of small creatures below it with a cold, clear-sighted and entirely self-interested gaze.

'Stupid fucking Tim,' she said when Ben had finished. 'What business has he got sniffing round here? I told Katherine she should deny him a permit, but apparently there was no way she could with a high-profile guy like him, much as she'd have loved to have done it. He's so annoying, that man, don't you think? He's so annoyingly, dumbly *benign*. I gather he's been talking about building a monorail to Amizad, right across the Delta. What kind of shallow fuckwit thinks of a thing like that?'

This news clearly shocked Hyacinth. 'A monorail? Really? He's actually seriously—'

But Ben interrupted her impatiently. The monorail seemed like a detail right now. 'Well, nobody could accuse you of being annoyingly benign,' he said to Jael. 'You seem to be quite happy to drive your boyfriend insane.'

Her gaze returned to him and she considered his face coolly for a second or two. It was a pretty damning thing he'd just said to her, but she showed no sign of being ruffled by it. 'You're a bit like Tim yourself, aren't you, Ben?' she observed calmly. 'Benign. Or no, actually – let me correct myself – you're not really like that at all, but you'd like people to think so. Tim really *is* benign, but I saw another side of you, the other night. Not exactly the regular policeman type.' She turned to Hyacinth. 'Where were you, by the way? I mean, I assume it was you he'd just come from?'

Hyacinth looked puzzled. 'I don't know what occasion you're talking about.'

'I hadn't just come from Hyacinth,' Ben said.

Jael shrugged. 'Anyway, to return to your point. I *made* Rico. He had no agenda when he came here. He was just going to slowly fall apart, being nursed all the while by Justine the Submissive, the patron saint of doormats. I gave him a purpose. I mean, what did you expect me to do? Persuade him to wear a suit and get a job on Wall Street? He is what he is, for fuck's sake. I can't help that. But I made him a scientist and a great explorer. I gave him a place in history. ' She stood up. 'Anyway. I'll see you guys later. Oh and by the way, Ben, if you ever want a new job, I reckon you'd be quite a decent explorer too.'

'What did she mean by that?' Ben asked when she'd gone. The waiter brought him his second glass of strong sweet wine.

'She was trying to unsettle you, Ben. Pay you back for criticizing her morals.'

'I can see that. But still, she must have meant something.'

'I don't know. Something similar to what I said earlier, perhaps. I'm sure she can see how the forest clings to you.'

'How can she see that?'

She leant towards him a little. 'Surely you've noticed how easy it is to read people here?'

'I suppose so.'

'And probably you've noticed that you can see things in other people that they don't seem to see themselves?'

'Okay, so what do you see in me that I don't see? Or more to the point, what does Jael see in me that makes her think I could do what Rico does?'

Very tentatively, Hyacinth touched his fingertips with hers across the table, not as a renewed move towards intimacy – somehow she made this clear – but as a small gesture of reassurance. 'I suppose what we see in you is a kind of hunger, a kind of gap you're trying to fill. You contain it well. You have a strong sense of how you ought to behave, and you're a clever guy, so you work round it and tell yourself it isn't there. But we can still see it, a gap, a place that you yourself don't know or understand.'

He bowed his head. Her words had an odd effect on him. He felt somehow purged, as if by tears. 'It's true,' he said, from this strange, unexpected place. 'There is a gap. And when I'm in the forest, it seems to heal.'

'That's because, when you're in it, the forest fills you up with itself. Or it does until the duendes come along, anyway. They're different, aren't they? They sort of prise you open, to make still more room for the forest to fill you, and that's not so pleasant, because they move too quickly and you can actually feel yourself being taken apart. But it seems that Rico has reached a point where even that feels okay to him.'

'What I don't get is that Mundinos are out there all the time, but that doesn't seem to happen to them. They don't end up like Rico.'

'Well, that's what's unique about them. They've learnt the trick of being in the forest, but not being overwhelmed by it.'

'Of which Rule One is: don't let the duendes get near to you?'

'It seems so, yes.' She sat up straight again, withdrawing her hand. 'By the way, what was Jael talking about when she said she assumed you'd been with me?'

'I met her in the forest. She could tell I'd been with someone.' Ben took a breath. 'She could tell I'd had sex with someone, I mean.'

Hyacinth's expression didn't change in any obvious way. It remained interested, it remained, at least ostensibly, detached and free of judgement. And yet it did change, and it seemed to Ben that it changed in the same way as his must have done earlier when he felt her to be shutting a door. People still wanted doors to be kept ajar for them, it seemed, even when they didn't want to go through them. But, however she felt, 'Oh,' was all she said.

'You're probably wondering who it was with,' he said. 'Jael actually mentioned her, funnily enough. It was Justine, you know, the—'

'Yes, of course I know her. Gosh. I didn't expect that, I must admit.'

She was deeply disappointed in him, he could see. The door was not only shut now, but bolted. 'I'm not saying it was a good idea,' he said. 'I'm not even sure I like her all that much, but …' He tailed off, recognizing that he wasn't helping himself.

Hyacinth shrugged. 'Well, funny things happen in this place. Be kind to her, please. Justine's not had much luck with men. Or with anything else, for that matter.'

'Yes, of course.' He stood up. 'Thanks for the drinks. I think I'll go now.'

'But not to the forest, right? Not on your own. Not in the night.'

Ben swallowed. He longed more than anything to be among the glowing pools and the spiral shadows. 'No. I suppose you're right.'

He downed his wine, stood up, and headed across the square towards the hotel. But beneath the clock tower he stopped. The white-hot ember shone in his mind.

'Who the fuck is she to tell me where I should go?' he muttered. 'Or who I should be with, for that matter?'

He'd leave the Submundo soon. He'd return to London, and resume his old life, and his time here would soon just be an embarrassing blemish on his hitherto impressive career. And that would be the end of all this. He'd never get a chance to come here again.

With his heart suddenly pounding so hard that it was like a kind of delicious sickness, he turned away from the hotel, refusing to consider whether or not Hyacinth was watching him or what she might be thinking.

The sky was glowing in the east with the light of the rising half-moon, and by the time he reached the track into the forest, the moon itself was shining softly through the trees, making those dim spiral shadows on the ground that he'd imagined and longed for as he sat outside the café with Hyacinth. On the far side of a pool, three harts stood watching him with their cold unblinking eyes. A ghost ray flopped its way through the trees. He flipped on his torch to shine in its direction and saw it for a moment head-on, its white body and fleshy wings seeming merely to frame the great, dark, gaping hole where a head should have been.

Keeping his torch switched on, he strode forward, sweeping the beam round hungrily each time he heard a splash from one of the pools or channels. Once a fat blue beetle rattled past him, one of those occasional strays from the world outside, and Ben followed it until it alighted on the trunk of a tree beside the path. At once, tiny, soft white tendrils flowed out from the smooth purple skin of the tree, embracing the creature so gently that it didn't even try to resist, but simply clung on there, twitching its antennae, while the tendrils flowed together to become a membrane. Only when this new white skin tightened did the beetle belatedly realize it was about to suffocate, and the membrane jerked slightly a couple of times as the creature struggled to free itself. But the tree held tight until the insect was still.

He knew Hyacinth was right. There were no predators in the Submundo, no poisonous snakes, no animals that bit or stung, but it was a dangerous place. It might feel benign to someone whose hidden heart longed to reach the surface and open itself up to the world, but it wasn't in any way concerned with human welfare, only with maintaining its ancient hegemony. It cared no more for him than it cared for that beetle, or for that poor bewildered lizard which the bluebirds had pecked to death.

Yes, Ben thought as he plunged on along the track, but that was part of the appeal of it, and that was why Justine's silly little duendes were so repellent. There were other forces in the world than kindness and fairness and you had to embrace them too if you were going to be truly alive.

He found a pool, stripped and dived in. The water was soft and cool against his bare skin as he swam down into the cathedral-like spaces under the forest. But when he surfaced under the root mass, he realized there wasn't going to be a repeat of his time in the wooden cave. He was at a different point. The coolness, the stillness, the merging of himself with the world around him was no longer soothing in the way it had been then because he knew it would soon be beyond his reach, and he would be back home in London, inside the dull little box of his own head, writing reports, attending meetings, punishing himself grimly in the gym. He climbed from the water, left the track and followed a small path south, away from the Lethe and deeper into the forest.

'Come on, you bastards,' he muttered. 'Where are you? You accuse me of hiding but here I am!'

He passed several groups of harts. They watched him silently, impassively, with their faceted eyes, with none of the poised, nervous tension of wild animals in the world outside. One of those flat white ribbon-like creatures flowed across the forest floor in front of him. And then Ben had a sudden sense of something immensely tall and thin walking alongside him, perhaps twenty yards off through the trees, its white face turned towards him. In a moment of pure, irrational terror, he imagined it to be the Palido of the Mundino legends, the ghost of Baron Valente, with his cold smile, his top hat, his embroidered waistcoat, come to capture and bury him. But his torch beam revealed a completely inhuman creature, with long, thin arms and legs and a spherical and headless body, from which the limbs appeared to dangle as if from a helium balloon that was almost but not quite light enough to float away. Bobbing slightly, just as a balloon would do, the thing stopped, extended its arms sideways, and turned the flats of its many-fingered hands towards him as if they were parabolic dishes. It stayed in that position for several seconds, and then, apparently completing its task, it turned and loped away through the trees with that same strange bobbing gait, as though it was walking on the moon.

The forest creaked softly.

'Where are you?' Ben shouted, sweeping his torch around to create a kind of kaleidoscope of spiral leaves and spiral shadows. But apart from shadows, nothing moved. He wondered if his torch was the problem and turned it off, plunging himself into a world so vague and undefined it barely existed. There were just vague spiral shapes in the dim grey light, and here and there the glow of a pool or a channel. The only thing that was clear and solid was the half-moon he glimpsed through the leaves, and the sharp black spirals silhouetted against it.

A series of small splashing sounds came from the distance and he peered into the darkness, resisting the temptation to flick his torch on again. But whatever it was that had emerged from the hidden sea, it appeared to have no interest in him, for nothing approached and the silence returned. He waited motionless for several minutes, then continued walking, the spiral shadows passing across his skin as if he was simply a wave of pressure moving through the shadowy fabric of this grey and tenuous world.

He came to a pool with a space on one side of it where, for no obvious reason, there were no tree trunks. Suddenly he had the sense once again of a tall, pale presence watching him.

'Who are you?' he called out. '*Quem é Você?*' The shape didn't move or answer him and when he flicked on his torch he saw that what stood there wasn't a living creature at all but a kind of tower, seven foot tall and covered all over in spirals and curlicues of fantastic intricacy. It was what the Mundinos called a castelo, but this time it was intact.

He walked over to it, reached out and touched its hard, shell-like surface. Mary Boldero had called these things beautiful, but that seemed to him now a kind of lazy and conventional piety. This thing triggered no associations, connected with nothing in his own experience, and was completely empty of meaning. Its incredible intricacy didn't seem beautiful to him at all but cold and almost mocking.

What was he doing here anyway? he wondered, his fingers still touching the hard, brittle surface. There was no point. There was nothing here in the forest that he could learn from and carry away with him. This place fooled you. It made you feel there was somewhere else it could take you to, somewhere more open and more generous than the cramped space of your own skull. But it couldn't really take you anywhere. He was stuck with himself, confined behind the taut facial muscles of Inspector Ben Ronson. He broke off a spiral, shone his torch on it briefly, then flung it out into the pool. He already had one, and outside the Delta it would just be a bit of shell.

And then he thought of Nus. It wasn't just behind him, but ahead of him too. He wasn't just stuck with Ben Ronson the policeman, he was also stuck with whatever Ben Ronson became when he was sure that even his own self couldn't see him.

'Why don't I know?' he whispered. 'Why don't I know who I am?'

Because you're a mummy's boy, he heard himself answer inside. You're mummy and daddy's good boy. You look straight ahead and pretend you can't see the sides. You run in the race, you torture yourself trying to beat your personal best, and you never, never, never look at bad things or think bad thoughts. Mummy's boy. Daddy's boy. Mummy and Daddy's little hiding boy.

He wheeled round and there they were. Two of them, twenty yards away, squatting by the edge of the pool, watching him with their black button eyes. Oh ho ho! If you go down to the woods today you are *sure* of … Not so nice when you actually found the damn things, was it, eh? He could feel the castelo behind him, see it in his mind. An image of eternity, on and on, infinitely intricate, infinitely empty. But that's what you ended up with if you weren't allowed to look at anything else.

'I don't *want* to hide!' he shouted. He could just make out the duendes in the glow of the pool, but he shone his torch straight at them anyway. 'Why don't you just fucking show me what I'm hiding *from*? I don't care what it is! I can take it!'

But of course they didn't respond. They just watched him silently. One of them held something in the palm of one of its long-fingered hands and gently stroked it. Ben's needs and struggles were no concern of theirs.

'You've come here to play with your pretty little tower, eh?' he shrieked at them. 'Is that it? It really is picnic time for teddy bears!'

The one with the object in its hand laid it gently on the ground and then dived into the pool with a plop. Ben was instantly dismayed.

'Hey, don't go! I've come here specially to see you.'

Plop. The turbulence briefly made patterns on the glowing water and then the pool was still again, and the second duende was disappearing, frog-like, beneath the forest floor and into the hidden sea.

He turned back to the castelo and began to kick holes in it until the whole thing collapsed to the ground.

(19)

Reaching his hotel room just before midnight, he went to the window to let in some cooler air. There were still a few people outside the cafés, but Hyacinth had gone.

He thought about himself with Justine in her back room, after the duende in the window. It was impossible to deny that the violence of it had excited him. He remembered a momentary vision – he could no longer recall where – of a blade in the sun, and bright red blood.

Violence. Was that it?

Impossible to know. There were glimpses and then nothing more.

But then he remembered his diaries, his notes from oblivion, just across the room in the drawer of that fancy desk. His palms sweating, his heart pounding, he fetched the blue notebook, removed the elastic bands, and turned to the final entry.

I'm sitting on the deck as usual, with insects whirling and flopping around the light above me. It's dark and warm. The

de Groots have retired to their cabin. Hyacinth is reading
on the other side of the deck. Lessing, the engineer, is in her
usual spot at the back, writing in her notebook, surrounded
by a thick cloud of cigarette smoke. The lights of the boat
shine on the water and the nearby trees, and our bow-wave
sparkles, but otherwise there's nothing to see out there but
shadows and silhouettes. The river winds this way and that.
For every one mile as the crow flies that we notch up, we must
be travelling ten miles at least. But I know we're nearly there
and at each bend I wonder, is this where we'll finally see the
lights of Nus ahead of us? I can't believe how excited I am. I'm
like a kid the night before Christmas. I wonder what presents
Santa Nus will bring?

I've been thinking some more about what I wrote
yesterday. Strikes me that a human being's future self is really
another, separate person from who they are now. The only
thing that's special about this particular other person is that
they're someone who one day you'll actually have to *be*. And
that's the beginning of responsibility, isn't it? We're about to
do something and we think, 'But will my future self be glad
that I did this? Or will he wish I hadn't done because of the
consequences that he'll have to deal with?'

I'm reminded of watching a pigeon once in Paris, that time
with Cynthia, trying to make its mind up whether to dart
forward and snatch the piece of bread from right underneath
the bench we were sitting on. (We'd run out of things to talk
about. We weren't having fun and were feeding the pigeons
because we had no idea what to do, and there was a lead
weight of loneliness pressing down on us. Funny to think you'll
remember that too, Ben Ronson of the future, every bit as well

as I do, and yet you won't remember a thing about writing this. Not one single thing.)

Yes, and of course, as well as our future selves, we're supposed to think about *different* people as well, the people with different names and different histories and different bodies who our actions will also affect. But in their case we know we'll never have to *be* them and whatever suffering they may face as a result of our actions, we ourselves will never have to experience it. And I'm wondering now whether we try to do right by those different people mainly because of the shame we know our future self will otherwise feel, or the condemnation our future self will have to face, rather than real concern for those people in themselves?

Yes, and I'm saying 'we' here, but really I should be saying 'you'. Because these things don't apply to me, do they? I'm inside the Zona. And okay, you who are reading this are my future self in the sense that you will inhabit this same body, and see this same face when you look in the mirror, and have the same memories as I do of things like that pigeon in Paris, but in another sense I – I as I am now – have *no* future self. In a few days' time, when the boat leaves the Zona again, I will simply cease to exist and no one will ever know what it was to be me. And that means that the awareness of consequences which normally constrains a person and makes them hold back from doing things that might be seen as 'bad', and even from thinking bad *thoughts* … well, that awareness is no longer a factor. I can relax. I can be the me that comes naturally, whether that me is 'good' or 'bad', knowing that either way I – this I that exists now – will never have to face what I've done.

So what am I going to do with this freedom? I really don't know. I can feel things stirring inside me but I don't yet know what they are. There are so many possibilities. For instance, I have always thought of myself as someone who doesn't like hurting people's feelings, but I wonder whether I'd care so much about that if I knew I wouldn't have to remember that wounded face, that reproachful look, those bitter, disappointed tears? It's too early to say yet, I am like a butterfly that hasn't yet emerged from the chrysalis and has never known what it is to spread its wings and fly. But who knows, perhaps in these new circumstances, I might even enjoy my ability to inflict pain?

However that, dear future self, is for me to find out, isn't it, and for you to never, ever know.

But here comes another bend. We're going round it now. And this time, oh yes, this time there are lights!

That was the end of the first diary. He took it back to the drawer. The purple and red notebooks lay there, wrapped in their elastic bands, but he couldn't bring himself to pick them up, for a new thought had occurred to him. The arch, teasing tone of what he'd read so far was hard enough to take, and it was very disturbing to be the butt of hostile teasing that came, not from other people, but from another version of himself, yet it seemed to him that by holding things back, that past self was still in a way protecting him, still demonstrating that, whatever he might say, the Ben who wrote those words still felt some sort of responsibility to his future self. But that Ben was still in a chrysalis. He'd said so himself. And it seemed to Ben now that this vestigial need to protect his future self would fade when his hidden self spread his wings and began to feel at home with the idea that he was really completely disconnected from his own future. It was clear, after all, that, even in the chrysalis, he was already enjoying the idea that what he wrote would make his future self uncomfortable. So when his loyalty to that future self diminished still more, why would he hold back at all? On the contrary, wouldn't he write down exactly what was on his mind, and what he planned to do, and what he did?

All of this was ridiculous, Ben quickly told himself, for what on Earth *could* that other Ben have done that would be so terrible?

But there was little comfort to be had in that. The very fact that he had no idea what that butterfly might do was, in itself, frightening. After all, this was himself he was talking about, himself whose motives and drives he seemed not to be any surer of than he would be if this had been another person altogether.

And at this point his body seemed to deal with his inner struggle by switching off the power. He felt utterly exhausted, with no energy left to think or struggle or do anything at all. He pulled off his clothes and lay down on the bed: it was too warm for any kind of cover. And, as he lay there in the darkness, he imagined that he'd grown up in Nus and lived there all his life, but had still chosen to become a policeman. A criminal was fleeing from him in a powerboat on the Lethe. Ben was chasing after him in a boat of his own, but he knew he was getting near to the edge of the Zona, and he knew that if he crossed over it, it wouldn't just be a few days that would be lost for ever but his whole life so far. His policeman's badge would have no meaning, nor would the boat racing away ahead of him. He'd be a man in a boat in the middle of a river, with no idea who he was, or where he was going, or how he'd got there. There would be nothing left of him. If he opened his mouth to speak, he'd find he had no words, no language, no means of making sense of the bewildering shapes and sounds all around him. And if, by some fluke (as it would have to be, for he would have no idea what the boat was or how to steer it), he turned back in the direction he'd come from, and crossed once more into the Zona, he would still find nothing that he recognized or cared for or understood, for once all that was lost, it could never come back.

He was beginning to drift down towards some kind of sleep when he heard something that would be familiar and commonplace in the world outside, but which no one expected to hear in Amizad: the pleasant drone of a light propeller plane. When he went to the window, the plane was right overhead and he couldn't see it, but it sounded as if it was only a couple of hundred feet above him. Then it had flown past, and he heard the engine tone change over to the west as it wheeled round above the slopes of the ridge. And now he *could* see it, very dimly, in the glow of its own winking lights and the light of the moon, banking steeply as it prepared to come back over the town. Meanwhile, a kind of snow was falling, a blizzard of little pieces of paper that the plane had strewn across the air behind it.

He pulled on some clothes and ran outside. The plane passed back over as he emerged, still buttoning himself, from the hotel. Several of the other hotel guests had also come out, including Tim Dolby looking very tall and handsome in a green silk bathrobe, and people from the cafés had left their tables to come out into the square. Rocking from side to side so that its wings seemed to wave at the people below, the plane headed off east again over the Lethe. In the stillness that it had left behind it, Ben looked around for one of the leaflets. Dolby had already found one.

'Ziggy, you mad bastard!' he laughed as he read it, and then he called out to the square at large. 'It's Ziggy Stamford! He's an old friend of mine! And he's completely mad!'

The last few leaflets were still fluttering down from the sky. Dolby noticed Ben and came over to him. 'So typical of him,' he said, 'so damn typical. He told me he'd do it, but I honestly thought he was joking. An *insanely* stupid thing to do.'

Ben looked down at the paper he'd just picked up:

To Tim Dolby, United Universal Oil Company.
Who says you can't fly into this place?
Ziggy
PS Back soon.

'That crazy guy.' Dolby laughed again and shook his head. 'That crazy crazy guy. That's how he made his money, you know. Doing stuff that everyone else said was just too risky to attempt.'

It seemed that this was exactly the antidote he needed for his earlier attack of doubt. 'This is a historic moment, people,' he called out to the square in general. 'A historic moment. This could change *everything*!' A small cheer went up in response.

'Is this Ziggy Stamford we're talking about?' Ben asked.

'Yeah, that's right! Amazing guy, absolutely amazing! If there's something impossible to be done, he's the one that'll do it.'

Ben knew of Ziggy Stamford. He'd read articles about him, heard him interviewed, seen pictures in colour magazines of his fearless, optimistic, freckled face, his country house, his Caribbean island, his clever, beautiful and equally famous wife, Athena Sharpe, who'd set up the cosmetics shop, the Skin Store, and made it a global brand. He'd seen Stamford's inspirational quotes on the walls of the chain of bookshops he'd launched, back in the days before he moved on to airlines and laptop computers, and became an advocate for the vast potential of the so-called internet which, so he said, would soon connect the entire planet in a single web of knowledge and collaboration. He'd even seen pictures, now he thought about it, of Stamford piloting one or other of his collection of planes.

'He was a friend of Jael's in our college days,' Dolby said. 'She introduced us. Jael fell out with him, of course – she always falls out with people – but he and I stayed in touch. Man, this is incredible! This could be an absolute game changer!'

But Ben didn't share his euphoria. His own feelings were more of dread, as if it wasn't simply the Submundo that Dolby's friend had broken into, but some much more personal sanctuary of his own.

'You okay?' the oilman asked, stuffing the leaflet into the pocket of his robe.

'Yeah, of course.'

Dolby nodded. 'We should have a drink to celebrate. I'll buy you one, Ben. A drink to the Delta finally joining the twentieth century, just in time for the twenty-first.'

Ben patted his arm. 'You have a drink for me. I'm exhausted. I need to sleep.'

Father Hibbert was standing nearby. 'A drink sounds like an excellent plan, Mr Dolby.'

Ben couldn't get back to sleep, though. He kept thinking about the purple notebook. He'd only seen the butterfly in its chrysalis so far, but there it would have emerged and taken flight. What colour was it? What patterns decorated its wings?

He went to the drawer and fetched the notebook, allaying his anxiety by telling himself that he wasn't necessarily going to read it, but that simply holding the thing would help to crystallize his thoughts. He sat naked on his bed, turning it over in his hands. 'It's best like this,' he muttered. 'It's best to keep it closed and sealed.' Opening the notebook would give it power, and once opened, it could never really be closed again, for when he knew what was there, he would have to deal with it.

But his hands were removing the elastic bands.

It was very different from the blue notebook. There was no date at the top of the first page, no proper paragraphs, just a series of notes scribbled hastily and almost contemptuously, in a barely legible scrawl:

You're reading this, aren't you, Inspector Ronson, wondering which of your sordid little repressed desires you actually dared to act on in Nus? I wonder how long it took you to pluck up the courage and look.

You'd be surprised how different it is when you're here. No need to repress anything. I'm letting it all hang out, and it feels amazing.

Nothing special about the place to look at, of course (but you know that), and the facilities, such as they are, are boringly predictable. All the people who've come here from outside know that they want to do something they'd never ordinarily dare to do, and a range of tawdry attractions are duly provided for them. But most of them are little more than kids. They know they want something but they really don't know what it is or how to make it happen. But me, with my police training, the things I've seen, the people I've talked to: it kind of gives me an edge, a head start, a layer of sophistication that most of them lack, and that makes me interesting and attractive.

So, for instance, I met this young Austrian backpacker: Dieter. Planning to study 'experimental theatre' when he got home and very very excited about the fact that he'd managed to get to Nus overland. (Quite a surprising number do, it turns out: there's a regular Ho Chi Minh trail through the jungle, with a little industry of local guides you can pay to bring you here illegally.) No one at home knew where he was, he told me, which I noted with interest. They thought he was on a trip up the Amazon. Silly, thrill-seeking creature, naïve as a little pampered toddler who imagines the whole world is just there to provide him with fun.

Know what I did, dear future self? I took him back to this room I've rented in a sleazy lodging house. And … guess what? No seriously, I mean it! Have a guess! This is your brain I'm thinking with, Inspector Ronson. This is your history I've got to work with. I know how ridiculously repressed you are, but you ought to have *some* idea, for Christ's sake!

No? No clue at all?

Okay, I'll tell you. I sliced his throat.

X. THE ANTHROPOLOGIST

(20)

Poor Justine, Hyacinth thought as Ben walked away from her. She knew Justine had given up a whole life to come here with Rico and it had always struck her as much braver than anything she'd ever done. She knew that, since Rico had abandoned her, Justine had been in a couple of other unhappy relationships with troubled and bitter men, who had mistreated her in various ways. It was as if, unable to find her own rage, Justine had tried to use the rage of men as a substitute, *even if that rage was directed against her.*

Hyacinth wouldn't have put Ben in the same category as those other men, but it seemed to her that Justine had a perverse instinct for these things, and perhaps had seen something there that she had missed. There must be some sort of weird, perverse chemistry. And Justine was so obviously easy to hurt, so obviously willing to be hurt, that the opportunity for cruelty was surely part of her attraction.

Hyacinth smiled wryly. She knew why she was thinking about Justine. It was because she didn't want to think about herself. There was a kind of ache inside her, a kind of focusless grief.

She glanced across at Ben as he crossed the square, and saw him stop abruptly and change direction. She shrugged and looked away. And then, thinking it might settle her a little, she took out her pad and began to draw the Bluebird Café across the square where people from the research stations were sitting at the aluminium tables, some of them talking, many of them busy with the screens of their laptops. She began to sketch some shapes and lines.

What was unsettling her so much? Where was the epicentre of her agitation? She was troubled in several different ways about Ben and Justine, but actually that turned out not to be the core of it. What had distressed her most this evening was what Jael had said about the monorail and, even just thinking about it now made her press down so hard on the paper in her distress that what had been supposed to be preliminary lines became deep trenches that couldn't be erased. She loved the Submundo. She loved its separateness. She loved the way the Mundinos had found their own unique way of living here. She loved the rich, fecund solitude that was possible in the forest, like dreaming while remaining awake. The whole place was a kind of sanctuary for her, an escape from the comfortable and self-satisfied banalities of the little academic enclave that she inhabited in the outside world. It had been painful for her at sixteen when her little bomb-created wood had been bulldozed to make way for the bland seventies architecture of Diski House, but her accidental wood with its odd little coalition of visitors had just been a diagram, a tiny hint, of what she had since discovered here in the Delta. To think that this might end felt impossible to bear.

She'd never met Tim Dolby but she'd read about him. She knew he was bright, well-meaning and liberal, an ardent advocate of personal self-improvement, social progress, and technological innovation, in an enlightened, secular and borderless world. She had always been sceptical of that kind of vision. Even if such a world were possible, it seemed to her, it would simply create still higher pyramids of power than those that already existed, with the brightest and the richest and most driven at the top, separated by an even greater distance than now from the rest of humanity.

Probably there was nothing to be done about it. How could the world not be run by those best able and most motivated to run it? After all, you could hardly expect those who preferred to daydream, or draw pictures, or tend their gardens to be the ones in charge. But still, that didn't mean you had to like it. The fact that *Homo sapiens* was always going to take over from *Homo neanderthalensis* didn't mean that the Neanderthals were obliged to welcome that fact, let alone help to make it happen. No, the best plan available to them was to carry on doing their own thing for as long as they could. After all, if the only criterion of value was survival, then *everyone* was a failure, every single creature that had lived or would ever live in this universe that would one day die.

And a *monorail* … No more slow boat journeys. No more Mundinos, for even if they weren't forced to move away, their descendants would soon play video games, and go to shopping malls, the same as everyone else. They'd work at whatever routine tasks were left for them by the people up there at the top of the pyramid, and in place of their own stories they'd have TV. And, as for the Delta, mined discreetly but very lucratively for interesting molecules, it would become a location for adventure holidays, with trained counsellors on hand. It would be added to the list of wonders that people felt the need to be photographed in front of. And it would become part of that helpless and pathetic 'fragile planet' that people were constantly exhorted to look after, like those sweet little African children in the charity ads with their big beseeching eyes.

Hyacinth looked down at her picture, which she'd been drawing more or less automatically. The tables and the figures round them were bold and bright, the surrounding world a thin and fading blur. She felt hollow with grief and loneliness.

Eventually she headed back to her apartment but found she couldn't settle there. Those little rooms normally felt comforting to come back to, but they now seemed oppressively confined. After an hour or two, she went out again and walked to the harbour. A big half-moon was rising from the forest on the far side of the water to the east. Little spiral branches of trees were silhouetted against the bright half of the lunar disc, a fringe of black lace in front of the craters and seas, as intricate as the fringe of coiled leaflets along the edge of a single magenta leaf, and a great band of moonlight extended towards Amizad across the swollen skin of the Lethe. Floating objects kept drifting into this strip of light, branches and clumps of root mass, broken from the forest by the storm.

Mr de Groot was sitting on one of the benches beneath a streetlamp, polishing his glasses. When Hyacinth stopped to ask after his wife, he put them on again so his huge watery eyes could look up at her. 'This trip has been a disaster, I'm sorry to say. I listened to someone I should never have listened to. And now my poor Sara is lying in a hospital bed, full of drugs, with a nurse keeping watch to make sure she doesn't rip out the tubes and run off. I will never forgive myself.'

She sat down beside him. 'You thought perhaps the Delta would heal her?'

'I was told it could free you from yourself.'

'Well, I think it does exactly that. Isn't that why she keeps going back to the forest whenever she can?'

'Yes, of course, but she can't stay there! I'm a fool, I know, and I've let her down, but I imagined that it would work like ...' He made a helpless gesture. Either the English language or language itself was an obstacle to what he wanted to say.

'You thought that it might be like a medicine that, once taken, would fix her for good, yes? So she could leave her pain behind her and begin a new life?'

'Exactly so. But ...'

'But you've discovered it isn't a medicine, right? The forest can relieve her of her pain, but only when she's in it, like a sieve fills up if you put it in a bowl of water, but empties at once as soon as you take it out?'

'Yes, that's it.'

'And when she's in the forest, it also relieves her of what you might call her sanity?'

'Yes. As I should have found out, of course, before we came here. You obviously understand all this very well but I'm afraid I didn't. I wish I'd spoken to someone sensible like yourself instead of relying on—'

'Has it occurred to you, Mr de Groot, that perhaps you should allow her to do what she wants?'

He stared at her. 'But she wants to go out into the forest and never come back!'

'It's warm in the forest. There are no predators. The duendes would be troubling, but only at the beginning. The honey-milk would feed her, and the Mundinos would let her be. It's been known to happen to some of their own people after all. You've perhaps heard of the loucos?'

'But this is madness!' The huge eyes filled with salt water, as if in some magnified textbook image of the operation of human tear ducts. 'I'd never see her again! My own darling Sara.'

'No. I understand. You wouldn't. Or not unless you joined her.'

Now he was angry. 'How can you say such a thing?'

'I'm sorry. I didn't mean to upset you. I suppose I was thinking about my mother. Her life was a burden to her, often almost unbearable. But I'm pretty sure she would have loved the Delta. I was thinking that, if it had been an alternative, perhaps letting her live in the forest here would have been quite a rational choice.'

But before he could answer, they heard the bumblebee whirr of the same small propeller plane that Ben was hearing in his room. Hyacinth was dismayed. 'Go *away!*' she screamed at it, jumping to her feet. 'You've got the whole damn *world*! Go away and leave us alone!'

Mr de Groot glanced across at her in surprise. The plane passed over them to continue across the town, its lights blinking white and red, and little squares of paper fluttered from the sky. The Dutchman stood up. It was very late, he said, and he should return to his hotel.

She sat there by herself for a long time, watching the broken bits of forest drifting through that band of moonlight, picked out for a second or two in silhouette before they disappeared back into the darkness and continued towards the Valente Falls.

The world looked after itself. She'd always found that comforting.

XI. THE POLICEMAN

(21)

Ben shook violently, his mouth so dry that his tongue seemed to have stuck to his palate. He flung the notebook down on the bed. He paced up and down the room, groaning. But finally he forced himself to sit down again and turn the page:

Ha! I bet *that* worried you. You know so little of yourself, don't you, you pathetic little man. What you call your 'self' is hardly you at all.

Do you really believe I cut his throat, you idiot? Maybe we just had sex. (You knew you were into boys as well as girls, right?) Maybe we engaged in a little S & M. Maybe we went to a dogfight together, and screamed with excitement along with the rest of them, as some poor brute got its throat ripped out and the sawdust was soaked with its blood. Or perhaps we did all of those things? I'll leave you to guess. Ask yourself whether or not you're excited by any of them. That ought to give you some clue. (PS I know the answer already.)

But then again maybe you were excited by the sliced throat too? (And do you know what, I think I know the answer to that as well. Let's face it, you've always been drawn to a decent blade.)

In which case, oh dear, that's kind of tricky, isn't it? Are you going to believe what I told you on this page, or what I told you on the page before? Or neither? You really don't know, do you? You have no idea. And that's what I despise about you. That's why I'm glad I'll never have to be you again.

But you will have to be me again, won't you? Or someone like me. You've got no choice but to come this way again, unless you decide to spend the rest of your life in the Delta.

(22)

Dolby was in the dining room in the morning looking happy and relaxed. He beamed and waved Ben over, but Ben declined to join him with as realistic a smile as he could stretch over his entirely uncheerful face, and went out to Mrs Fantini's for some coffee. He needed caffeine to keep him going – he hadn't slept at all – but he didn't want to sit in the square where everyone could see him. He felt like a man made of glass that anyone could look right through.

There were no other customers in Mrs Fantini's shop, and she and a younger woman called Ana were sitting at one of the tables when Ben arrived. It seemed that Ana was some sort of cousin of hers from a village to the south.

'This is the English policeman who's going to stop us killing duendes,' Mrs Fantini told Ana.

Ben was starting to develop an ear for the language and the ways in which it differed from the Portuguese he'd studied, and Mrs Fantini had slowed down her speech to help him.

'Oh, and how are you getting on with that?' asked Ana, regarding him sceptically, as her relative went to make a fresh pot of coffee.

She was a very plump and rather attractive woman in her early thirties with amused, combative eyes.

'I'm not actually here to stop duende killings,' he told her. 'I'm here to write a report for the people in Geneva about how they might be stopped.'

'Ah.' Ana smiled sarcastically. 'The people in Geneva. The ones who protect us. And then *they'll* come and stop us, will they? It'll be nice to get to meet them finally.'

Behind the counter, Mrs Fantini laughed. 'Maybe they'll come in a plane, like the one last night. What a thing! I've never seen one of those in the sky before. Like a car with wings!'

'As long as they don't come in a plane like the one near my village,' Ana observed sourly. 'That one ended up nose-down in a pool. My grandpa told me the man inside was cut in two.'

'Do you know if the plane last night made it back across the Zona?' Ben asked.

Mrs Fantini chuckled. 'How would we know that?'

'You people seem to find out what's going on pretty quickly.'

'In the Delta we do, maybe,' Mrs Fantini said, bringing his coffee and setting it out in front of him on the red and white checked tablecloth. 'But who knows what happens in the Zona?'

'Have you ever been there?' Ben asked.

'She can't remember!' Ana called out, as if it was the punchline of some old Mundino joke.

'No, of course I've never been there,' Mrs Fantini said a little sharply. 'What would be the point?'

'Lots of outsiders go there,' Ben pointed out. 'They pay a lot of money for it, too. And take quite a risk.'

'Well, they're mad,' she said flatly. 'Why pay to see something you won't remember?'

She left him his coffee and returned to talk to her friend. Without Ben in the conversation, they spoke much more quickly and diverged much more widely from the standard Portuguese he'd learnt. He could no longer follow them at all.

He drank the coffee in a strange, numb state, a tightrope walker over a pit of dread. The Nus diary, having teased him with the possibility that the first knifing hadn't really happened, had then gone on to catalogue a whole series of killings, each time pointing out that it might or might not be true. So now he asked himself, over and over, the questions that his own disconnected self had put to him: did he find the idea of cutting throats exciting? Would he be tempted in any way to cut the throats of young men and women, if he thought he could get away with it completely? It was impossible to tell because though he felt revulsion and horror now, he knew very well that the exact same physical response could be ascribed different names and different meanings depending on the circumstances, just as the exact same temperature can be experienced in winter as 'warm' but in summer as 'cool'. So was this feeling *really* horror, or was horror just what he chose to call it now, when he was frightened of being exposed? Perhaps in Nus, where he didn't have to care about the future, he would have experienced this same feeling as a deep, dark thrill of almost heart-stopping intensity?

But this was silly, he told himself. Surely it wasn't really conceivable that all these crimes could actually have happened? There were police in Nus after all. They might not be able to leave the place, but they could still send letters and reports on the boats that passed through the Zona on the way to Amizad. Surely people here would have heard by now if there had been a string of killings there?

That thought provided a certain precarious comfort. But even supposing that the killings he'd boasted of hadn't really happened, it was still shocking to discover that he had to rely on external evidence to know what he'd done and what he hadn't. This was what his Nus self had taunted him with, this was what that other Ben hated him for: he didn't know himself at all. No wonder people found him a little stiff and bottled-up. What they were dealing with wasn't really him at all, but a kind of robot that acted in his place.

Still, he told himself, better to be a bit of a robot than a serial killer. And relaxing slightly, he listened to the women talking, the pleasant slightly African cadences of their idiosyncratic version of Portuguese. He knew that the people who lived in the Zona also spoke a Portuguese Creole and had a similar history to the Mundinos, being the descendants of indentured labourers brought in to harvest the latex from the trees. But it occurred to Ben that, in spite of these similarities between the Zona and the Delta, the Zona would be an even more mysterious place to non-literate Mundinos than it was now to modern outsiders, for without writing or photography, no news at all could travel between the Delta and the Zone of Forgetfulness that surrounded it. In theory, people from each side could walk to the boundary and shout across it, but who from within the Zona would risk that when the precise position of the boundary fluctuated all the time, and a few steps too far might mean forgetting everything?

And then, like an eruption of icy water inside his chest, the dread returned. He really couldn't know for sure that he didn't commit those crimes. That was the truth. Bodies could be hidden. He could have hired a car and taken his victims out into the jungle.He could have rented a place where no one would look until long after he was gone. He could have got hold of a boat and—

No, he told himself. This was stupid. He was panicking needlessly. There might be sides of himself that he didn't know, but he wasn't a killer. In fact, if anything, he was more of a voyeur (which perhaps said something about why he'd joined the police), and it was easier to imagine himself getting a kick out of claiming to have done these things, creepy though that might be, than to imagine himself actually doing them.

There was some reassurance in that thought, but not very much.

'Would you like some more coffee, Mr Ronson?' Mrs Fantani asked, bringing over the pot.

'The reason people go to Nus,' he said as she filled his cup, 'is that they find it exciting to think that they could do things there that they won't have to remember later.'

'Well, what *would* they do?' she asked.

'I guess things they'd enjoy but would be ashamed of.'

'I can see the point in that,' Ana said, 'if I could get Horga the boatman over there. I wouldn't mind a couple of nights of—'

'Really, Ana!' Mrs Fantini clucked. 'You're a married woman! You shouldn't even *think* such things.'

'Come on, Maria,' her friend teased her. 'We're only playing here. There must be something you'd be tempted to do if you knew you'd not remember it?'

'*I* might not remember it,' the shopkeeper retorted primly, 'but Iya would. She knows everything I do, and she'd know I'd let her down.'

'Well, of course.' Ana resigned herself with a mildly disappointed shrug to her friend's piety and stood up to go. She looked across at Ben. 'But outsiders don't believe in Iya, do they?'

'No, they don't,' Mrs Fantini said, 'nor in the other saints either, apparently, these days. They really are truly alone. How awful that must be.'

'There's something in what you said,' Ben told Mrs Fantini, as soon as Ana had left. 'We are alone. And in the Zona even more so. To be honest with you, I'm a bit anxious about going through it again.'

She was behind the counter, washing up some cups. 'Why? You seem like a good man.' She hesitated. 'You seem like a man who tries hard to be good,' she qualified. 'So why should you be troubled by it?'

'It's exactly what you said. I don't have Iya to watch over me, and I don't know anyone there, so it'll just be me, just me alone, and a me that I'll soon completely forget. What happens if the only reason I normally try to do the right thing is that I want to seem good in the eyes of others?'

She came over and sat down at his table, patting his hand kindly. 'But you must *know* why you do things, surely?'

He laughed without humour. 'I would have thought so in the past, but coming here has made me doubt it.'

She studied his face with a troubled expression. 'Stay on the boat,' she finally said. 'That's what they tell you to do, isn't it? Just stay on the boat. What harm can you do there?' She squeezed his hand. 'And can't you find someone you trust to travel with you? Surely you don't have to be alone?'

There was a small office by the harbour where, in another dim brown room, a middle-aged official kept an eye on the comings and goings of boats, collected mooring fees, and sold tickets for journeys to Nus and the world outside. He was asleep and snoring behind his desk when Ben entered, and jerked awake with a start when he pressed the bell. Ben asked when he could next travel back to the outside world.

'All being well, a boat will arrive this evening,' the man said. 'It will leave tomorrow afternoon.'

As Ben was leaving the office, Justine came in. They greeted one another awkwardly and Ben waited outside for her. 'I thought you said you would stay here in Amizad.'

She stood at an oblique angle to him, seemingly anxious to walk away. 'Probably I will.' She gave a bleak shrug. 'What would I be outside, after all, but a sad middle-aged woman who has done almost nothing with her life?'

'But you threw away your clay duendes. You cut your hair! And why did you go into the office anyway, if not to ask about boats?'

'I've been asking about boats for the last ten years,' she said, without turning towards him or meeting his eyes. 'The man in there knows me very well. These days he barely even bothers to pretend that there's any possibility of my actually buying a ticket. I'll never leave Amizad. I'm too afraid. I can't bear the idea of spending days and nights on the river, surrounded by the forest. Those awful mocking bluebirds, those twisted flowers. I'm afraid of Nus too. God knows what I did there in the past with Rico and Jael, but I can't bear to face that place again. And most of all I'm afraid to face the world outside. Not now, not all alone, not after all these years. So much shame waiting for me, so much disappointment. I've left it far too late.'

'So what you said in my room about this being where you belong ...?'

'Oh, it *is* where I belong. A hiding place, a place where I can't be seen by ordinary, competent people with real lives.'

'I'm afraid too,' he said. 'I'm afraid of Nus especially. I'm worried about what I might become there without anyone to watch me.'

She looked at him in some surprise. 'You? But you're a policeman ... You're—'

'Perhaps we could travel together? As far as the other side of the Zona, anyway. We could watch out for one another.'

She flinched when he said that, but didn't respond at once. When she finally turned towards him, her eyes were filled with tears. 'I don't know,' she said. 'It's nice of you to—'

'Please, I'm not being nice. I'm afraid, just like you are. But if we agreed to support one another, don't you think that would make things a little easier?' Ben attempted a laugh. 'I mean, I know you don't ever want to find yourself with another man who asks you to look after him and then gets angry with you for doing just that, but I promise you that's not what I—'

She interrupted him impatiently. 'I can assure you my fears are nothing to do with you.' She wiped the tears away – a quick functional swipe of the back of her hand – and glanced at him, just for a moment, warily and without warmth. 'But I will think about it, okay? I'll think about it and let you know.'

'Yes, of course. You know where I am.'

As he watched her walk off, he felt almost euphoric. He had a plan now. He was sure Justine would come round to his idea and he knew, with her help, he could get through Nus. And then, when he was out of the Delta, he'd write a report, a detailed well-thought-through report about the kind of place the Submundo was, and why the practice of duende killing was a problem too complex to be addressed by policing alone. It wouldn't be a matter of him trying to get out of the job he'd been sent to do. It would be a case of him explaining why the thing he'd been asked to do had made no sense. People would understand that.

Of course there was still the question of what he'd got up to last time he was in Nus but in his euphoria he came up with a plan even for that. He would contact the police in Nus. He would show them his purple diary. He would tell them he doubted that any of these things had really happened, but if there was evidence to the contrary, he'd willingly face justice. It was one of those shallow kinds of resolution you make when you are trying to bargain your way out of guilt, but it did its job. If he'd done anything wrong, he would bear the consequences. What more could anyone offer?

And then, having constructed this plan for his exit from the Delta, he told himself that he should go out in the forest one more time.

He started off at the usual place, but this time veered over to the left and north, towards where the forest met the Lethe. And there, after perhaps half an hour, he met Jael, standing smoking a roll-up of local tobacco and looking out despondently over the wide waterway, the warm, treacly smoke blending with the mysterious Submundo smell.

'Rico hasn't come back yet?'

'No. No sign of him,' she said. 'I thought I'd walk round some of the places I know he likes.' She was visibly worried. In her hunger for him to experience what a mind was like without its human mask, she had driven Rico right out of her own orbit and into the orbit of the duendes, and she had no idea what that might mean for him. Perhaps he'd try to follow them under the water and drown? Perhaps he'd forget to feed himself and starve?

Jael looked accusingly into Ben's eyes. 'Are you judging me again, policeman?'

And of course she was right, he *was* judging her. Preposterous as it might seem, considering what he'd written in the purple diary, he was thinking how selfish she was, and how irresponsible. He was thinking that she was the most extreme case he'd ever seen of a certain type of clever person, arrogant, contemptuous and self-indulgent, who imagines they are so superior to the rest of the human race, as to be entitled to do as they please.

She was still studying his face. 'You're an utter prig. You're judging something you have no comprehension of, when you don't even understand your own self.'

'I know you're super-intelligent, but I don't think being very bright is an excuse to—'

'It's not an excuse for anything, and that's not what I'm talking about. But, since you mention it, I'll tell you something about being super-intelligent: it's a drag. I figure things out at once that other people spend a whole happy evening discussing. I know what people are going to say before they open their mouths. I watch people cheerfully mangling logic and have to bite my tongue while others applaud them and tell them how wise they are. But, seeing as you obviously think I'm just out to exploit other people for kicks, Mr Self-Righteous Policeman, perhaps you might like to consider the fact that I could have used my talent to make myself very rich and famous but I made a different choice because I don't think those things are worth shit. I chose to do something which you don't even have to be that bright to do, something you could even do yourself, you smug bastard, if you were willing to sacrifice your entire life to it as I've done. And the reason I did it was that I realized that my intelligence wasn't worth shit either. Being smart means you get to look at the fractals at a higher magnification than everyone else, that's all. You still see essentially the same pattern, and the pattern still goes on for—'

'So what do you think's happened to Rico? He told me he wasn't going to be your diver any more.'

She winced at that, but said nothing, just narrowed her eyes and drew in a final lungful of smoke before throwing the cigarette stub out into the river. Some bluebirds gathered on a nearby tree, forty or fifty of them, watching the two humans with their identical jewelled eyes, their mouths curled in sardonic smiles. It occurred to Ben that, if they wanted to, they could easily kill Jael and himself as they'd killed that green lizard, just by ripping and tearing at them until they bled to death.

'Most likely he's sitting by a pool somewhere,' she said with a shrug, 'strumming on his guitar and giggling, with a bunch of duendes at his feet. And if that's what he wants, well, so be it.'

She looked round at him appraisingly. 'People have a choice, you know, Inspector.' She snorted. 'Or insofar as that stupid word "choice" means anything at all, they have a choice. They can choose to be themselves, or they can pretend to be someone else. Rico's no more than averagely bright, and his schooling didn't take him much further than learning to read and add up, but what he and I have in common is a need to be ourselves. A *need*. But of course you see this as mere self-indulgence because you belong to the other type. The type where someone's told you who you ought to be, and you've dutifully tried to become that imaginary person.'

Ben looked away from her to avoid a gaze that seemed to bore straight through him. The bluebirds watched him, smirking, all their heads tilted at the same angle.

'Fuck knows what someone like you does with all the needs and wants you've had to suppress,' Jael said, 'but I suppose they're in there somewhere, shackled in some dark cell, screaming, and rattling the bars, and going slowly mad.' She sniffed. 'Let me guess. You went ashore at Nus, right?'

That question scared him very much, and of course she could see he was scared. She could have seen it even in London, so powerful was his reaction, but here in the forest he knew his fear must positively be shining out of him. She laughed. 'I thought so,' she said. 'That's where your sort go to let your prisoners out, and give yourself respite from their screaming.'

'Well, you go there too!' he burst out defensively, like a very small child. 'Justine told me that you and—'

'Ha, St Justine! Of course! I might have guessed you and her would get together! Yeah, sure we go to Nus. How could anyone with any imagination at all live near the Zona de Olvido and not want to experience the mystery of going in there and coming out again? But hey, never mind that, eh?' Her tone changed and she tipped her head on one side slightly and looked up into his face, inviting him to turn towards her again. 'Never mind that. I am what I am, and you are what you are, and I don't want to quarrel with you. I'm going back to the apartment to see if Rico's turned up If you run into him out here, tell him I'm looking for him and would be pleased to see him if he felt like coming back.'

She missed him, Ben realized with an unexpected pang which might have been either pity or envy. For Jael, this wasn't just about guilt. However peculiar and unhealthy their relationship might seem to an outsider, she and Rico had connected in some way that she valued. Probably she had assumed at the beginning that she would be the one who would grow tired of it first, but now it was beginning to look as if the opposite was true. He had found someone or something else, and she was the one who'd been abandoned.

'Okay,' Ben said. 'If I see him, I'll tell him that.'

'And come and tell me if you do find him, yeah? Here, look, I'll write down where I live.'

She headed back to Amizad. Ben stayed by the Lethe. After a few minutes, a sudden flapping sound made him start. It was the bluebirds, all in unison, heading back eastwards along the river, as if responding to a summons.

What did it even mean, to 'be yourself'? he thought. Wasn't that just more New Agey nonsense? And was it even consistent with what Jael herself had said to him about what human beings really were, that time he met her by that softly glowing lake?

The forest had crept into him. Last night it had been hard to let it in, knowing that it was about to be taken away from him, but somehow this morning it had crept back in. Being Ben Ronson didn't seem so important now, with these big spiral leaves hanging down all around him, those quivering white helices opening their crimson mouths … And what was Ben Ronson anyway? He imagined a kind of web which linked up objects out there in the world with memories and nodes of feeling in long branching chains. At any particular moment almost all of this web was in darkness, and if he had a self at all, it was a kind of spotlight that swept back and forth through these hundreds of millions of branching chains, searching for some kind of meaning, some kind of sense that he was connected to something he wanted.

But there were some strange connections in there, that's what his purple diary had shown him, connections that linked cruelty to pleasure, and connections that were hidden in some way from the light of that sweeping beam and yet seemed to carry on their own separate existence. He wondered how they'd formed and why? It would make sense if he'd had an unhappy childhood, but his childhood was perfectly ordinary. It wasn't like Hyacinth's, for instance, where, from what she'd told him, she'd been more or less left to bring herself up. It wasn't like Rico's, as Justine had described it. He'd been well-fed, and well-clothed. He'd never been beaten, or locked in his room. His parents bought him presents for Christmas and always showed up for parents' evenings.

But now, as he stood by the Lethe, immersed in that strange forest smell and the silence, he wondered if there was a kind of childhood which he'd never considered before: one that mimicked the form of a happy childhood but was made out of the wrong stuff, like a meal that looked colourful and nutritious but was moulded out of papier mâché, so that it had no flavour and no nutritional value, so you remained hungry, however much you ate.

This thought disturbed him so much that he looked around to see if there were duendes near. There weren't, though, or not unless they were under the root mass beneath his feet. 'But they'll be here soon,' he muttered, and a fragment of a song came into his head: 'They'll be coming back again, those nasty grumbly grimblies … they'll be trying to get in.' It came from his teens. It wasn't a song he'd liked particularly, and he couldn't remember the name of it, if indeed he'd ever known, but it was one he'd heard a number of times. And now that he'd remembered it, all at once the tune activated one of those long chains of connected events and feelings and that same fragment of memory came back to him of something that had happened by the waste ground opposite the Scout hut. But it was a much larger fragment this time. He'd been sixteen. He was in his Scout uniform, walking with his father back to the car that was parked in a nearby street, and they were passing that mesh fence with the warning signs. Inside the fence, and three or four yards back from it, Ben saw a girl and boy in the gap between two remnant pieces of an old brick wall. They were about his age. The girl was leaning back on the brickwork on one side (and, for all he knew, she could have been Hyacinth). The boy was sitting on a lump of masonry in the gap itself, with the green leaves behind him of shrubs and trees, deeper in and lower down. Ben couldn't remember what they were wearing, but he knew it was what he thought of as hippy clothes – one of them, he was fairly sure, had a yellow T-shirt with Jimi Hendrix on it – and both had long hair. They were smoking hand-rolled cigarettes and, from some hidden spot, below and further into the greenery, a cheap cassette player was blasting out that song about the grumbly grimblies with its loping rhythm and its summery dreamlike sound. Neither of them smiled at Ben as he briefly caught their eyes. They didn't smile in a friendly way, but nor did they smile in the mocking and knowing way he half expected, they just observed him, without much curiosity, and the girl exhaled a cloud of smoke. Ben didn't smile either. He just hurried past. 'Silly kids,' his father said. 'They'll give themselves cancer, and that's if they don't set off an unexploded bomb.' Ben said nothing, but he felt ashamed that those two had seen him like this, wearing his Scout shorts and following his dad back to the car.

The memory petered out at that point. His father would no doubt have held forth about something that he disapproved of all the way back to their suburban semi where his mother would greet them both in that determinedly cheerful way she had, as if family life was something you just jolly well had to get on with, like the Blitz. But he did remember a pang of longing for the freedom of that boy and that girl.

Looking back now, it didn't seem so much, the freedom to smoke a cigarette with a friend of the opposite sex, behind a sign that said 'DANGER! KEEP OUT!', but it felt at the time that a huge gulf lay between what was possible for him and what they calmly took for granted. And that made him angry. How dare they take something from the world with such ease that he was forbidden and could never reach?

He felt that anger now, flaring up inside himself and directed not at the boy and the girl behind the mesh fence but at Jael. *Be yourself.* Oh yeah, it sounded so noble and brave! But it was easy for her. She joked about those prisoners going mad in their cells but what did that stupid cow want him to do with them? And what if they were too dangerous to let out?

He came to a village. He didn't learn its name. It sat on the banks of the Lethe, a small, intricate patch of sunlight and shadows, huts, bean-rows, tobacco plants and ripening corn, surrounded on three sides by the magenta forest, and on the fourth by the water. He felt like he was in a painting. Some men were butchering a pig, surrounded by brilliant green maize. In front of one of the cabins three young woman were smoking while one of them suckled her baby. A group of children was playing some kind of hopscotch beneath the shiny black figure of Iya whose long sharp shadow cut right through the village and continued towards the Lethe.

Two men sat on the jetty and one of them called out: 'Hey, Inspector Ronson!' He was a big man in his late sixties and it took a few seconds to recognize him because he was wearing only a pair of shorts, and the last time Ben saw him he'd been wearing a stylish three-piece suit. But as he walked towards him, Ben saw that it was Branco Muti, the chair of the Legislative Council. His companion, who was wearing a crumpled cream-coloured linen jacket and clerical collar was the priest, Father Hibbert, his red face shiny with sweat.

'Don't worry, Inspector,' called Branco, 'we're being good. No dead duendes here!'

'Ha ha,' shouted the priest. 'We're all being *very* good. I can vouch for that.'

They'd been sharing a bottle of bourbon and gestured that Ben should join them. He sat down beside the priest. 'Not my concern any more,' he told them. 'I'll be leaving on the next boat. It was a mistake to think that duende killings could be dealt with as a police matter.'

'That makes sense,' Branco said, picking up the bottle and reaching behind the priest to offer it to him. Ben declined, so Branco gave it to Hibbert instead, who took it with enthusiasm and shuddered as he took a swig.

'So you're going home, eh?' Hibbert said. 'Back to the outside world. I barely remember the place! I know it's out there, of course, but it seems so … I don't know … a kind of grey blur. I can vaguely remember people but I can't recall their faces, and hardly any names at all.'

'I would have thought, as a churchman, you'd have to go outside from time to time to … I don't know … meet with the bishop, or the cardinal, or something?'

Hibbert laughed and shook his head. 'I did used to get invitations at one time, now you mention it. Ecumenical conferences, that kind of thing. I don't recall exactly. They seem to have dried up now, in any case. Haven't received one for years. I suppose they've pretty much forgotten me.'

'That's the Zona for you,' Branco said with a chuckle. 'It shields the Submundo from the world. I almost forgot the place myself when I was in London, and I was born here and had lived here for forty years.'

'That's the Zona indeed,' Hibbert agreed with a sigh. 'They say it extends above us like a dome – that's what makes the sun and moon seem so big – and I like to imagine it extends beneath us as well, so as to make a sphere. The whole Delta enclosed, so to speak, in a shell of oblivion. Almost like an enormous human skull.'

'So what brings you to this village today?' Ben asked him.

'He's our parish priest!' exclaimed Branco and, rather startlingly, he suddenly switched to a rather good music hall cockney: 'We all love a visit from the dear old vicar, know what I mean? We all love the old pie and liquor.'

The priest laughed and took another swig before passing the bottle back to the politician. 'They're always very welcoming in the villages, but of course they don't listen to a word I say.'

'You don't make many converts, then?'

'None,' said Hibbert. 'Not one. Folk are very happy to take part in services, and they sing with great gusto, and cross themselves and kneel and all the rest of it. They'll knock back the communion wine happily enough as well. But I'm under no illusions. Iya watches over them, so they stick with her. And, when you think about it, why wouldn't they? They have a god whose presence they can actually feel, while the one I offer them comes from within the pages of a book. Not much of a contest! I've tried from time to time to adapt my message.' He produced from his pocket a crumpled leaflet on whose cover a Mundino Christ was crucified on spiral branches with magenta leaves, showed it briefly to Ben, then scrumpled it up and tossed it out into the Lethe. 'But …' He leant forward confidingly, as if what he had to say now was for Ben's ears alone, although Branco could hear him perfectly well. 'But let's face it, why do they need me, when they have their own god to crucify for real, over and over again?'

Leaning behind the priest, Branco caught Ben's eye and conveyed in sign language first that the priest had drunk a great deal, and secondly that he was crazy. The priest turned to look at him as he was completing this little pantomime, and they both laughed and pretended to punch each other.

'That's what they all think about me,' Father Hibbert said, 'and I suppose they're right. I've let things go a bit. I used to worry greatly for people's souls when I first came out here. Folk would listen to me politely and then, when I'd finished, they'd say they were sure what I said was true in the world outside, but things were different here in the Delta. And back then I'd try to argue: No, I'd tell them, truth is truth, and whatever deviates from truth must be a lie. But you know …' he made a sweeping gesture that took in the great purple spirals that surrounded the village, and the huts with their murals of grinning skeletons and monsters and people in cages, 'things *are* different here! *Everything's* different. There's no denying that! And maybe there's something a little arrogant about trying to insist on a truth that will apply everywhere.'

'You know what they say,' Branco said with a chuckle, 'when the Palido told his corpses to bury us here, we cried out to all the saints to come with us, but they all refused because they were much too comfortable where they were. They'd had fine houses built for them, and pictures painted of them, and all their words were safely locked up in a little box which dumb people like us didn't even know how to open. So why would they come with us, they said, when all we could offer them was a few scrawny chickens now and then, and the odd song?'

'Ah yes, I've been told that story many times,' Father Hibbert said. 'The corpse servants laughed at you, didn't they? "Even the saints have deserted you," they jeered. "And look at us! We may be dead bodies, but we walk the earth while you languish under the ground."'

Branco nodded. 'But there was just one small saint who whispered that she'd come with us, if we promised to make her our god, and feed her and give her eyes to see with.'

'Iya, I assume?' Ben said.

Hibbert nodded. 'It was Iya indeed, Iya whose twin sister Boca, so we're told, lives in the dark water beneath us, controlling everything with her many arms, seeing everything with her thousand higgledy-piggledy eyes. "All the creatures of the Delta belong to Boca," Iya told the Mundinos, "and without my help, she'll—"'

'Exactly.' Branco yawned and jerked a thumb at the priest. 'He knows this stuff better than we do, you know, and it's not even his religion! But anyway, how have you enjoyed my wife's hotel, Inspector Ronson?'

'Your wife?' A story began to construct itself in Ben's mind about the relationship between needy, bitter Nicky Martin and this charming player. Nicky wanted a prince to rescue her, after all, so it wasn't hard to see how, in the context of London, a handsome man from the mysterious Delta might have seemed like a prince from fairy land.

But his thoughts were interrupted by the sound of hundreds of wings. A huge flock of bluebirds was pouring out of the forest behind the village, and climbing up into the sky over the Lethe. And now they were looking in that direction, the three men could see more flocks in the distance, rising from the forest on the far side of the water, twisting and turning in the sky.

Ben glanced at Branco. He'd been born and grown up in the Delta, but it was obvious from his face that this wasn't something that was familiar to him. Then a flurry of flapping sounds made them all look round at the river to their left where another huge flock was streaming straight up from under the water in a strange un-birdlike way, among a mass of exploding droplets. And now they saw patches of similar turbulence appearing, one after another, across the whole surface of the Lethe, as still more birds emerged from below the surface and climbed up through the air to join the countless overlapping skeins of birds stretching across the sky.

And into all this, from over to their right, arrived the plane, the same small low-winged plane as last night, coming from the direction of the outside world.

XII. THE ANTHROPOLOGIST

(23)

Hyacinth was down by the harbour when the plane came over this second time. It flew right over her head, climbed at the ridge, and wheeled round to pass over the town again and out over the Lethe. But this time, instead of heading off at this point, it banked round, rolled over playfully, swooped down to skim the surface of the water, and then climbed up to hang there on its prop, high, high up in the clean, fresh, rain-washed blueness of the sky, before diving down to come in once more over the town.

Quite a number of people had already gathered to watch the bluebirds. She saw Tim Dolby, in black jeans and a white T-shirt, and Nicky Martin from the Hotel Bem-Vindo. Even Katherine Tiler had emerged to see the spectacle from the dim brown depths of the Town Hall.

Hyacinth walked over to talk to Horga, who'd been working on his boat when the birds began to gather, and had climbed up on to the quay to watch them. He told her that he'd never seen birds gather in such large numbers. But of course there was no reason why, up there in his cockpit, Ziggy Stamford should know that something strange and unprecedented was happening beneath him, even supposing he'd noticed the birds at all. He did two loops and then swooped down over the harbour to perform a victory roll and release another snow-cloud of paper before heading back out over the Lethe. Hyacinth guessed his fuel must be running low by now and he needed to return to whatever rainforest airstrip he'd started out from, but his leaflets were still fluttering to the ground:

You see? Yesterday wasn't just a fluke!

Dolby punched the air and gave a big cheerful shout of triumph. 'Stamford, you bastard! You've done it again!'

Never mind a monorail with an airport at the end of it. This was *way* better. For a tiny fraction of the cost, an airport could be built right here on the Rock of Amizad, and then you'd be able to fly in directly from New York or London or Tokyo in a single hop.

Above the far bank, the plane climbed steeply for one last parting loop. As it did so, the birds in their thousands converged to form a gigantic swirling cone beneath him like a kind of tornado. Oblivious to this, Stamford climbed more and more steeply until, just for a moment, his plane was heading vertically upwards. Hyacinth expected it to turn right back on itself and loop over as it had done very elegantly a few minutes before, but suddenly and for no obvious reason, the plane toppled sideways instead. She could still hear its engine, so it clearly hadn't run out of fuel, but Stamford no longer seemed to have any control over it, because it lurched upwards one final time and then, from that high point, twisted and tumbled from the sky like a kite with a broken string, to crash into the forest way to the south of the Lethe. A small cloud of white smoke came up. The birds followed it down like a flight of arrows.

After a stunned silence, a kind of low wail went up from the people who'd gathered there. They knew they'd almost certainly witnessed a death taking place right in front of them, and Hyacinth supposed that this stirred up in everyone, as it did in her, a strange, atavistic emotion that mingled horror and fear with a deep, dark, dirty thrill, like the feeling people might have looked forward to in days gone by when they set out to watch an execution.

Dolby took charge. 'Do we have a helicopter?' he demanded of Katherine Tiler. She told him no. 'How about police boats?' They were all out on patrol, she said, and of course radio didn't work in the Delta so they couldn't be summoned, though most probably some police officers would have seen what happened and would set off to help on their own initiative. After studying her face for a few seconds, Dolby seemed to make a decision that she had nothing to offer, and simply moved on from her, sending two people to get the doctor and supplies from the Amizad hospital, someone else to seek out Captain Strugatsky who he'd hired to pilot his launch, and another again to run to the bookshop to get him a largescale map of the Delta.

'We've got to get a fix on where that smoke is coming from. Yeah, and let's get a second party heading that way on foot in case that proves to be quicker. The plane's not on fire, that's the key thing. There'd be more smoke if it was. Ziggy could still be alive. If anyone's going to survive a crash like that, it's him.'

Hyacinth held back. If she'd been the only one there, she would have helped, but there were plenty of volunteers already. And she was struggling within herself between her sense of horror at the crash and a rising feeling of elation that Ziggy Stamford had not, after all, been able to defeat the Delta. Horga had sat himself down on the quayside, his legs dangling, watching all this without expression, and noticeably not offering his own boat.

A man had just crashed his plane and was either dead or likely to die, she had to keep reminding herself, and Dolby was this man's friend, behaving just as she would behave if it had been a friend of hers. But the reason she had to remind herself of this was that her main feeling was one of exultation. Two clever and successful and very modern men had tried to turn the entire Delta into a backdrop for their own story, noisy with heroism, but the story had not gone the way they planned.

'Tomorrow when this is over,' she said to Horga, 'how about you take me across the water again?'

XIII. THE POLICEMAN

(24)

Ben, Branco and Father Hibbert watched the plane's final ascent at the pinnacle of a cone of birds, and saw it lurch sideways and tumble across the sky above their heads to crash into the forest behind the village, perhaps half a mile back from the Lethe. They were all standing now, having scrambled to their feet in case the plane came towards them. In a matter of seconds after the impact, birds were swarming over and around them, hurrying hungrily towards the crash.

Branco made an exasperated gesture. 'The Delta is full of crashed planes! What made that idiot think he was the exception to the rule?'

'There's something obscene about a death like that,' Father Hibbert observed, looking into the forest beyond the village in the general direction of the crash. 'A live, vibrant, enthusiastic human being, reduced in an instant to a mere lump of meat, like some fly swatted against a window.' He looked around for the bottle, then noticed Ben watching him, and turned his attention back to the forest.

'We don't know he's dead,' Ben pointed out.

'Oh surely,' Hibbert protested, 'after an impact like—'

He was interrupted by a swishing sound beneath him as a single wave, radiating out from the impact, emerged from under the forest to spread across the Lethe.

Ben became a policeman then. He took command and, with Branco's help, organized the adults in the village into a search line.

It was slow progress because of having to walk round pools and lakes and find a way across channels, and as Ben came nearer to the crash site he encountered another difficulty: the world began to dissolve, the spiral-branched trees becoming diagrams of trees, the ground a diagram of interlocking roots. And as the world dissolved, so did he. He was a stick man, a hieroglyph, a symbol, moving among other symbols through a kind of colourless, bodiless matrix. 'You must prove yourself, you must prove you're worth something,' a voice seemed to whisper to him, bodiless as the matrix itself. Only vaguely, as if through frosted glass, could he see the actual forest, his actual hands and feet.

'Ugh! Duendes!' he heard villagers calling to each other along the line in tones of disgust. 'A whole lot of them.' Then one of them shouted. 'This way! Tell the foreigner it's this way!'

Ben ran towards the voice. It was a young man. He pointed through the trees ahead of him, and Ben saw the white shape of the plane through the leaves and branches, nose down in the forest floor. The young man squatted down where he was – he'd done his part and had no intention of going any nearer to the duendes – but Ben hurried forward, though there was barely such a thing as Ben Ronson any more, only a small and temporary node connecting together a cluster of sensory impressions and emotional responses which he might have called memories except that that would imply a past and a present and a future, and it was obvious that there were no such things. There was no time. There was no space either. The apparent scale of the universe was just a misapprehension. Mars, the Andromeda galaxy, they were all right here where he was. You could step over to them in a single stride if you knew how, and to any one of countless other Earths that were just like this one except perhaps with no Delta, or no London, or no something else. It was all as small and intimate as a single room.

'But however small the world,' the voice said, 'you must still prove yourself.'

Why? Prove what?

'You know! You must know! You must prove that you're good!'

To whom?

'To ... you know ... to ... *them* ...'

Them? Who's them?

'Well, I don't know but ... but ...' And here a silver band began to play: cornets and trombones, saxes and sousaphones ... but every bear that ever there was is gathered there for certain because today's the daze the daze the daze ... Trumpets glinted like knives in desert sun as the sound disintegrated into blinding blare ... today's the daze, today's the daze, the daze, the daze, the dazedazedazedaze daze ...

With a huge effort, he forced his attention away from the echoing labyrinth inside his head and back to the hazy, fleeting, insubstantial place beyond his skin. The plane had plunged into the forest floor right up to its smashed cockpit and its wings were stretched out across the ground like the hilt of a giant sheathed sword to form a kind of wall. The large letters painted on them shouted out a message that couldn't be heard or pronounced or understood while, up among the branches, wreathed in purple spirals, the tailfin whispered those same silent letters.

Beneath the plane squatted Rico with the pilot's bleeding body across his lap. This part of the scene was very clear, even exaggeratedly so, as if lit up by studio lights that brought out its three-dimensionality and colour so as to transform the two figures into a kind of *pietà*. The world swirled around them – the diagrams of trees, the endlessly spiralling branches – while duendes squatted at Rico's feet and on either side of him, grinning their identical V-shaped grins as they reached out to touch the body of Ziggy Stamford. There was a stink of hot oil and the sound of something dripping. And, in a blur of colour that resolved itself momentarily here and there into a sneering mouth or a crystal eye, bluebirds watched silently from every branch.

'Rico?' Ben called out from twenty yards away. 'Hello there, Rico. Remember me? Ben Ronson? The policeman from the boat?'

Rico looked up but his eyes didn't focus.

'Last time I saw you, it was in the harbour in the rain,' Ben tried again. 'Perhaps you remember that?'

Rico smiled vaguely, his face and hands smeared with blood.

Ben continued forward, a thin stick man in a crudely drawn diagram, pushing through thrumming lines of force. The duendes turned towards him and watched him with their black button eyes. He tried to ignore them as he approached and reached out to Stamford, his hands and the whole scene in front of him dissolving at once into jagged, fizzing, flickering forms, as if he'd stepped into the wrong spot in front of someone's poorly tuned TV. It was almost a surprise when his fingers made contact with the familiar texture of a real human body and not just a framework of sticks and lines.

He felt the billionaire's neck for a pulse … Today's the daze, the daze, the daze, today's the daze … But never mind all that, his legs, his face, his arms were all broken … Teddy bears, teddy bears, teddy bears have their … Something had pierced right through his cheek but, after some initial bleeding, shock had pulled his whole circulation deep down into his core, leaving his exterior flesh empty and grey and bloodless … Picnic time for teddy bears, dee dum-dum diddle dee-dee, dee dum-dum diddle dee-dee … But Stamford was still just alive. After checking that his airways were clear, Ben lifted him from Rico's arms and carried him thirty yards away to the bank of a small channel …Today's the daze, the daze, the diddly daze … In spite of the din inside himself, in spite of his having lost all sense of where he was, or what kind of world he inhabited, he still tried to think through how best to do this. For instance, he knew that normally you'd try not to move someone in Stamford's state, for fear of back or neck injuries, but he reasoned that Rico must already have dragged him out of the smashed cockpit window and there seemed to be a significant danger that whatever was dripping from the broken plane might at some point ignite. Rico and the duendes followed, gathering round Ben as he tried to examine Stamford's wounds.

'Rico?' Ben tried again as he worked. Dee dum-dum diddle dee-dee, dee dum-dum diddle dee-dee. 'Can you not hear me? Don't you know who I am?'

Rico glanced sideways at one of the duendes with an embarrassed giggle.

'Did you make this happen?' Ben asked him. 'Did you make the plane crash?'

At this point, Rico seemed to see the policeman for the first time, although his eyes focused not so much on his face as on a point several inches inside it. 'Cage head,' he muttered in an odd, stumbling voice, like a man trying to speak after a stroke. 'Ha ha! Cage head.'

Father Hibbert arrived then, his face shifting randomly from blue to grey to green to red, his watery eyes hovering in the air.

'Is he ...?' The priest's hands were continually disintegrating into scribbles, although somehow they never quite stopped being hands.

'No, he's still alive, but ...'

And suddenly Branco charged into the scene, bellowing with rage and laying into the duendes with a heavy stick, not caring where or how hard he hit them. They hopped and skipped away and dived into the pool. As if he was a duende himself Rico too scurried out of Branco's reach and crouched to watch what happened next from behind a delicate quivering screen of dangling helical flowers.

XIV. THE ANTHROPOLOGIST

(25)

'So. More stories?' Horga asked, as he and Hyacinth left the harbour on the morning after the crash.

He'd never been able to understand why she felt it necessary to gather up stories and store them in writing, and she privately thought he had a point. Very few people read the articles on Mundino folklore she published in the few obscure journals that would take them. She was only able to fund her work because of the Protectorate's small budget for 'preserving the Delta's unique cultural heritage', but she knew she couldn't really preserve a heritage, even with a budget a hundred times the size. A story that needed protecting had already died. It was an animal in a zoo, an Egyptian god in a glass case, there to be drawn with crayons by schoolchildren.

'You know what,' she said, 'just take me across the Lethe, will you, and leave me there for the day.'

So he left her on the shoulder of forest opposite Amizad, where the Lethe came from the east and turned towards the north to avoid the Rock. She sat there for a while watching Horga making his way back across that smooth expanse of water to the little town of Amizad. And as she watched, Dolby's launch, the *Jimmy G*, emerged from the harbour and began to cross the water in the other direction, heading towards the Zona and the outside world beyond. Ziggy Stamford, she knew, had died that night in hospital, and so his friend Tim Dolby was taking his body home, along with the news of his death. Who knew what consequences that would have for the Delta? Stamford was famous and the whole world would want to know how and where he died.

But for now, at any rate, the Delta carried on as before. Small waves splashed against the tree trunks underneath the forest floor. The great wooden mass creaked, fell silent, creaked again.

She turned and began to walk, leaving the Lethe behind her and surrounding herself with magenta spirals and dangling helical flowers. There was a track running parallel to the river which connected several villages and she began to walk along it, sometimes stopping to sketch. She was not enjoying the forest as much as she usually did. Stamford and his plane had made her sanctuary feel less safe, but it was more than that. She felt tired of her life as she'd lived it so far and, for the first time she could remember, she found herself thinking about what it would mean to grow old.

At one point, after walking for an hour or two, she left the path and walked through to the riverbank to sit and drink some coffee. A boat came by, the kind that ferried goods and people between Amizad and the outside world, with a passenger deck at the front and a cargo hatch behind the bridge and the stack. It was heading towards Nus and there were a couple of men she didn't recognize sitting on the hatch, but on the deck, a little apart from one another, she saw Ben and Justine. After all these years, Justine was finally leaving the Submundo Delta, and Ben was the one going with her.

Ben was looking down at his hands, twisting them about in his lap. Justine was staring out at the water. Though she couldn't have said why, exactly, Hyacinth hated the idea of them seeing her there, and shrank back into the trees. She felt another stab of grief, and asked herself why. Did she wish she could be with Ben? No, not really. Did she envy them their relationship, if that's what it was? No. If it existed at all, it hardly seemed likely to last. But perhaps it was just the fact that something was happening to them, they were moving forward, and their lives would never be the same again.

Through the trees ahead of her, surrounded by a cloud of white flowers, she saw a little Mundino hut of the kind used for chicken sacrifices, such as you found in the forest all over the Delta. She went inside. There was the usual floor of packed and bloodstained earth, with assorted earthenware pots and plastic cooking-oil bottles in one corner, and the usual vivid murals with their bright comic-book-like images. (The Mundinos had once worked with pigments they made themselves, but they'd taken with enthusiasm to imported paints.) Here was the Palido with his curly moustaches. Here were the jeering corpse servants with their spades. Here in a cage were the poor Mundino forebears, waiting to be lowered into their living grave. And there, right at the bottom, beneath the ground, beneath the fringe of pink that represented the forest, Boca was waiting in the secret sea, her many eyes looking in every direction all at once, and her many arms reaching out to feel and caress her surroundings.

Hyacinth could understand why, once they discovered it would support them, the Mundinos would choose to stay in what they believed to be an underworld, for they knew that outside, beyond the Zona, the Palido waited with his corpse servants. But what if you knew that the ones who sent you down there had long since gone, she thought, and could no longer reach you or harm you? Would it make sense then to stay in Boca's realm?

When she returned to the door of the hut, she looked from the dim, windowless interior into a kind of sunlit bower packed with many thousands of white spiral flowers dangling down from the trees and gently spinning this way and that on their axes, showing and then concealing again their crimson saxophone mouths. Hyacinth stood still, so as to experience the silence of the place, undisturbed by the sound of her own footsteps. There was no reason to think she couldn't come here again, or that the Delta would change in any major way for a good long time to come, but she still felt as if all this was to be taken from her. It was almost as if she was grieving over time itself, constantly devouring each moment without respite, or pause, or any possibility of going back.

After a few minutes standing there, she became aware of a growing patch of darkness somewhere in the midst of all those flowers. It grew, became more distinct, assumed a definite shape until, pushing through the last dangling flowers, a full-grown jaguar emerged. It stopped just ten yards in front of her, twitching its tail and regarding her with its yellow eyes. She'd never encountered a jaguar before, but she'd come across them often in Mundino folklore. In some of these stories, like the one she'd been told in Boa Sorte, the jaguars were wise and gentle allies of humankind. In others they were unhinged killers, maddened and disorientated by the Zona.

She had no idea which kind this one was but she felt surprisingly calm. She would know soon enough, after all, and meanwhile there was nothing to do but continue to be alive.

'But if I survive this,' she whispered, almost as if in prayer, 'I will do something new. Why otherwise would I need more life than I've already had?'

XV. THE POLICEMAN

(26)

Apart from Ben and Justine, there were just two passengers. Their names were Todd and Chad and they were both physicists returning to Boston from their second trip to the Rock. Todd was short and plump with a beard and glasses. Chad was tall and blond, and did fifty press-ups on the deck every morning. They both kept talking in reverential tones about the death of Ziggy Stamford.

'Terrible thing to happen,' Todd said, half an hour out from Amizad, as he and Chad joined Ben at the bow railing. 'I mean, he was taking a big risk, of course, but that's a good thing to do. In fact, that's what you have to do if you want to progress.'

'A great man,' said Chad. 'A pioneer. There'll be a statue of him in Amizad one day: the guy who just refused to accept that the only way to get to Amizad was *this*.'

He gestured back at the deck, its metalwork encrusted with layers of flaking paint. The boat was growling and smoking as it slowly negotiated one of the Lethe's tight coils.

'He'll inspire others,' Todd said. 'Sooner or later someone will crack it and we'll finally join the Delta up with the rest of the world.'

'Which will be great,' said Chad, addressing Ben now rather than Todd. 'Because, to be honest, coming to the Delta is not far short of career suicide right now. I mean, we do it anyway, of course, because we love it, but it's crazy that things are still like this.'

'So, Ben,' Todd wanted to know, 'what is it you're working on?'

'This is the police guy, Todd!' Chad said. 'Don't you recognize him? The guy who came here to look into the duende killings.'

'Oh wow, that's fantastic,' Todd said. 'And wait a minute, didn't I hear that it was you that got to Stamford first?'

'Really?' Chad was impressed. 'It was actually you?'

'Yes. He was alive then, but I'm afraid he was on his way out. There were duendes gathered all round him.'

'Duendes?' Todd exclaimed. 'Wow, that's amazing. It's almost like they appreciated what he was trying to do! They appreciated he was on their side.'

'I guess that must have been a pretty moving thing for you to see, Ben,' Chad said, 'when you'd come here yourself to help the duendes?'

Ben couldn't avoid them at meals, but the rest of the way to Nus, he did whatever he could to keep out of their way. Luckily, sensing his unfriendliness, they gravitated to the cargo hatch.

This journey back was very different from the journey in. There was no elation. The magenta forest was the same as it had always been but he was saying goodbye to it. Soon he would have to face Nus and then the outside world, and he dreaded them both.

'It's been years since I so much as stepped off the Rock,' Justine told him, after they'd been travelling for an hour or so.

'And how do you find it?'

'It's easier to face the Delta from the water than on the land. I'd forgotten that. I'd grown afraid that the forest would gobble me up completely if I so much as looked at it. And the scary thing was that part of me wanted that. To be gobbled up. Like some people are afraid to go to the edge of a cliff because they know they'll feel a need to jump.' She glanced briefly towards him. 'And then, of course, there were the duendes and the horrible things they made you think about.'

'They don't really put anything in your head, though. They only—'

'Yes. I know that,' she snapped, and Ben remembered he'd only been in the Delta for a couple of weeks and she'd been there for years.

'I ask myself where those voices *do* come from, though,' she said after a while. 'Who said those things that we hear in our minds?'

'Well, *we* do, don't we? We say them to ourselves?'

'But why would we say horrible things to ourselves, if someone hadn't said them to us first? What would be the point?'

Ben shrugged. He had no idea. It had never occurred to him to ask the question. But for some reason that bright blade flashed in his mind: silvery, and razor sharp, and the crimson blood spurting from its bite.

'Oh, look,' said Justine. 'Wasn't that Hyacinth?'

He jumped up at once and went to the railing.

XVI. THE POTTER

(27)

Assuming Ben would soon sit down again, Justine gathered various thoughts together in her head that could if necessary be offered as the basis for conversation. But Ben stayed where he was at the railing. They passed a village of no more than ten huts. Children yelled and waved from the jetty. A wizened old woman sat playing a guitar in front of a flaking mural of the skeletons burying a cage into a hole in the ground. (The thin man in the top hat was watching the scene, and he too was playing a guitar.)

Ben went to stand at the front of the boat after that, so Justine released those thoughts she'd kept tethered for him. Never mind, she thought, with a little flash of anger, he wouldn't have been interested anyway.

That she wasn't very interesting was an idea very deeply engrained in her: she wasn't very interesting and should try her best to be someone else. So deeply engrained in her was it, in fact, that she had almost no sense of what she might have been like if she'd somehow managed to ignore what others wanted her to be and simply been the person that came naturally to her. It was as if she had buried that other self so deeply and so long ago, that she could no longer locate the grave.

But perhaps in Nus she might find something. Perhaps when she knew that no one would remember, not even her …

'It's Nus that worries me,' Ben said, suddenly reappearing beside her. He was very agitated. He couldn't bring himself to sit down or keep still. 'We'll only be there for two nights but—'

'You're worried what you'll do, you mean?' She knew those worries herself, of course, but for her they seemed to be diminishing as time went by. 'Well, what *can* you do there? Go to a cock fight? Visit a brothel? Not nice things I know, but … still … in the scale of things, does one sordid escapade of that kind really matter so very much?'

'I won't go ashore at all, that's the only way. It's just one day, after all. I'll stay on the boat. There are books here to read. There's a bar. Yes, stay on the boat, that's the best thing. Can you remind me of that, please, when the time comes? Can you remind me of this conversation?'

She shrugged. 'Of course, but—'

'Thank you, I'm very grateful.' And off he went again to the front of the boat.

He kept coming back to it, over and over. 'I really do need your help, Justine,' he told her five or six days into the journey. She knew that the previous night he'd been ashore, because she'd heard him talking to the crewman on deck, promising to be back before the morning. 'I'm not just saying it, I really do need you to remind me what I said about staying on the boat.'

'Okay,' she told him, as she'd already told him several times. 'I can certainly remind you. But you've spoken about it so often that I don't see how you could possibly forget.'

He could never sit still when they had these conversations. He would pace up and down on the deck. 'I know, I know, but it'll be just words that I remember, and words can be chucked away like … I don't know … like scraps of paper. I need you to remind me that I really meant them.'

Justine laughed, though actually he was getting on her nerves. He seemed to have forgotten that this was supposed to be a mutual arrangement and that they were going to look after one another. 'Well, you'll remember you really meant it too,' she said to him. 'You'll still have all your memories in Nus, don't forget, and you'll remember this conversation. You'll know it really mattered to you that you should take this seriously.'

'I'll remember saying it, and I'll remember thinking it, but please, Justine, remind me anyway.'

'Okay. If that's what you want.'

'Oh, and I have an envelope to give to the captain for him to deliver ashore. Don't let me wriggle out of that either. Remind me that I promised you I'd do that when the time came.'

'I can't make you do things, Ben, or stop you doing things either. If you decide to wriggle out of something, that's up to you.'

'Yes, of course, I'm sorry. It is up to me, I know that, but I think it'll help if you remind me.' And he went through the points again like a shopping list: 'Remind me about not going ashore, I mean, remind me I really meant it, and remind me about the envelope.'

She didn't ask what was in the envelope.

•

She watched the trees go by: spirals growing out of each other, spirals in front of each other, spirals bigger than people and as tiny as grains of sand. Why had she become so afraid of all this as to never leave the Rock? It was hard to remember, for now this felt like what was familiar to her, and comforting, and it was the world outside that was frightening and unknown.

One time, when the boat was moored at night and she was the only one still sitting on the front deck, three duendes crept into the edges of the light. She saw their little black eyes looking at her, and, amidst the chaos and din of her own mind, voices asked her what on Earth she was doing. Did she really imagine there could be a place for her outside? A place for someone like her who had already thrown away her youth, without qualifications, or special talents, or friends?

She couldn't sleep afterwards, even though three of the crew had gone ashore and thrown sticks at the creatures to drive them away. But even duendes didn't frighten her as much as the idea of being in Paris again, or some other town, with cars everywhere and people, and television, and advertising, and noise.

She was nearly forty, she thought as she lay there in the dark, listening to the woody creaking of the Delta forest. What kind of life could she possibly build for herself now?

Eventually it became impossible to contain these worries while lying still, so she got up and went back on to the deck. A crewman was sitting up on the cargo hatch, ready to drive the duendes off again if they came back, and it seemed that Ben had been unable to sleep as well, because he was up there too, leaning on the railings on the port side of the deck, and looking out at the faintly glowing river.

Surprised by her own boldness, she walked up to him, put her hand on his shoulder, and asked if he wanted her to go down with him to his cabin. And then, on the narrow cot, whispering and trying to muffle the sounds they made so as not to disturb their neighbours in the other two cabins, she and Ben had fierce and desperate sex for the third time: sex that temporarily turned fear into a tension that could be discharged. It was just an illusion, though, an illusion that barely lasted longer than the time they were actually grinding against each other. The fear came back almost at once.

And loneliness came back too, because she didn't know if she liked him all that much, and she had no sense that he liked her. She could see a certain similarity between them, it was true. She imagined he had a story that was a bit like hers, and she could tell there was a streak of cruelty and punitiveness in him – perhaps there was in all policemen? – which part of her felt at home with. But having things in common with people was not much help if they were the very things you disliked about yourself.

When she climbed off the cot to return to her own cabin, she noticed the envelope Ben had told her about, lying on the top of his opened suitcase. It was a fairly fat envelope, not just a letter but a package containing something the shape of a slim book, and it was addressed to 'The Delta Protectorate Police – Nus'. And so that was another thing to turn over in her mind as she lay sleeplessly on her own cot. Ben had something he felt he needed to tell the Nus police, but he knew he might want to wriggle out of doing so. So what could that be? And why, if he was so sure that it was the right thing to do, had he not given the envelope to the captain already?

XVII. THE POLICEMAN

(28)

On the final day before the Zona, Ben took out his red notebook, the last of the three diaries he'd kept on the journey out, and carried it up to the deck.

Justine glanced across at him as he turned the notebook over in his hands. 'You're going to write something?'

'No, I wrote this before, on the way here. I just thought I'd have a look at it.'

The huge Delta sun burnt in the white sky above them, fringed with glints of broken glass. He was tempted for a moment to tell her the whole story: the things he'd written in the purple notebook, and how he didn't know whether they were true or not, and his decision to hand the whole thing over to the police. She'd been to Nus many times he knew, back when she was with Rico, and he knew she also feared she'd done things she'd be ashamed of.

'But not murder, I don't suppose,' he murmured to himself, turning away from her as he rolled the elastic bands off the notebook. There were only three pages of scrawled handwriting:

For some time now the green rainforest trees have been
interspersed with strange pink spiral growths that aren't

like trees at all, and seem to come straight from a nightmare.

I say that approvingly, by the way. A nightmare, but in a good way. I am awash with darkness and I feel alive as I've never done before. All my life, I've been dutifully paddling round on the surface in my water wings, and finally I've been down into the depths.

It won't last, of course. Korzeniowski came round a few minutes ago to tell us that in about an hour we will be through the Zona and in the Delta itself. 'An hour minimum,' he said. 'Eighty or ninety minutes at most.'

'So I'm about to cease to exist,' I said to Jael. I've grown to really like her since we met in that bar in Nus. I don't particularly like Rico, though I find him *very* attractive – he's dangerous and vulnerable and beautiful all at once and that is an amazing combination – but Jael I actually like. I admire her directness, her willingness to speak out loud whatever seems to her to be true. And I think she likes me too, because she often chooses to come and speak to me.

She laughed. 'That's right,' she said. 'Pouf! And all this will be gone. Isn't that great?'

'You won't like who I become after that,' I told her. Of course the only me she knows is the one she met when I'd already adjusted to Nus.

'No? Why? What will you be like?'

'Nothing like this,' I said. 'Almost the opposite of this.'

She examined my face, her eyes narrowed in that way they have. 'You're really *that* divided, are you? Jesus, that must be hard work. I don't think I change all that much. The me you see now is pretty much the me I was before I came into the Zona.'

'Hyacinth doesn't seem to have changed either.'

'No, she hasn't. I know her from before and she's pretty much the same as ever.' Jael smiled, looking over at Hyacinth standing there at the front of the deck, looking out at the river ahead. 'She doesn't like me in Amizad and she still doesn't like me here.' She looked back at me. 'My guess is that most people do stay more or less the same when they cross into the Zona. If that's not true of you, you're one of the exceptions.'

'It's *definitely* not true of me.'

She smiled. 'So I wonder what that other you will make of me when we've left the Zona?'

'Oh, there's no doubt about that. I'll disapprove of you. I'll think of you as irresponsible and self-indulgent. And I won't like you at all.'

She laughed incredulously at that and that made me laugh as well. 'You seriously mean that? *You'll* disapprove of *me*?'

Inwardly I smiled. She was very sharp, but she didn't know even the half of it.

'I know,' I said. 'But I won't remember what I was like in Nus.'

There's nothing to fear about it. It won't be like death. I won't even know when it happens. And anyway the whole point of *this* me, the me that's writing this now, is that there is no future. Without that knowledge, I wouldn't have existed in the first place.

It's not what I *did* in Nus that's important, by the way. I know that's the thing that will obsess my future self, and I'm going to leave him to stew with that because he's a coward who doesn't know himself and he damn well ought to try, but actually what precisely I did is not the point. What was best about Nus was that sweet, deep darkness, and that just came from knowing that I could do what I liked.

More and more of those strange magenta trees now, and the forest is completely silent without the hoots and shrieks of monkeys and birds that were always coming from one direction or other in the green forests further back.

   Hyacinth is up there at the front of the boat, thinking her own thoughts. She's not into this whole Nus thing. 'People make such a cult out of it,' she said over breakfast. 'I mean, yes, okay, we'll forget this moment, but so what? We forget moments all the time! And it's not like memory is the only way we maintain continuity between the present and the past.'

I just looked at my watch. If Korzeniowski has it right, there could be as little as fifteen more minutes left inside the Zona. I let the second hand sweep round. Once. Twice. Only thirteen more times round the dial perhaps, and that will be me done. This same body will be sitting there, of course, and Ben Ronson will still look out of my eyes. It just won't be this Ben Ronson.

   I suppose it'll feel strange for him, suddenly finding himself in the Delta without knowing how he got there. Not that I care.

A few minutes left and I've had a new thought.

   I was wondering how come I'm bothering to write this, if I really don't care about the other Ben Ronson? And I've just realized that actually I *won't* cease to exist when we cross the line. I will just lose control of this body, and return to where I was before, buried and forgotten deep inside, but I will still be there. I'm more than just what happened in Nus, I'm the Ben that always exists when no one is watching him, not even Ben himself.

And the other Ben is my jailer. Those taut policeman's muscles in his cheeks are the bars of the cage that keeps me in.

So I'm writing this for me.

One thing I'm sure about is that he won't succeed in what he's supposed to be doing. He won't be able to stop those killings. You only have to look at those trees to know this isn't that kind of place. You'd need someone like me as I am now to make the most of it. Someone who's at home with darkness. But he won't understand that. He'll carry on trying to make the world into something that it's not, and never can be, and never should be.

Because the truth is

He closed the book and dropped it into his canvas bag. He had a mango in there. He'd bought at the last village they'd stopped at because someone badly wanted to sell it to him and it was easier than saying no. He took it out and offered half to Justine. And as he opened his pocket knife to slice it open, the sun caught on the silvery blade and, just for a moment, blinded him.

XVIII. THE POTTER

(29)

The captain came to say that they'd be entering the Zona soon. Maybe thirty minutes, maybe a little longer. Justine rather liked him. He was a humorous man, a middle-aged Argentinian with a very large nose, who'd been going back and forth along the Lethe for twenty years.

'So if either of you were planning to propose marriage,' he said with a wink, 'or to conclude a business deal, or explain the meaning of life, may I suggest you do it now?'

Todd and Chad were up on the cargo hatch, reading science fiction novels. As the captain went back to speak to them, Justine turned to Ben.

'Of course I can do this again when we've reached Nus,' she said, 'but I'm going to say it now so you'll remember later that I did what you asked. You wanted me to remind you of three things.'

She resented having to do this. This boundary they were about to cross was at least as significant for her as it was for him. He'd only been in the Delta for a matter of weeks, after all, but she'd been here for fifteen years, and this would be the last time she'd see these spiral trees, or smell that smell, or feel this presence all around her, pressing insistently into her mind. She should have been free simply to experience it.

Justine sighed, not even trying to conceal her irritation. 'The first thing was that you decided you shouldn't go ashore at Nus. The second was that—'

She broke off because he was grinning broadly. His whole face had relaxed. That haunted desperation had gone.

'Don't worry, Justine,' he said. 'Thanks anyway but you enjoy your moment. I can remember that stuff just fine. But we're grown-up people, aren't we? I'm sure we can both manage a little bit of time in Nus.'

He leant forward and kissed her, quite slowly and lingeringly, though what this was supposed to express she couldn't tell, and then, still smiling to himself, he went forward to stand at the bow.

ACKNOWLEDGEMENTS

I am grateful to my friend Tony Ballantyne and my son Dominic who read and commented on drafts of this book, and to my editor Sara O'Keeffe and copyeditor Alison Tulett for their valuable contributions to the final version.